By Vivienne Lorret

Daring Miss Danvers

Daring Miss Danvers

Tempting Mr. Weatherstone
(Novella)

The Wallflower Wedding Series

The Debutante Is Mine (Coming Soon)

By Vivienne Lorret

Daring Miss Danvers
"Tempting Mr. Weatherstone" in
Five Golden Rings: A Christmas Collection

DARING MISS DANVERS

The Wallflower Wedding Series

VIVIENNE LORRET

AVONIMPULSE
An Imprint of HarperCollinsPublishers

Excerpt from "Tempting Mr. Weatherstone" copyright © 2012 by Vivienne Lorret. Originally published in the anthology *Five Golden Rings*.

Excerpt from *Winning Miss Wakefield* copyright © 2014 by Vivienne Lorret.

Excerpt from *Falling for Owen* copyright © 2014 by Jennifer Ryan.

Excerpt from *Good Girls Don't Date Rock Stars* copyright © 2014 by Codi Gary.

EPub Edition MAY 2014 ISBN: 9780062315748

Print Edition ISBN: 9780062315755

JV 10 9 8 7 6

CHAPTER ONE

Emma Danvers prided herself on her cool head. She frequently held fast to propriety, even when the world around her turned to complete chaos. This time, however, she was being tested to her limits.

Opening the parlor doors, she expected, as anyone would, a parlor. Instead, she found a disaster. Paint-speckled tarps lined the floor. The furniture was piled in the corner. A wine table was perched precariously atop a pair of walnut chairs, stacked with backs angled together on the upholstered sofa. The chaise longue stood, upended and resting against the monstrous heap. Then, as if someone had thought the mound untidy, grayish sheets were strewn over the mess. Now, it resembled a granite monolith in the corner of the room.

Yet, in the center, the real horror stood. Every beam of sunlight streaming in through the windows centered on the unmolded block of clay sitting atop a fat wooden pedestal.

Celestine Danvers, with her untidy calico hair and bright copper eyes, grinned madly at Emma. "What do you think?

It's simply divine! The light is so much better in here, with the bank of windows along the south wall."

Emma responded the only way she could. Her expression, she was sure, spoke the words she wouldn't dare say aloud for fear of them coming out with far too great a volume. *Mother, what have you done to the parlor?*

However, as usual, she kept her mouth closed. Then, for sanity's sake, she took a step backward, out of the room, closing the door as if it had never been opened in the first place. *If only.*

"*Oh, Emma,*" her mother said with a sigh from the other side. Doubtless, her birth certificate now read "O. Emma Danvers," given the frequency of the "*Oh, Emma's*" expelled and exhausted throughout the house.

Closing her eyes for a moment to gather her composure, Emma pressed her forehead against the door and began to count. "*Unus . . . duo . . . tres . . .*"

She wasn't worried about what Parker would think, should he return to his post, guarding the door—although, whether he was keeping them safe inside or sparing the rest of the world from the madness of the Danvers clan remained an Oracle's mystery. He'd seen her counting thusly on too many occasions to be surprised. At least twice daily for the past three years, ever since her mother had followed her father's example and taken up *the arts.*

Those last two words were always said with dramatic flips of the wrist and an effervescent joy that, if Emma were honest with herself, made her a tad jealous. She'd often wished to have her three-syllable name said with the same excitement. "*Oh, Emma! You've made us so proud.*"

Instead, she was a perpetual disappointment to them both. Which was completely unfair, since she was the only sensible person living in the entire house. Well, her brother, Rafael, had his moments of sound mind, but lately they were few and far between.

"Are you praying?" The all-too-familiar voice came out of nowhere. Oliver Goswick, Viscount Rathburn, had a way of appearing out of thin air, like a carnival magician behind a puff of smoke. This, of course, brought her directly back to her brother's sanity—or lack thereof—due to his choice of friends.

"I'm counting," she said without turning from the door. She still felt too unsteady to face the rest of the world without screaming: *"The parlor! Why did it have to be the parlor?"*

Where exactly did her mother expect Emma to entertain friends? Or even a gentleman caller, unlikely though he may be?

"In Latin?"

Giving up, she lifted her head and glanced to the stairs to see if her maid was on the way. "Counting in Latin is like praying, but without the risk of eternal damnation for my actual thoughts."

Rathburn let out a sound that wasn't quite a chuckle, but signaled his amusement all the same. He didn't chuckle like other men, a fact that had always annoyed her. Instead, he gave a low hum, deep in his throat, as if his amusement were a delicacy he didn't want to share with anyone else.

Most of all, it annoyed her that the sound made her want some for herself.

Tucking that disturbing thought away, into the pile of

similar thoughts that resembled the monolith in the parlor, she faced Rathburn. He was, indeed, grinning at her. Not like other men, of course. This, too, was kept under close guard—a grin that was not a grin or even a smirk, for that matter, but something dark and delicious that he kept to himself. The intensity of it resonated in his gaze. His irises were the color of moss-covered stones, with a few fireflies lounging on that lush, mossy bed near the center.

More disturbing thoughts. Soon, she'd fill a room with them.

"Rafe told me you were on your way to Number 3 for your needlework circle," he said, amusement lingering in his gaze as if he were privy to her thoughts. "Since I need to speak with Ethan Weatherstone, I thought I might accompany you."

"I'm just waiting for Maudette." Her voice came out as a rasp, making her realize she hadn't taken a breath or swallowed since she'd turned to face him. She swallowed now and, needing a distraction, reached to the marble console for her gloves.

That low, decadent hum vibrated in his throat again. "Surely, you can walk down six doors without the risk of impropriety."

He was laughing at her, and therefore didn't deserve an answer. She pulled on the first glove and began to push the pearl buttons through the eyelets in the soft leather.

"Would you like me to retrieve your needlework from the parlor?"

The parlor. *Ugh.* "Trust me, Rathburn, you don't want to go into the parlor." She glanced at the door and held back a shudder. "No. I have a spare needle and brown thread in my reticule. I'll simply begin something new. I could embroider these gloves, for instance. It's a good thing that nearly everything I own is in shades of brown."

"I've often wondered why that is."

She sincerely doubted he spent any time wondering such things, but this time she humored him. "I like brown. It matches my hair and my eyes, and when I wear it I feel . . ." *Normal. The only sane person living in an asylum.*

"Monochromatic?"

"Yes, of course." She fought the urge to laugh. "Color coordination is my highest priority."

"Then you must do better at choosing your thread in the future. Your hair isn't brown, but more of a mahogany, with the same luster of a newly polished handrail," he said, surprising her enough that she lifted her gaze to his. He shook his head. "And brown isn't the correct color for your eyes either. They're more like . . .," He tucked his finger beneath her chin and tilted it upward. "Like cups of chocolate on a rainy morning."

Emma did not blush. The heat in her cheeks came from a sudden rise of annoyance, she was sure. It certainly did not come from any wayward romantic notions she may have once had about him. "A rainy morning implies a lack of light. Not enough to discern a brown liquid amongst the shadows. Essentially, you're saying my eyes are rather dim."

There it was, that *almost* grin. "Quite the contrary, they're warm and lovely. The perfect complement to a rainy morning. Have Maudette bring you a pot of chocolate before she opens your curtains tomorrow morning. You'll see that I'm right."

This time she did blush.

"I am an unmarried woman. It would be unsuitable for me to demand chocolate in bed. I'll have mine, as I always do, in the well-lit breakfast room."

"Ah, Emmaline." He clucked his tongue at her in mock disapproval while his lips curved, flashing his teeth in a grin that was irredeemably rakish. "You don't know what you're missing."

For an instant, the fireflies in his eyes looked alive, taking flight. They seemed to find their way directly beneath her breast, where they buzzed around for a few turns, creating havoc with the beat of her heart. She ignored his words, or at least tried to, and focused on buttoning her other glove. "Kindly stop calling me Emmaline. It is not my name, as you well know."

Seeing her fingers fumble with the eyelets, he moved a step closer and took her hand. A shock of warmth radiated from the center of her palm to the tips of each finger, tingling and pulsing. She fought the urge to jerk out of his grasp, or worse . . . to curl around it.

Instead, she kept perfectly still.

"Yes, but 'Emmaline' sounds so buttoned up, as you obviously are."

She watched his dexterous fingers fasten each tiny button at her wrist, marveling at his efficiency. It was as if he did this all the time . . . for *other* women. The thought disturbed her, even though she knew he was not shy when it came to other women or his involvement with them. That was how she knew his flirtations were never serious. She'd be a fool to lose her head over him.

When he finished, she tried to pull her hand away, but he kept it.

She glared at him, ignoring the swarm of fireflies, ignoring the fall of ash blond hair over his forehead, and especially ignoring the deep cleft at the base of his aquiline nose that drew her focus to his perfect and unrepentant mouth. "If you persist, I will call you Oliver. I know how much you hate it."

"I do detest that old-sounding name, as if I'd been born a septuagenarian. Yet, somehow, from your lips it rather makes *me* think of rainy mornings and a pot of steaming chocolate on *my* bedside table." He lifted her gloved fingers to his lips. A fresh surge of heat penetrated the soft leather. Her fingers tingled, curling automatically into his palm. "Some of the best things happen on such mornings, when the rain is pattering on the balcony and the barest light fills the space."

He was only trying to shock her, she knew. However, this time he'd succeeded.

She tugged her hand free as she heard the unmistakable shuffle of Maudette on the stairs. Thankful for the interruption, she took a step back from Rathburn and waited for her maid.

The woman in question paused on the third stair to press a hand to the pile of gray hair atop her head. Possessing the most eccentricities of all the servants, she fashioned it into a large bun, crested with a smaller bun, and topped off with a tiny white kerchief, which Emma had always suspected had come from a doll in the attic.

Maudette's paper white cheeks lifted in a smile of small, worn teeth. "Good morning, dear. I see you're up and ready. In a hurry, as usual," she scolded with the familiarity of a grandmother rather than a servant. Her parents weren't the only unconventional people beneath this roof. It was as if the nonconforming manner of her parents had spread like a plague to everyone . . . Everyone, except for her.

The thought unsettled her, making her feel like an outcast, like she didn't fit in any longer. That could be the reason she felt so edgy lately, uncomfortable in her own skin. It was as if there was something inside the darkest recesses of her being churning with impatience to be set free. If she weren't careful, soon she wouldn't know who she was anymore.

She shook away the disturbing musings and smiled fondly at Maudette without responding. Her maid could hear only from close distances and even then only when it suited her.

For the most part, Emma was her own lady's maid. She didn't mind it. In fact, she preferred styling her own hair and choosing her own clothes. If she needed something pressed, it was easy enough to ask her mother's maid. Besides, while she was immensely fond of Maudette, the woman was a terrible chaperone.

As if to prove it, Rathburn stepped forward and took her hand again, this time tucking it neatly beneath his arm before he proceeded to walk toward the door. "It's like I have you to myself all the same."

She tugged to retrieve her hand, but he refused to let her go. Parker had not returned to his door-guarding duty, which kept her from the luxury of reminding Rathburn about propriety in front of an audience. "I'll not leave without her, or walk too far ahead of her. So, don't get any ideas."

"Ideas, my dear Emmaline, are what separate man from beast." He shifted his hold of her captive hand to open the door.

"Not in your case," she said, and then added with an all-too-sweet smile, "my dear Oliver."

He chuckled in his way and led her down the stairs to the sidewalk.

The early spring sky was less gray than usual. She'd even go so far as to say it was a grayish shade of blue. A grand day, indeed. The clouds overhead were thin and wispy, like a veil that had been caught on the breeze. To top it all off, it hadn't rained today . . . yet.

She glanced over her shoulder to see if Maudette was on her way. Sure enough, she shuffled along a mere six steps behind them. Rathburn kept them at a slow, meandering stroll, which gave her far too much time to think about her hand on his sleeve and the way the muscles of his forearm bunched and flexed beneath her palm.

"Speaking of propriety," he said, out of the blue. "We were, weren't we?" Which, apparently, was a rhetorical question, because he continued immediately. "My grandmother will arrive the day after tomorrow. She'll remain at the townhouse for the next two months."

Emma fought the urge to cringe. Never was there a more severe woman in matters of propriety. While Emma prided herself on her decorum, the Dowager Duchess of Heathcoat had made her feel like an ill-mannered street urchin the last time she'd had the *fortune* of being invited to tea. "How nice for your mother to spend time with her for a lengthy stay."

"Yes. Of course, my mother is one of the only people my grandmother is truly fond of. That being said, I suppose a woman ought to be fond of her own offspring." He cleared his throat, an uncommon enough occurrence to gain her attention. "She's also fond of you."

"Of me?" Taken aback, she blinked owlishly at him and then suddenly reasoned that he was pulling another one of his jokes to make her feel gullible and foolish afterward. "You're teasing me again. Clever. You managed to catch me off my guard this time."

He drew in a breath, severe as an undertaker. "Not this time, I fear. She genuinely approves of you."

"Approves of me?" She felt a sudden rise of anxiety at the prospect. Her temples started to throb. No good could come of the dowager's approval, she was sure, and she quickly sent up a prayer *not* to be invited to tea.

Rathburn made no effort to elaborate or put her at ease. Instead, he stared ahead as if the lamppost had stolen his undivided attention. "Ah, look. Here we are. Number 3. Please do give my regards to the new Mrs. Weatherstone, as I'm certain I'll be gone before your needlework circle is finished. You'll have to rely on Maudette to see you home safely."

She glanced at his profile as they ascended the stairs to the door. The hard angles of his countenance gave nothing away. "Somehow, I shall manage."

"Yes," he offered, observing her, his gaze serious enough to make her wish he'd say something rakish and outrageous so she could shake the uneasiness that had settled over her. "You are adept at managing seemingly difficult situations with aplomb, wouldn't you agree?"

The edge of mystery in his voice made her uncertain whether to agree or not. Yet, she found herself nodding all the same.

"Good, I'm glad to know it," he said with a peculiar expression of relief. On the tail end of his compliment from his grandmother, Emma had the disturbing suspicion that she didn't want to fully understand it.

Could there be something worse than an invitation to tea with the Dowager Duchess of Heathcoat?

No. Certainly not.

"*Why* . . . are you glad to know it?"

Rathburn frowned, his brow furrowing as if he were about to reveal some horrible calamity. In all honesty, his serious expression was starting to alarm her.

Just as he opened his mouth to speak, the door to Number 3 opened.

Rathburn appeared far too relieved for her liking. "Hinkley, how good of you to come to Miss Danvers's rescue," he said with a quick wink and squeeze of her fingers as he escorted her over the threshold. "And just in time, too."

CHAPTER TWO

Merribeth Wakefield stepped into the Weatherstones' cheery yellow parlor shortly after Emma. She untied the periwinkle ribbon of her bonnet and removed it from her raven tresses. "What a gorgeous day! I'm tempted to suggest we hold our first official needlework circle of the Season in your lovely garden, Penelope," she said with a smile brightening her cerulean eyes. "But I would hate to freckle before the wedding."

Penelope gasped in delight and stepped forward to embrace Merribeth. "Mr. Clairmore proposed! Oh, that is wonderful news."

Emma embraced Merribeth, too. "I'm thrilled for you."

Her friend had spent the entire Season last year embroidering her wedding dress with the certainty that her childhood sweetheart, William Clairmore, would finally ask her to marry him. It was a common understanding that they'd been unofficially engaged for the past five years. However, Mr. Clairmore's studies had put their *official* engagement on hold.

"I wouldn't say he actually proposed," Merribeth said as she glanced away. "It's more like he proposed that he would be proposing very soon. It will happen any day now, I'm sure. Perhaps even after the Sumpters' musicale later this week." She retrieved the large satchel she carried with her, which Emma knew was filled with the wedding gown.

Emma and Penelope exchanged a look. "I'm sure he will."

"Any day now."

Merribeth turned to face them and drew in a deep breath. "He's probably only waited this long to make an entire scene of it. A grand romantic gesture." For the first time, the ever-present dreamy gleam in her eyes dimmed. "Those take a great deal of planning, after all."

Emma took Merribeth's hands and led her to the settee. "That is exactly what he's doing. Never fear."

"After all, look how long it took Mr. Weatherstone to finally realize he couldn't live without me." Penelope smiled, brightening the mood with her usual grace and good nature. While her long-standing affection for Ethan Weatherstone had been no secret to the members of the needlework circle, their sudden wedding over the Christmas holiday had been quite the surprise. But a pleasant one.

Emma was delighted to see her friend settled, as well as truly and completely in love. In fact, Penelope fairly glowed with happiness. Marriage certainly agreed with her.

One day, she hoped to find the type of affection and respect the Weatherstones shared. Of course, her own parents had a deep love for each other, even if it had addled their brains over time. Her marriage, she knew, would never cause her to go mad. For, if she were to go off to bedlam, her husband would be the kind of man to bring her back to sanity.

If only.

The sound of a commotion in the hall drew their eyes to the parlor doors. Then, with a glance at one another, they all said in unison, "Delaney."

They were right, of course. In the next moment, Delaney McFarland swept in, closed the door and leaned against it. Her lids closed over violet eyes. Curling wisps of her sunburst red hair snaked out from beneath her bonnet. "Younger sisters should be raised by grandparents to avoid the risk of being murdered by their older and much wiser siblings."

"What has Bree done this time?" Penelope asked. Even though she was the only other one to have a younger sister, they all giggled.

Her eyes flew open. "It isn't her—well, not entirely. I mean, it's *always* her. But this time, it's Father as well." Since she hadn't bothered to tie her lavender bonnet ribbons, she simply pulled her hat off and let it dangle from her hand, freeing a tumble of wild, corkscrew curls. "He let her come out. Out! She's only seventeen. I had to wait until I was twenty—practically on the shelf, thanks to that retched *decorum instructor*, Miss Pursglove."

Emma and Merribeth had delayed their debuts, as well, making the three of them the same age, with Penelope only two years older. While Delaney blamed Miss Pursglove and Merribeth had been busy waiting for Mr. Clairmore, Emma had delayed hers by a year out of respect for the death of Rathburn's father.

"This will be my second Season," Delaney lamented. "With Bree out, you know what this means. I'll never marry."

They gathered around her in a supportive circle and guided her toward an upholstered chair amid a constant flow of *"never fears"* and *"I'm certains."*

"You don't understand. She's perfect in every way that matters. At least on the outside," Delaney added with a grumble. "They'll take one look at her perfect complexion and perfect golden hair that curls in an *acceptable* manner and wonder why I even bothered to show up this Season. Especially, after last year." She lowered her face into her hands. "I'm a virtual pariah."

The group exchanged a look and shook their heads. They'd each vowed never to speak of *the incident*.

In the chair beside her, Penelope reached out and patted her shoulder. "There, there. If you're lucky, Bree will find a husband at her first ball as Eugenia did."

"If I'm lucky, the Duke of Fiddler's Green will sweep her off her feet and take her to his far-off land before she sets foot in the Dorset ballroom next week." She sank even farther forward, which one could only do if one weren't wearing her stays. Then again, Delaney was not fond of propriety, and no wonder, with Miss Pursglove breathing down her neck every moment. The decorum instructor was even more severe than Rathbun's grandmother, though she held less clout in society.

Imagine having to deal with such a woman on a daily basis. Emma suppressed a shudder.

"I'm certain any gentleman would prefer you over your sister," she said, wanting to cheer her friend.

Another round of *"never fears"* followed.

Delaney grunted and sat up. "They didn't prefer me last year. With Bree around this year, she'll be the toast, while I'll be . . . the crust." She made a face. "Burnt crust at that. I'll be lucky to have two dances this entire Season, and those will be with my cousins."

"Then we'll have to trade for every other set," Emma decided, not quite certain she could manage it, especially considering she hadn't danced at all last Season. She still hadn't forgiven Rafe for his part in her lack of partners. "Your cousins will take a turn with Merribeth and me, while my brother takes a turn with you, and Rathburn . . ." she added hesitantly not sure why the mention of his name made her feel those fireflies again, "will take a turn with Penelope, if her husband will allow it."

Penelope smiled again, a peculiar light in her eyes. She reached into the basket beside her chair and retrieved a bundle of white satin attached to her embroidery hoop. The others followed suit, settling their needlework on their laps, as she spoke. "While we'll be attending the musical, I'm not certain we'll attend the ball."

"You'd miss your first ball as a married couple? But I so want to see you dance with Mr. Weatherstone," Merribeth added with a rather romantic sigh.

"I want to see his face while you're dancing with the ever-dashing Lord Rathburn," Delaney said with a broad grin that Emma tried to ignore, though why it should bother her that her friends found Rathburn handsome, she didn't know. After all, half the *ton* thought so as well. "Is he a jealous husband?"

"Jealous?" Penelope said, glancing at the door as if she could see through it to the study across the hall. "I'm not certain. However, I do know he is quite overprotective. Especially now."

Concerned, Emma looked over at her friend. "Why now?"

Penelope smiled, as if secretly, and then unfolded the scrap of white satin in her lap. It was in the shape of a gown. A very small one.

"Oh, Penelope!" they cried as one, followed closely by, "A baby!" and "My goodness!" and the absolute certainty that she and Mr. Weatherstone deserved every happiness in the world.

After admiring the christening gown, they settled in their seats again and took up their needlework. The maid knocked on the door and brought in a tray of tea, scones, and clotted cream.

"Begging your pardon, ma'am," the maid said, bobbing a curtsy beside Penelope's chair. "Mr. Weatherstone said to thank you for the tea and especially the orange marmalade."

Penelope blushed. "Very good, Sally. Is Lord Rathburn still with him?"

"Yes, ma'am." Now, Sally turned to Emma. "The Lady Danvers sent a message down for Maudette to return. And this is for you, Miss Danvers," she said, handing over a folded missive before she quit the room.

"Thank you," Emma said, hiding the dread she felt before she even read the note. Then once she skimmed the words, she refolded it and tucked it into her reticule. With all eyes on her, she managed to keep her embarrassment in check. "My mother needs Maudette's assistance with her latest"—she took a breath—"project."

As if overtaking the parlor wasn't enough, now her mother had to take her chaperone and use her as a model. Fond though she was of Maudette, Emma did not want her bust on the table in the center hall.

Like Delaney's calamity last Season, the *cut direct* her father had received years ago was a topic they'd vowed not to discuss. During her second Season, she'd lamented that if a gentleman were to show interest enough after learning of her abysmal dowry and her father's disgrace, surely after meeting her parents, the question of insanity running in her family would take highest priority.

"Third Season or not," she said as she stabbed her needle through the petal-soft leather. "If my parents continue like this, I will never marry." The sense of urgency that had plagued her of late returned like the threat of a storm on the horizon. If she didn't find a well-grounded husband soon, she feared her own brand of madness would overtake her.

Her friends, the best in the world, she was sure, gathered around her with a chorus of "*never fears.*"

Yet, even then, she had her doubts.

Ledger in hand, Rathburn walked to the study window, as if better light would somehow alter the figures on the page before him.

Unfortunately, not. They were still the same. Still not enough.

"As you've doubtless noted, the sum has nearly doubled from last quarter," Ethan Weatherstone commented, jotting down an equation on a fresh sheet of parchment before handing it to him. "If everything goes as planned, this should be your profit next year."

He took the paper, impressed by the sum and having enough confidence in Weatherstone to count on its accuracy. In another year, he'd have all the money he needed. The only problem was, he didn't have another year. He needed the money now.

"That is fantastic news," he said, though his tone lacked enthusiasm.

"But it does not improve your immediate circumstances," Weatherstone said, understanding.

Rathburn handed back the paper and the ledger. "Collingsford decided to alter our agreement. He wants the balance paid in full before he releases the funds to finish." He gritted his teeth. "Somehow, he learned about my grandmother's most recent refusal to release my inheritance. Now, with mere months to completion, all work has stopped."

"On Hawthorne Manor or the . . . *other* project?" Weatherstone asked, keeping his voice low. He was one of the few people who knew about the hospital Rathburn was building in memory of his father. And for now, it was important to keep it that way.

"Both," he said, angered.

After losing his father in the fire that had destroyed half of their home nearly four years before, Rathburn wanted nothing more than to honor his father's memory by building a teaching hospital that would aid in the study of treating severe burn victims, among other things. However, he didn't want anyone to know about it. At least, not yet. Not until the possibility of his reputation tainting it diminished. He'd even disguised the true purpose of the building and paid a handsome sum to keep his name from being associated with it.

"I know I've no right to be angry with the man for wanting payment. If our positions were reversed and I'd lent a fortune to a reputed ne'er-do-well, then I might want guaranteed assurance I'd get paid too."

"You're hardly that. Not anymore at any rate," Weatherstone added with a chuckle as he stood and clapped a hand over his shoulder. "You must know how much I admire what you're doing. When I think of all the people who will be saved and treated with the care they deserve for years to come, I am in awe of you."

"Don't say that, please." Rathburn shifted, uncomfortable by the compliment. He'd put so much pressure on himself, this only made the situation worse. People, even the ones who didn't know about it yet, were depending on this hospital. What if he let them all down?

It would be like disappointing his father all over again.

Weatherstone closed the ledger and placed it inside the desk drawer. "You'll have to get used to taking a compliment, my friend. Of course, if you're willing to accept my offer for funding . . . we could both share the burden."

He shook his head. "I have to do this alone."

He needed to prove himself. However, now, his goal appeared out of reach. If the hospital wasn't finished in two months, he was going to lose the surgeon and physician from Germany.

Dr. Friedrich Kohn had made it eminently clear that his expertise in working with burn victims was in such high demand that he was considering other offers: from a well-established hospital in Paris, as well as in Geneva. He refused to consider relocating his family without the assurance of a finished hospital and a salary by June.

Rathburn had researched and interviewed surgeons from all over the world, and he felt that Dr. Kohn's ideas were the most promising. For the sake of his father's memory, and for the servants who still carried the burden of scars from that terrible night, he had to have the best.

Now, he needed enough money to pull off a miracle. He wondered if he should take up gambling as a true occupation. Many a Rathburn had fallen down that path. In fact, his father had spent most of his life repaying the debts incurred by previous titleholders in the family.

Rathburn hated that some of the debts his father had repaid had been his own, as well.

"Perhaps you could use something a bit stronger while we consider all other options?" Weatherstone gestured toward the decanter of brandy perched on the fall-front secretaire on the far wall.

"Thank you. No," he answered with a shake of his head. "I'm not chancing a single drop before my grandmother arrives. If she catches even a whiff, I'll be confirmed a drunkard and certainly not up to snuff." No drinking. No cards or horses. And no more mistresses.

Weatherstone chuckled. "You're still not willing to tell Her Grace of your venture?"

"No. Since she never liked my father, I doubt it would matter to her, anyway. Besides, she loves nothing more than keeping tight rein on the inheritance that should have been mine upon my majority." He was seven and twenty, now. How much longer would he have to wait? "I still can't believe how she managed to cajole a clause in my grandfather's will stating that I must earn her approval before inheriting."

"Then we'll find the funds another way." Weatherstone resumed his seat and pulled out a fresh sheet of parchment. Across the top, he scribbled the title *Venture Capital* and underlined it. "I suppose the obvious should be stated first. You could marry an heiress."

"True." He nodded. Weatherstone was always practical. "However, time is certainly a factor. The problem is, I am not currently acquainted with any heiresses. One would have to allow time for the inevitable courtship, along with funds with which to woo said heiress . . ."

Weatherstone put a line through option one. "What else will it take to earn Her Grace's approval?"

Rathbun cringed. He nearly wished he couldn't answer the question. "During the most recent conversation when I approached her in regards to my inheritance, she mentioned a few things, not the least of which was aligning myself with a young woman who met with her approval."

His friend chuckled. "Is there such a creature?"

"Apparently, yes." He let out a breath. "However, before I tell you, I'd rather give you the list of these characteristics and see if the same name pops into your head."

Weatherstone drew a box on the paper beneath the title of *Qualities of Rathbun's Bride.*

Rathbun began with the most general. "She must have enough sense not to laugh at my inane humor. She must possess a degree of beauty, but not enough that allows for conceit. She must be demure and yet not wilt in a crowd." He waited a beat and then continued. "She must engage in activities that are acceptable in all circles of society and refrain from any flamboyance. She must be of excellent character, even more so if her parents don't always display the best judgment."

Suspicion marked Weatherstone's features as he jotted down the last requirement. "I'm beginning to form a picture."

"I thought you might." Rathburn watched his friend move the quill across the bottom of the page.

"It says quite a lot of this young woman's character that Her Grace would approve of her despite her parents."

He linked his hands behind him and stared out the window. "I suppose it does."

"During this conversation, did she happen to mention the young woman by name?"

"She did. She even went so far as to mention that she would think highly of any gentleman who managed to earn this young woman's favor."

Weatherstone turned in his chair and regarded him. "I'm curious to learn what your response was."

Rathburn swallowed, recalling his rash choice of words that day. The lie had tripped so easily off his tongue that even he'd believed it. "I told her that this . . . certain young woman . . . and I had an understanding."

"An understanding."

"Yes." Rathburn frowned. "Is that so difficult to believe?"

"Quite the contrary," Weatherstone said as he pointed to the name he'd written at the bottom of the page, proving that they were of like mind. "However, since I've heard no word of this *understanding* through her friend, who happens to be my wife, I'm wondering how you plan to proceed."

"Simple," he said, his confidence already wavering. "I'm going to propose to Miss Danvers."

Brows lifted in patent speculation. "I imagine her brother would not find this plan of yours all that *simple*."

"No." In fact, Rafe Danvers would flay Rathburn alive if he found out. Emma's brother was his closest friend and as such knew too many of his worst traits. Specifically, how he would do *anything* to gain his inheritance. "I see no reason to bother him with something so trivial," he added, offhand, guilt niggling at the corners of his conscience.

Weatherstone chuckled. "Then, it's fortunate he's leaving town tomorrow."

True. It was almost as if fate were stepping in to aid his quest rather than thwart it this time.

He brushed his hands together, holding on to that last thought. "And by the time he returns, this will all have blown over."

CHAPTER THREE

After a horrendous night's sleep, Rathburn lumbered into the breakfast room. "Good morning, Mother," he said on the tail end of a yawn.

On the way to the buffet, he squinted against the cruel sunlight streaming in through the diamond-paned windows. It was the second sunny day in a row. Quite an astounding occurrence. One he was trying hard to appreciate at the moment.

At least, it boded well for the laborers at Hawthorne Manor *if* he managed to convince them that their wages would be paid soon, no matter what Collingsford had told them.

At the far end of the polished oval table, his mother poured milk over a bowl of berries. "I'm surprised to see you still here."

He picked up a plate and began with a neat pile of kippers. "When I am here breakfasting nearly each morning? That wounds me more than you'll ever know," he said with a dramatic sigh, teasing her as he added a slice of ham and a mound of buttery eggs. "I would prefer to put forth some effort in order to surprise you. Yet, clearly, all it takes is showing up for breakfast day after day. All these years wasted, I see."

He glanced over his shoulder and caught her hiding a grin behind her napkin.

"You're usually off on some errand for the length of the day by now."

He shrugged before he set his plate down and slid into one of the fiddle-backed chairs that surrounded the table. "I slept later than usual."

Ever so casually, she dusted her berries with sugar. "It wasn't because you came in over-late last evening. So, then there must be a reason you still look tired this morning."

He reached for the teapot and filled his cup with the steaming elixir that would make him feel human. "Mother, are you having Stewart inform you on the schedule I keep? Perhaps I should assist you both and begin to sign a ledger for each time I leave and then list the time I return."

"As you will," she said with a flip of her wrist. "I thought, perhaps, you were losing sleep because of your grandmother's arrival this afternoon."

Slicing into his kipper, he paused briefly. "I dearly love Grandmamma. There is no reason why her visit would cause me to lose sleep," he lied smoothly. Or at least he thought he had until he saw the look his mother leveled at him.

Her pale brows lifted. "Nothing to do with your declaration of how you planned to prove yourself worthy of your inheritance, then?"

"An inheritance I should have received on the day of reaching my majority," he answered with more calm than he felt. "That was years ago. Since then, Grandmamma has made the reason she altered the original contract quite clear. I have done my utmost to stay out of the scandal sheets. I keep schoolboy hours . . ." He was about to go on, but the scoff from his mother stopped him.

"You forget. I remember you as a schoolboy, and that statement certainly does you no credit."

True enough. "Nevertheless, I have done nearly everything she's asked of me. Yet, when I approached her last month, it was still not enough."

"Then bringing Miss Danvers into the mix was an act of sheer desperation?" She dabbed the napkin to the corner of her mouth in a look which stated quite clearly that he should know, by now, he couldn't keep secrets from her.

"You've said nothing."

She smoothed the napkin over her lap. "I thought the matter would sort itself out."

In place of his appetite, the heat of injustice and determination roiled in his stomach. "You know very well that if I confess the lie to *your mother* and the reason for it, she may never hand over my inheritance. She'll simply add it to the heaps of money your brother already possesses."

This earned him a sigh of exasperation. "Your uncle is a duke and a powerful man. If he wanted to add the money my father left you to his own fortune, he would have done so by now."

"Then what is she waiting for?"

"You already know the answer."

Yes. He would have to marry someone of excellent character. Someone of whom his grandmother approved. The trouble was, he knew only one person who fit both requirements.

His appetite left him and he pushed his plate away. He desperately needed a distraction from his thoughts. There had to be another solution, surely. That thought had plagued him the past two nights. Yet, each morning he awoke with the same conclusion.

"You're whistling again," Emma said to her brother as he stepped out of his chamber and into the hall. "Which can only mean you're going on a trip."

With Rafe's lips pursed, it drew her attention to the fashionably angled cut of his side whiskers. The style emphasized the definition of his cheekbones and jaw, two things their mother had commented on repeatedly while imploring him to model for her. His dark, wavy hair was artfully unkempt and a tad too long, but it seemed to suit his devil-may-care manner.

He winked at her and touched the tip of her nose as if she were still in leading strings. "You think you know me so well, do you?"

As confirmation, his valet stepped out from behind him. Under each arm, he carried a satchel and proceeded down the hall to the servants' stairs after a hasty nod of acknowledgment.

Rafe lifted his shoulders in a careless shrug. "No more than a month, I'd say. Are you going to miss me?"

Of course she would, but she wasn't about to feed his ego by telling him so. "You promised to be here for the beginning of the Season."

He'd missed all last year while away in the north of England, supposedly seeking a country estate. What he hadn't realized was that she was old enough to know why he was really leaving town, and it had more to do with the widow Richardson than finding a place to hang his hat.

"You know very well that the idea of attending balls and parties, enduring the company of simpering debutants and their oppressive mothers, is the last place I want to be," he said as he cast a glance over his shoulder to his room. "Which is precisely why I've arranged for Rathburn to look after you. Although, I pity him—his title puts him at a *severe* disadvantage and forces him to attend these tedious events all for the sake of—*What?* Why are you glaring at me with such contempt?"

His expression only displayed concern for an instant before he grinned, proving he wasn't bothered by it. "I didn't say *you* were a simpering debutante. However, I could hardly remain solely in your company. I can only presume you'll want to dance, which will leave me with the obligation of either finding my own partner or enduring a conversation with one of those oppressive mothers I mentioned." He touched the tip of her nose again, unaware of how close he was to losing that finger. "Surely, you would not wish such a fate on a most beloved brother."

Emma expelled a breath and tried to keep the trace of hurt from her voice. Not that he would notice. He was too busy preparing for his journey. "Is a brother who would abandon his sister to the care of a gentleman—whose surly attitude frightened away every possible dance partner last Season— beloved? I think not."

Apparently, Rafe thought she was joking, because he laughed. Draping an arm around her shoulders, he began to stroll companionably down the hall toward the stairs. "I had Rathburn give his word that he wouldn't allow you to waste your time on unworthy candidates. After all, I don't want to be saddled with a simpleton for a brother-in-law."

"Because of *him* there have been *no* candidates."

Of course, it went without saying that her father's reputation might have had something to with it, as well. At one time, her father had been a respected portrait artist among the *ton*. Being a member of the peerage, and with most of society more comfortable sitting for one of their own, he'd been in high demand. Then, one day, that had all changed.

Her father had done the unthinkable. He'd begun painting portraits of the servants. And not the polished servants in their stately livery either, but groomsmen covered in muck from the stalls, and elderly kitchen maids in dirty aprons, with flour caked into their wrinkled faces. His portraits had been far too real for the *ton*.

When Lady Philomena Fitzherbert had allowed him one more chance to prove his worth by commissioning him to paint a portrait of her spaniels, Cuthbert Danvers agreed. However, he wasn't interested in gaining her approval or going back to the way things were. He wanted freedom to create his art. So, instead of gracing her with a divine portrait of her precious angels, what she'd received was a painting of the spaniels biting the hands of the maid who groomed them, along with a sizeable bill. After that, her father was given the *cut direct*.

Neither he nor Emma's mother received invitations to

societal events any longer—none other than from the close
friends who'd stood by them.

In fact, if it hadn't been for Lady Rathburn and her support, Emma never would have had a Season.

While she admired her father's work, part of her wished
he'd kept those paintings a secret until *after* she had been
married. But perhaps she was the only one who fully understood the vital importance of keeping secrets.

"*No* candidates?" Rafe teased with an overly dramatic
gasp, which apparently gave him no end of amusement. His
robust laughter echoed off the walls. "Perhaps this year's crop
will be different."

Hmph! Or perhaps, this year, it was time to take matters
into her own hands.

CHAPTER FOUR

Emma should have known that being summoned to her father's study on a perfectly sunny afternoon would spell disaster. Normally, he used the third-floor studio to paint on days like this. And, of course, Mother had *the parlor*.

Therefore, when Parker opened the door, revealing her father *and* mother, in addition to Rathburn of all people, she should have taken a step back and dashed out of the townhouse. Or at the very least asked him to close the door so that she could begin a stream of counting in Latin to calm herself.

There was no reason Rathburn should be alone in a room with her parents, especially when her brother had left town this morning. She sincerely hoped this wasn't about the missing paints and canvas she'd heard her father railing about this morning.

Her nerves climbed closer to the edge of an unknown precipice.

After a hasty glance down to make sure there wasn't a single speck of paint on her hands, she stepped into the study. "Good afternoon," she said, greeting everyone in turn and lingering close to the doorway, just in case she needed a quick escape.

Perched on the edge of the loveseat, as if ready to spring at any moment, her mother smiled broadly at her. The combination of brown, red, and silver in her hair looked even more shocking against the orange flowers of her yellow day gown. "There she is."

Emma swallowed. "Yes. Here I am."

"Playing in the shadows as usual," her father said with a chuckle, an unlit pipe clenched in his teeth. In addition to little flecks amid the waves of silver hair brushed back from his forehead, his large hands were spotted with paint. While his cerulean blue coat remained pristine—as he usually painted in his shirtsleeves and an apron—the bottoms of his trousers and tops of his shoes were splattered as well. Then, as if he were one of his outrageously bold portraits come to life, he wore his signature paisley silk cravat. "Come into the light, child."

She preferred the shadows. The light made her feel lacking in the eyes of her flamboyant parents, especially with Rathburn here.

Even though he leaned casually against the edge of her father's desk, his glossy Hessians crossed at the ankle, she sensed a distinct amount of tension from him, as well. Of course, on the outside, he appeared the perfect specimen— buckskin breeches that fit his muscled thighs like a second skin, a buttery-colored waistcoat with a pristine white shirt and cravat beneath a hunter green morning coat. Though his tailor must put padding into the shoulders, because she refused to believe he was *that* perfect.

However, his eyes gave him away. Faint purplish smudges told her that he hadn't slept. Above the bridge of his nose, his flesh puckered, revealing strain. And the fact that he didn't hold her gaze for any length of time spoke of uncertainty. Though what he could be uncertain about, she hadn't a clue. And that made her even more nervous.

She moved slowly into the room, her hands clasped before her.

Her father nodded approvingly. "Emma, you always do the right thing. It's a wonderful characteristic to be said about anyone. You are bright, charming, and a great asset to your unconventional parents."

She always prided herself on her cool head, yet now she felt a swift bubble of panic climb up her throat. What could he mean? Her gaze darted from her father to her mother's bright eyes, and then to Rathburn, who now studied the paperweight on the corner of the desk. "Thank you, Father," she managed.

"Rathburn, here," her father continued, using the tip of his pipe to point at Oliver as if she'd never laid eyes on him before and had been wondering all this time who the man standing in the room was, "is in a pinch. The boy's like family, Emma. And you know how I feel about family."

"*A prize above all others,*" she quoted in whisper to herself, having heard him say those words her whole life.

While she was contemplating the proper way to excuse herself without causing anyone in the room, including herself, embarrassment, her father went on about Rathburn's predicament. Since he was, as her father said, part of the family, she already knew of his withheld inheritance and the many stipulations the Dowager Duchess had set on his gaining the funds. He must earn her approval. No gambling. No drinking. No indiscrete affairs.

However, she truly had no idea why this had anything to do with her. If she thought about it for too long—the reason for him being here with her parents when Rafe was away, her father stating he was in a pinch, and that he was like family— her temples began to throb.

Nerves already frayed, she quickly decided there was no reason to stay.

"Yes, that's very interesting, but you see . . ." Just as she was about to make an excuse of a previous engagement to walk in the park with Penelope Weatherstone, her father said something that struck a familiar chord. Too familiar.

"So far, you're the only one who's earned the dowager's approval."

Rathburn had said something just like that yesterday. *She's also fond of you . . . She genuinely approves of you.*

Emma suddenly had a terrible suspicion that Her Grace's approval meant something more than an invitation to tea.

"For what purpose?" she heard herself asking and instantly wanted to take the words back. By asking the question, it was akin to agreeing to go along with this conversation, which she most certainly was not.

All the same, she felt like she'd stepped into a carriage that was headed to an unknown destination.

She looked to Rathburn, narrowing her eyes.

He tried to charm her with a smile. "In order to release my inheritance, she wants to ensure I have my feet on solid ground. That I'm dependable. That I'm . . . settled."

The carriage jolted in to motion. "Settled."

"With someone of whom she approves," he added, lowering his chin in a way that forced her to focus on his gaze, making it impossible to ignore the beseeching look he gave her. *Please, Emma*, it said. *It's just one small favor.*

Finally, she understood. Only, she wished she didn't. Then again, he couldn't be asking what she thought he was asking. "You're not . . . proposing . . . *marriage*, are you?"

"Actually . . ." He drew in a breath and slowly nodded. "Yes. Mostly."

And with those words, the driver of her proverbial carriage fled.

Emma braced herself. "Mostly?" Confused, panicked, she looked to her father.

His shrug didn't help. He pointed his pipe at Rathburn as if he were the star attraction of the carnival that her carriage was speeding toward. Downhill. At an alarming rate. There was little hope for survival.

"A mock-courtship, if you will," Rathburn said as if this made all the difference. "It would only be for the length of her stay."

"Which will be . . .?" Again, she knew she shouldn't ask.

"Two months."

Two months! "That's nearly half of the Season." Her third and final Season before she would be on the shelf.

Her mother suddenly leaped up from the sofa and wrapped her arms around her, apparently unable to rein in her excitement a moment longer. "Oh, Emma! I'm so proud of you!"

At last, those words. Not said in disappointment, but with that effervescent joy she'd craved.

More than anything, she wanted to let the words sink in to repair the frayed strands of their relationship. However, the sensation of tilting end over end as her carriage crashed to bits, kept her from feeling the joy she's always expected would come at this moment. "For this? For deliberately deceiving the Dowager Duchess of Heathcoat and ruining my chances for a suitable match?"

Her mother was still smiling, bright tears shining in her eyes as she pressed a kiss to her cheek. "No, my dear girl, for rushing headlong into certain disaster, no matter the consequences."

Emma blinked. Was that supposed to make her feel better? Or make any sort of sense at all?

Before she could ask, her mother released her. Then, together, her mother and father headed toward the door. "We'll leave you alone to sort out the details," her father said.

Her mother wiped away a tear. "You're finally coming out of your shell. I'm so happy for you."

The door closed.

Coming out of her shell? Coming unglued was more like it.

Emma made her way to one of the windows that banked the fireplace on the far side of the room.

"You've agreed, then?" Rathburn asked, never sounding less certain to Emma than he did at this moment. "It's difficult to tell. Your parents seem to think you've made up your mind; however, I'm still waiting for a definitive response."

"I can't believe we're even discussing this," she said in disbelief, staring outside. A row of daffodils lined the narrow path between the house and the garden wall. New glossy shoots of ivy climbed up the rust-colored brick. The world outside was bright and blooming, not a cloud in the sky. It seemed unfair, really. Her mood all but demanded a rumble of thunder and dark, threatening clouds. "You realize, don't you, that you're ruining my chance for a normal, happy marriage?"

"We'll make sure it doesn't go that far."

We'll make sure, as if they were in this together. *Ha!* She turned to face him. "How?"

He stared down blankly toward the Axminster carpet, his brow furrowed as if he'd been wondering the same thing. Then suddenly, he looked up, his eyes alive with fresh perspective. "Perhaps we won't even have to attempt a mock betrothal. We'll simply have an understanding. Or, at most, be formally engaged for the duration of her stay. Then, after a time, we'll have a disagreement that separates us." He brushed his hands together as if the entire ordeal were a pile of crumbs easily dislodged. "Simple as that."

Hmph. *If only.* "Since you seem to have this all figured out, what happens if she wants to wait until *after* we are married before she hands over your fortune?"

She expected to see all the color drain from his face at the prospect. Instead, he held up a finger and grinned. "I've thought of that, as well. We'll simply get an annulment. I'll settle a small fortune on you for a trip abroad. Then, when you return, it will be like nothing ever changed. You'll procure a husband readily enough, I'm sure, once they realize you are wealthy."

"Precisely what I've always wanted. To be loved for my money." Oh no, she was starting to sound like her father. His exact reason for keeping her dowry so low was to keep fortune hunters away. She'd always felt cheated because of it before. Yet now, when threatened by the probability of having a man marry her for her money, luring him in such a way seemed tawdry.

Rathburn didn't respond. Not that she'd expected him to. He was still waiting for her answer.

Emma drew in a deep breath as if preparing to dive off a cliff into dark, murky water. "You're confident this ruse won't get that far?"

He nodded. "We'll make it perfectly clear that we're incompatible. That scenario shouldn't be too difficult to present."

"True." Was she actually considering this? Perhaps insanity did run in the family. Although, if everything went as planned, it wouldn't be too terrible a venture. After all, she finally had her parents' approval, a feat indeed. In addition, Rathburn had come to her—*her*—for help. How could she turn her back on him?

Still, if this had been anyone other than *him* . . . "I don't know why I'm doing this."

"But you are . . . doing this?"

She closed her eyes, knowing that if she agreed there would be no turning back.

After a moment, Emma met his gaze and nodded.

His shoulders sagged in visible relief and he tilted his head back as he let out a breath. The tight cording of his throat bunched as he whispered his thanks to the ceiling. His Adam's apple lifted above the knot of his cravat and then disappeared beneath it. For reasons she couldn't fathom, the sight held her attention. Her own hand lifted to her throat as she swallowed, leaving her to wonder why her pulse was suddenly so quick.

When he resumed a proper stance and regarded her with a wide grin, she quickly averted her gaze and lowered her hand. "Then it is settled." He strode forward, his pleasure in the outcome of their conversation evident in each confident step. "Shall we shake hands to seal our bargain?"

Not wanting to appear as if she lacked confidence, she thrust out her hand and straightened her shoulders.

He chuckled, the sound low enough and near enough that she could feel it vibrating in her ears more than she could hear it. His amused gaze teased her before it traveled down her neck, over the curve of her shoulder and down the length of her arm. He took her gloveless hand. His flesh was warm and callused in places that made it impossible to ignore the unapologetic maleness of him.

She should have known this couldn't be a simple handshake, not with him. He wasn't like anyone else. So, why should this be any different?

He looked down at their joined hands, turning hers this way and that, seeing the contrast no doubt. His was large and tanned, his nails clean but short, leaving the very tips of his fingers exposed. Hers was small and slender, her skin creamy, her nails delicately rounded as was proper. Yet, when she looked at her hand covered by his, she felt anything but proper.

She tried to pull away, but he kept it and moved a step closer.

"I know a better way," he murmured and before she knew his intention, he tilted up her chin and bent his head.

His mouth brushed hers in a very brief kiss. So brief, in fact, she almost didn't get a sense that it had occurred at all. *Almost.*

However, she did get an impression of his lips. They were warm and softer than they appeared, but that was not to say they were soft. No, they were the perfect combination of softness while remaining firm. In addition, the flavor he left behind was intriguing. Not sweet like liquor or salty like toothpowder, but something in between, something . . . spicy. Pleasantly herbaceous, like a combination of pepper and rosemary with a mysterious flavor underneath that reminded her . . . *of the first sip of steaming chocolate on a chilly morning.* The flavor of it warmed her through. She licked her lips to be certain, but made the mistake of looking up at him.

He was staring at her lips, his brow furrowed.

The fireflies vanished from his eyes as his dark pupils expanded. The fingers that were curled beneath her chin spread out and stole around to the base of her neck. He lowered his head again, but this time he did not simply brush his lips over hers. Instead, he tasted her, flicking his tongue over the same path hers had taken.

A small, foreign sound purred in her throat. This wasn't supposed to be happening. Kissing Rathburn was wrong on so many levels. They weren't truly engaged. In fact, they were acquaintances only through her brother. They could barely stand each other. The door to the study was closed— *highly improper.* Her parents or one of the servants could walk in any minute. She should be pushing him away, not encouraging him by parting her lips and allowing his tongue entrance. She should not curl her hands over his shoulders, or discover that there was no padding in his coat. And she most definitely should not be on the verge of leaning into him—

There was a knock at the door. They split apart with a sudden jump, but the sound had come from the hall. Someone was at the front of the house.

She looked at Rathburn, watching the buttons of his waistcoat move up and down as he caught his breath. When he looked away from the door and back to her, she could see the dampness of their kiss on his lips. *Her kiss.*

He grinned and waggled his brows as if they were two criminals who'd made a lucky escape. "Not quite as buttoned-up as I thought." He licked his lips, ignoring her look of disapproval. "Mmm . . . jasmine tea. And sweet, too. I would have thought you'd prefer a more sedate China black with lemon. Then again, I never would have thought such a proper miss would have such a lush, tempting mouth either."

She pressed her lips together to blot away the remains of their kiss. "Have you no shame? It's bad enough that it happened. Must you speak of it?"

He chuckled and stroked the pad of his thumb over his bottom lip as his gaze dipped, again, to her mouth. "You're right, of course. This will have to be our secret. After all, what would happen if my grandmother discovered that beneath a façade of modesty and decorum lived a warm-blooded temptress with the taste of sweet jasmine on her lips?"

She was saved by another knock, this one on the study door. Parker entered the room, a burnished bronze salver in hand. By this time, they were a respectable distance apart and her expression was back to its usual cast of disapproval. The butler presented her with an invitation. "This just arrived, Miss."

"Thank you, Parker." And when he exited, he left the door open. *Bless his soul.*

Apparently, Rathburn found that amusing as well. "That will be an invitation to tea from my grandmother. Her seal's on the back."

Tea with the dowager. Engaged to Rathburn. Could her day get any worse?

Before she could open the missive, he took her hand and bowed over it, lifting his head just enough to wink at her as he pressed his lips to her knuckles. "Until tomorrow, Emma—"

She yanked her hand out of his grasp. "If you call me Emmaline after what I've done for you, then so help me, I'll toss this invitation into the fire."

He laughed, the rich sound tingling inside her ears and along the soles of her feet simultaneously. The sensation took her by complete surprise and left her staring after him as he walked toward the door.

Before he left, he turned and bowed once more. "Until tomorrow, Emma—*mine.*"

CHAPTER FIVE

"What do you mean, you're not going?" Emma said, the following afternoon.

Her mother pushed away a fall of hair from her forehead. "My muse is calling me." Then she turned and took a sharp, scoop-shaped tool from the tray and scraped the clay off her sculpture. As she moved around the unidentifiable mound, long beige ribbons fell to the floor, where she stepped on them, much like Emma's hopes for an ordinary day. "The purpose isn't for the dowager to learn more about me, anyway. She wants to size you up and see if you fit the proper mold."

It was difficult for Emma to remember back to a moment ago—the moment before she'd opened the parlor door to find her mother with her face spotted with bits of dried clay, her smock and apron in even worse shape—when she'd actually thought that having tea with the dowager wouldn't kill her. After all, she'd worn her most sedate day gown, a lovely wheat-colored muslin. In addition, she'd fashioned her hair in braids to frame her face and pulled them together in a twist in the back. All in all, she'd felt quite good about her chances of having the dowager find fewer things wrong her.

If only.

"Of course she does," Emma said, unable to hold back her exasperation. "But you didn't think I'd want support?"

Her mother stopped and stared at her. "From me?"

Was that so difficult to believe? "Yes, from you. You are my mother, after all. You did help me into this mess. The least you could do would be to help me through it." She closed her eyes.

"Emma, I've never heard you say such things before."

That's because I've been holding them in for years. Some of them were bound to bubble out eventually. She shook her head and drew in a breath. Clearly, the Danverses' insanity was starting to affect her too. She must work harder to rein it back in. "You're right. I'm sorry, Mother. It must be my nerves—"

"No, don't apologize." Her mother's face broke into a grin. "I like it. We're finally talking. Of course, we used to talk all the time when you were little. We used to sit and draw pictures for hours on end, chatting about this and that." As if they were playing a parlor game of copying each other's gestures, her mother shook her head and drew in a breath. "But every girl needs to separate from her mother in order to find the woman within."

Emma relaxed. "Then you'll go."

"No, dear," she laughed and went back to her sculpture. "You don't need me to face the lioness in her den. This tea is all about testing your mettle." She pointed the scraping tool at Emma and smiled as if she had every confidence in the world. "Well, let them test you and find that you are the genuine Emma Danvers."

Didn't her mother realize that she was the only person in the room who possessed that confidence? "But—"

"You'd best not be late, dear. It will take Maudette an age to get from the door to the carriage and then to the door of Rathburn's townhouse."

Emma started counting in Latin before she left the room.

The entire mock courtship was a disaster waiting to happen.

In his own defense, Rathburn had never thought Emma would agree in the first place. Quite honestly, he thought she had more sense than that. He'd counted on it. Because if she'd have refused, he would have been forced to find another way out of this predicament.

Not that he'd had other options. He'd gone over all the possibilities until every single one was eliminated. Every option, except one: his sham betrothal to Emma Danvers.

Now he was left with the all-too tempting possibility of perpetuating the lie he'd told his grandmother months ago. Not that lying tempted him. No, in fact, he loathed it. The tempting part was Emma herself, and her surprising response to his kiss.

He should've known better than to give in to impulse.

Yet, if he were honest with himself, the impulse had been there for years, chipping away at the barrier between his sense of honor and his . . . *less* honorable intentions.

In truth, he'd never thought Rafe Danvers's sister *would* tempt him. After all, she did everything she could to blend into the woodwork. Quite literally, with her constant parade of cream dresses with brown trim, brown bonnets, brown shawls. At society functions, even her actions and words were wooden, almost always upholding the highest degree of propriety.

Yet, it was the *almost* that intrigued him. It was the *almost* that made him tease her, to see what she might say or do. Like yesterday in her father's study.

Rathburn closed his eyes and considered counting in Latin, but that would only remind him of the way her mouth moved when she chanted the numbers over and over. He needed no reminder of her lips. He'd lain awake all night tasting sweet jasmine and wondering why he'd ever been so stupid.

Now, warning bells rang in his ears each time he thought of her. He feared that this mock courtship would turn into far more than he bargained for. It wasn't as if he could avoid Emma while his grandmother was here. No, he was obligated to wait on her, take her to assemblies and on drives through the park, attend family dinners . . . and all the while, he would be thinking about the taste of her kiss and the sweet sound of her pleasure.

An unexpected development, to be sure. One that he had no idea how to resolve without risking everything in the process. His inheritance, for one thing, but more important was his friendship with Rafe and his relationship with the entire Danvers clan. Since his father's death, they'd been a second family to him, and Rafe like a brother.

Rathburn scoffed in self-derision. *Like a brother, and yet I have every intention of deceiving him, of keeping this mock courtship from him, knowing full well that he would never consent? I am a prince among men, to be sure.*

He scrubbed a hand over his face, shutting the guilt away for the moment.

Strangely enough, her parents hadn't been surprised by his plan. In fact, they'd seemed eager to grant their approval, merely upon his word that he would do everything within his power to keep Emma's reputation spotless.

Yesterday, their easy acquiescence had both honored and relieved him. However, today, he felt like a fool for not foreseeing this sudden complication. Her kiss had awakened the rake within him from obligatory slumber. For the first time in months, he didn't close his eyes and see the incomplete structure of Hawthorne Manor, or even the future Goswick Hospital. Instead, he saw her eyelids drift closed and the rosy tip of her tongue dart out to taste the dew on her lips.

How could he have been stupid enough to give his word, only to put her parents' high regard in jeopardy? Clearly, he hadn't considered how a simple kiss to seal a bargain could complicate his entire plan.

A *simple* kiss? He scoffed again.

By the time he returned to Grosvenor Square, part of the day had gotten away from him. He'd spent most of the morning south of town, making a list of all the unfinished projects at Hawthorne Manor.

Now, as the servants delivered the tea trays to the drawing room of the townhouse, he realized it might be too late to speak with Emma privately.

However, there was another option. He walked around to the second entrance of the drawing room with the hope of gaining her attention without causing a scene. Once there, he stepped through the gallery and toward the adjoining door opposite.

Listening at the door, he heard their cordial greetings and breathed a sigh of relief. It wasn't too late, after all. He could still back out of this ruse. Perhaps he would simply try groveling at his grandmother's feet and see how far that got him . . . again.

"Miss Danvers," he heard his grandmother say, her voice ringing up to the coffered ceiling of the drawing room as if she were the queen addressing her court. "I'm told you have an understanding with my grandson, yet there's been no formal announcement of betrothal. Would you care to explain this?"

He gritted his teeth. Leave it to his grandmother to cut through all niceties and plow directly to the most important issue in her mind. He had no idea how many ladies were in attendance, but if his formidable grandmother began with a question so direct, it was bound to get worse.

"We were waiting for an appropriate time," he heard Emma say, her voice calm and self assured as usual. He felt a surprising swell of pride in his chest, knowing that if anyone could handle the Dowager Duchess of Heathcoat, it was Emma.

Carefully, he turned the handle and opened the door an inch, then two. He held back from pushing it too far, then waited a moment, listening to see if they'd noticed the movement.

"When he receives his inheritance, no doubt," his grandmother said, never one to keep her judgments to herself. "Is the reservation with him, that he may find a better prospect once he is wealthy? Or does it lie with you, in that you are uncertain of his character?"

Curious about Emma's answer, farce or not, Rathburn

peered through the crack. The view only afforded him the reverse image of the room by way of a wide, framed mirror along the back wall. Yet, from there, at least he could see the group.

Although, *group* wasn't exactly what one would call it. There were only three ladies in attendance—Emma and his grandmother and mother. They flanked Emma on either side, with a low oval table between them. It seemed less an afternoon tea and more an inquisition.

"Neither, Your Grace," Emma said before she took a sip from her blue-laced cup. Even after the insult to her character, she was the epitome of poise. Surely, his grandmother could find nothing wrong in her manner or appearance. Not a single strand of her lustrous mahogany hair was out of place. Her flawless skin invited the eye to admire her features, the subtle arch of her brow, the rich brown of her eyes, the straight line of her nose, the gentle slope of her cheeks to her chin, and her mouth . . .

The mouth that preferred jasmine tea over black, and sugar over lemon.

He could still taste her. Still feel the way her slightly plumper upper lip nestled perfectly between his. Still hear the way she'd purred. Had he ever heard a sound so indescribably erotic? Of course, he'd made many women purr, moan, groan, cry out in ecstasy, but none had ever sounded quite like her. He wanted to taste that sound, devour it, devour her . . .

Damn. He drew in a shaky breath. Where had that thought come from?

A dark, dangerous place, he warned himself. Thoughts such as those were likely to get him into trouble. And he'd spent the past few years steering clear of trouble.

He drew in another breath and cleared his mind. This was no time for distraction.

"I'm on pins and needles awaiting your explanation." His grandmother lowered her own teacup, angling her chin the way she did when keeping a person under scrutiny. Her wavy, dove gray hair was pinned at the base of her neck. Never one to be called flamboyant, she wore a modest amount of jewelry, and a sedate lavender frock with a white ruffled collar.

Emma swallowed, her slender throat clenching and releasing. "Since your grandson and my brother have been friends for so many years, we thought it wise to tread carefully in new waters," she said, keeping her tone steady and managed to smile. "So to speak."

Yes, tread carefully, he mused. She was his friend's sister. If Rafe Danvers found out that he'd drawn her into his ludicrous scheme, he'd be furious. Then again, if Rafe found out that he'd kissed her, he'd demand Rathburn's blood in payment.

Clearly, this mock courtship was not a good idea. There was too much at risk now. Now that he'd kissed Emma. Now that he wanted to kiss her again . . .

No! He couldn't think about that. After all, he'd promised her and her parents that she would get out of this farce unscathed and still marriageable. If nothing else, he was a man of his word. Wasn't he?

His grandmother picked up her tea again and nodded. "That is wise, I suppose, though you cannot truly know what marriage is like until the deed is done. I see no true reason to tread. No, you must dive in headfirst . . . *So to speak.*" She turned to address his mother. "What about you, Victoria? Do you get along well enough with Emma's mother, even though she considers herself an *artist?*"

"Celestine Danvers is a lovely woman," Rathburn's mother said with a small smile. She hadn't actually smiled, not like she used to, in years. Not since his father had died. In fact, she still wore gray as if on the fringes of mourning. He hoped that once Hawthorne Manor was repaired, her smile might return. "While we don't often attend the same functions, when we've had the Danverses over to dinner, I've found them quite charming. Regardless, none of that matters. Oliver will be marrying Emma, not her parents."

His grip on the door handle froze. *Oliver will be marrying . . .* He'd never heard those words before and certainly never imagined that Emma's name would follow. He expected an icy flood of panic at any moment.

"He's marrying into her family as much as she is into ours," his grandmother interjected. "Their children will be a product of both houses, whether we like or not. Although there must be *someone* respectable in the line, or else Miss Danvers would not be here."

Their children. He waited for the swift dampness of his palms, or, in the very least, a headache.

Yet, as the minutes ticked by, he felt perfectly calm. The only sound he heard in the pause of conversation was the steady beating of his heart inside his chest. He wasn't sure what to make of that.

"Emma has merit on her own," his mother added smoothly. "Besides that, Oliver is fond of her. That should count for something."

He caught himself nodding in response to the statement,

as if it were a well-known fact. Of course, he was fond of her and her family. Yet, he couldn't help but notice how the way his mother had said it gave the words an entirely new meaning.

No. He shook his head. This was not how this was supposed to go. He'd come here for a purpose and then found himself lingering like a fool who didn't know his own mind.

"Merit enough for you and I, perhaps," his grandmother added. "However, that isn't to say he isn't using the poor girl to gain his inheritance."

"Mother!" His mother sent Emma a look of apology.

"It's all right," Emma said, not displaying an ounce of the panic he knew she must be feeling. "Lord Rathburn's interest left me suspect as well. At first." Perhaps only he noticed the slight tremble in her hands as she set her teacup and saucer on the table.

It was time to stop lingering in the shadows. He only hoped the right words would form on his lips that would save them both from certain disaster.

"He is quite my opposite in both appearance and unreservedness," she continued, without noticing that he'd opened the door to the gallery. "When he first approached my parents and then me with his intentions, I thought he was joking, playing a trick to tease me and see how gullible I was. However, those thoughts were more from my own insecurities than from his true self. Once I pushed those aside, I saw him clearly for the first time. He requires my company *because* I am his opposite, not despite it."

"So true," he announced, striding toward the group. Emma sounded downright convincing. Once he got them out of this, he would buy her a new pair of gloves. "She is the chain at my ankle that keeps me tethered to the earth. Hello, Grandmamma." He bowed formally and then leaned in to buss her papery cheek. "Mother." He repeated the action after stepping around the table. Then he simply smiled at Emma. "The incomparable Miss Danvers."

She blushed, granting him a poetic greeting without saying a word. A convincing response for their audience. Perhaps she deserved a new bonnet as well.

"A chain, did you say?" His grandmother chuckled. "You have the queerest way of complimenting your bride to be."

"Ah, but she understands me," he said as he exchanged a look with Emma, hoping she understood that there was still a way out of this. "As for her brother . . . well, that's another story." He cleared his throat and widened his eyes, certain that ought to plant the seed of discord.

Beside him, his grandmother ignored his efforts and lifted her hand to the servant standing near the door. "Make sure a formal announcement of my grandson and Miss Danvers's betrothal is in the *Post* in the morning. See if Saint George's is available four weeks from tomorrow."

"*Wait—*" he started to say, but the word stuck in his throat, scratching the flesh surrounding his vocal cords. He coughed in an effort to dislodge it, but before he could, it was already too late. The servant bowed and summarily disappeared through the doorway.

Emma went still, her gaze fixed on him. *Stop coughing and say something*, he could almost hear her saying.

Four weeks? He could hardly think. He thought he'd have at least two months of playacting ahead of him. Now, panic finally set in as he scrambled for what to say.

Perhaps, he could list a previous engagement. A . . . an appointment for throat surgery to get rid of his damnable cough. In an impatient gesture, he reached down for Emma's teacup and drained the last of it. Black tea with lemon, because his grandmother frowned upon sugar. He felt an odd twinge of sympathy as he swallowed the bitter brew. He'd done this to her, and now . . .

They were in this together.

"The perfect day for a wedding," he said in place of any other excuse. Besides, there was no tactful way to get out of it this instant. He would need to prepare a speech for his grandmother. In the meantime, they'd have to use a backup excuse. Set the stage for discord, or simply state that they still weren't certain they'd suit because . . . *Hell*, if she didn't have reservations regarding his character, she should. "I'm looking forward to it."

Emma swallowed. "As am I."

"Then why do you both look like you're ready to jump over a cliff and smash yourselves onto the rocks below?"

"Not at all," he said, concealing the sudden bubble of amusement that threatened to come out as a maniacal laugh. He was fairly certain Emma didn't find this the least bit funny. He thought of a quick excuse. "It's just . . . there's so much to be done. I'll . . . need to arrange a wedding trip."

Emma's gaze stayed with him, as if holding onto a lifeline. "There are so many things to consider. After all, I haven't even thought about a dress, or my maids of honor, or the flowers. Perhaps more time—"

"The dress!" His grandmother exclaimed, taking her pearl handled cane from the arm of the chair. "My dears, we must call upon Lady Valmont this instant. Her *modiste* makes the most remarkable gowns. Truly, Valmont wouldn't be half the rage she is if not for the way her clothes make her look. Abominable posture, you know."

His mother stood and rang for a carriage. He made the mistake of looking at her and seeing a true and genuine smile. His mother was happy about this wedding. Happier than he'd seen her in years. She lifted her gaze to his, and he saw her eyes glisten with unshed tears. In that moment, he knew he was doomed.

Only a fool would let her down.

As his mother and grandmother made their way to the door, Emma stood. "I hope you know what you're doing," she implored in a whisper.

He nodded by way of reassuring her. Yet, to himself he added, "So do I."

CHAPTER SIX

**The esteemed Dowager Duchess
of Heathcoat announces a much
anticipated and happy union . . .**

Emma stared at the morning's *Post*, and looked for any sign that this was indeed a mock betrothal. Unfortunately, it seemed far too real. After all, betrothal announcements rarely made it into the newspaper. No doubt, this would cause quite a stir. Not only was it staring baldly back at her, but it was worded in a way that gave every impression that the dowager had designed the match herself.

Now Her Grace's reputation was on the line as much as Emma's.

Briefly, she wondered if her parents would feel an ounce of guilt upon reading this. After all, they were part of the ruse and should—

The door to the morning room opened. Emma hastily tucked the copy between the cushions of the mauve loveseat.

She'd managed to swipe it from Parker before he ironed it, hoping no one else had seen it first. She didn't want the servants to know what a liar she was. After all, they knew Rathburn came over only to visit Rafe. His sudden interest in her must seem highly suspect.

Lucy placed a tray with a steaming pot of tea, a cut glass dish of biscuits and buttered scones, and a stack of flowered plates, along with several cups. Before she left, she bobbed. "Mrs. Newman expected you might have callers, Miss, considering the announcement in the *Post* and all. She also wanted me to offer congratulations from the entire staff."

Emma studied her expression, but surprisingly didn't find even a hint of astonishment. Hmm ... Perhaps the servants weren't as observant as she'd always assumed.

"Thank you, Lucy," Emma said, and questioned why she'd even bothered to hide the paper. The moment the door closed, she snatched it up, smoothing out the wrinkles and read it again.

She drew in a breath, hoping a gulp of air would chase away her sudden lightheadedness. What she wanted to do was go back to bed, close her eyes, and see if the next four weeks could pass quickly so this entire affair would be nothing but a memory. Unfortunately, she possessed enough sense to know avoidance wasn't a solution.

No sooner had she heard a knock on the door and tucked the paper beneath the cushion once more than the door opened. Penelope, Merribeth, and Delaney filed into the room. Without a word, they sat amongst the overstuffed chairs opposite the loveseat.

Oh, dear. One look at her friends told her that she wasn't the only one who awoke early and read the society pages. Though their expressions were carefully reserved—no doubt, a chastisement for not hearing the news firsthand—their eyes were bright and brimming with unfounded excitement.

"Good morning," she said, affecting a cheerful smile.

Merribeth withdrew a cutout from her reticule and placed it in the middle of the table. Emma knew without looking that it was the announcement of her engagement to Rathburn.

Her head went hazy again. What would she tell them? The entire truth was out of the question, since it pertained to Rathburn and his personal financial matter. Yet, she didn't want to lie to them either.

"You said nothing the other day. Not an inkling. Bree knew before I did," Delaney grumbled and reached forward to snatch a biscuit from the tray. "She came bounding into breakfast waving the paper madly. It thrilled her to no end to see the surprise on my face."

Emma felt ashamed. "I should have sent word to each of you. However, if it makes any difference, it surprised me, too. In fact, I'm still trying to decide how I feel about it."

"I don't know why any of you were surprised," Penelope added, grinning mysteriously as if she held the answer to the Sphinx's riddle. "It's been clear for ages how they feel about each other."

Emma stared at her friend as if she'd grown two heads. The only thing that could have been *clear for ages* regarding Rathburn was how much he strove to irritate her. She knew for a fact that she never said flattering things to her friends about him. She'd been careful not to make slightest mention of how his inappropriate flirting stirred her imagination.

After all, he was a notorious rake—or at least he *had* been—and any sensible woman knew not to lose her head over a smooth-tongued devil.

"You're joking," Delaney said, taking the words out of Emma's mouth. "I didn't have a clue, and I don't feel like a dunderhead admitting it either. I always thought Emma disapproved of Rathburn and his reputation."

She nodded, opening her mouth to respond, but Merribeth spoke first while brushing the crumbs from her lap. "Of course, he's vowed to change all that. He must have, otherwise Emma would never have accepted him. It's quite romantic if you think about it."

Romantic? Hardly. But she couldn't come out and tell them the circumstances. After all, word must never get back to the dowager or this entire charade would be for naught.

Now, they were all waiting for her to speak, gazes glued to her.

"Tell us what it was like," Merribeth said on a wistful sigh. "Did he ask your father first?"

At least with this, she could tell the truth. "He spoke with both my parents. And then they called me into the study."

Delaney took a biscuit. "Were you surprised?"

That was putting it mildly. "Oh, yes. For the life of me, I couldn't fathom why they were all together, watching me carefully as if I might suddenly break out into song."

"And then . . ." Merribeth had stars in her eyes. *Oh, if she only knew the truth.*

"Then, my father spoke and stated the reason for Rathburn's visit." She drew a breath, feeling her pulse rise as if it was happening all over again. "I could hardly believe it."

Penelope tutted. "Oh, come now, you must have suspected something. Especially with the way he looks at you."

She shrugged. "He looks at every woman that way." *As if he were slowly peeling off the layers of their clothing with his eyes,* she thought crossly.

"Not the way he looks at you."

Again, she stared at Penelope in complete disbelief. "He's a terrible flirt."

"True. He does have a way of offering a compliment that makes one feel . . . exposed." Merribeth blushed but received a nod from Delaney.

Even Penelope laughed. "But he's easily forgiven when it's obvious he isn't serious. Not like the way he is with Emma."

Emma shook her head. Because of the announcement, they were seeing things that simply weren't true. "He likes the game. The play of back and forth."

"Now that I think on it, when he teases and flirts with you, his entire demeanor changes," Merribeth said as she took a chocolate biscuit and nibbled the outer rim. "He turns serious."

"I would say predatory," Delaney added in a scholarly tone, as if the notion had been hers from the beginning.

"Or maybe possessive."

"Oh, yes," Merribeth agreed with Penelope's statement. "That is the perfect description. After all, he kept away your other suitors last Season."

A fact for which Emma would not soon forgive him. "That was Rafe's fault for asking Rathburn to look after me while he was away. He simply took matters too far by hovering over me at every ball." And glowering at every gentleman who came near.

"That's when he introduced you to the dowager." Delaney tapped her finger against the side of her mouth thoughtfully. "He was laying the foundation to build on later."

"No. It was to keep me occupied and on edge so that he had the freedom to flirt with other ladies."

She received three headshakes. "Surely, you can no longer deny it now. He must have expressed how he truly feels about you when he proposed."

Emma hesitated. She hated lying to her friends, so the only thing she could do was focus on what actually happened. "He did say that his grandmother approves of me."

Her friends gasped in unison. "The dowager . . ."

"Approves of you."

"Of course she would." Penelope leaned forward and squeezed her hand. "You could see it plainly in the announcement."

"She doesn't approve of anyone," Merribeth added in an awed voice as if she'd taken a sip of the elixir of life instead of tepid tea. "That only means one thing."

"He's completely in love with you."

"I wouldn't say that," Emma said, swallowing down a sudden rise of nerves. Her friends were sure to be heartbroken once their false betrothal was over and they knew the truth.

"Has he tried to kiss you?"

Leave it to Merribeth to turn this into a romantic saga. Nonetheless, Emma blushed furiously.

"More than tried, I'd say," Delaney snickered.

"What was it like? Was he swept away in the moment? Were you?"

"Certainly not," she lied. "It was a mere formality to seal our bargain."

"A woman does not kiss and tell when it comes to her husband, ladies," Penelope added with a secret smile of her own. "Besides, whatever is between Rathburn and Emma, you'll witness at the Dorsets' ball."

The three women nodded, as if the knowledge were a common fact. "Nothing will happen at the ball. I've more sense than that."

"Have you danced with Rathburn?" Penelope already knew the answer. They all knew the answer, but Emma humored them with a shake of her head. Her newly married friend toyed with the fringe of her shawl. "Dancing changes everything."

She mulled it over and made a quick decision to avoid dancing with Rathburn at all costs.

"Too bad there won't be any dancing at the musicale this evening," Delaney said with a wink. "Do you know what you're going to wear?"

Emma's nerves were still focused on what Penelope had said about dancing and didn't give much thought to the question. "The fawn evening gown, I suppose."

"The plain one with the brown sash?" Merribeth wrinkled her nose in distaste.

Emma considered the sash more of a russet, not that it mattered. "Then the cream one with the lace filigree at the neck and sleeves."

"Oh, that one is lovely." Penelope reached for the last biscuit on the plate.

"Yes, but is it enough? After all, she's essentially making her debut as Rathburn's viscountess."

"Delaney is right," Merribeth added. "What about pairing it with that beaded ivory shawl you wore at the end of last Season?"

Emma looked at her friends, grateful for the distraction from her previous thoughts. "I could wear my hair in a Grecian knot."

"And your mother's emeralds, to match Rathburn's eyes." Merribeth sighed and they all laughed.

At least with this entire courtship being make believe, she could allow herself to be immersed in the fun of it. But heaven help her if she started to prefer this lie over the truth.

Rathburn knew instantly that something was different that evening. He felt it keenly at the base of his skull, a sharp sense of awareness that made everything seem slightly foreign.

He'd been to the Sumpters' musicale in years past, usually attending as escort to his mother. Yet, even then he couldn't quite remember so many nods in his direction. Not to mention—*Wait*. Did his uncle, the esteemed Duke of Heathcoat, incline his head in approval?

He shook himself. Surely not.

It seemed strange that a single announcement in the *Post* could spawn this. That words printed on a page could make every expression, every sound, every scent seemed more vivid than ever before. He felt as if he were truly living in the moment, present in his skin, not focusing on the future and the list of objectives he had to complete in order to get there.

He liked this sensation even less than yesterday's anxiety.

With Emma by his side, he stepped into the music

room. The Sumpters' musicale was a popular event, one of the first in the Season. The large room opened into the parlor through a set of pocket doors. Aside from the rows of chairs down the center of both rooms, upholstered settees and loveseats were positioned on the fringes of the room and angled toward the musicians. He was fortunate enough to procure a loveseat at the back of the parlor for himself and Emma.

Taking their seats a moment before the music began, Rathburn drew in a breath.

Instantly, he stilled. Something was definitely different.

For starters, he'd never thought a spray of tiny white flowers would bring him to his knees. Or else, he never would have sent them in the first place. Now, he couldn't stop thinking of them, or wanting to pluck them from where they rested in Emma's hair.

Emma glanced up at him from beneath her lashes. "Is something amiss?" Her whispered words blended in with the first strains of violin and cello, but they were seated in close enough proximity that he could hear her plainly. Close enough to catch the sweet scent of jasmine perfuming the air around her.

"No," he said, shifting in his seat. "Nothing. It's just that . . . you're quite lovely this evening."

When he'd arranged for the flowers to be delivered to her earlier, he'd done so as a lark, playing his part of the besotted beau mostly out of the need to rile her. Their verbal parries always served to brighten his mood. He'd been certain that by the time he saw her this evening, she'd have daggers at the ready. He assumed she'd have tossed the flowers into the bin and prepared to give him an earful. Or, at the most, accept them blandly and put them into a vase.

He never thought she'd wear them.

To make matters worse, she'd fashioned her hair in a stylish mass of curls drawn up from the nape of her neck, and in a spill of rich, glossy tresses over one shoulder. Besting him at his own game, she'd woven the flowers into her hair with the last little buds nestled in the curls against the curve of her breast.

Now, he couldn't stop thinking about jasmine and her. Mostly her. Of how her lips tasted of jasmine tea, and how lovely she would look on a bed of white flowers, her dark hair spread out over the coverlet, her body bared to him . . .

She frowned, the flesh between her brows puckering. "Then why do you look as if you're in pain?"

He laid the program for this evening's music on his lap, hoping no one would notice swell of his erection in his form-fitting evening clothes. He didn't know what had come over him, or why everything seemed so alive and new to him. This foreign sensation was overriding the semblance of better judgment he'd adopted these past years.

He only knew one cure for it . . . to unsettle Emma as well. After all, she was too cool and calm, taking all this in stride as if certain of how it would end. Damn it all, but she gave every appearance of trusting him.

"If you must know, I was contemplating whether I would prefer cups of chocolate or jasmine flowers on a rainy morning." Flirting was good, he told himself. It was a behavior he knew better than breathing. Right now, he even needed a reminder on how to do that.

Catching his meaning, she blushed. Quite prettily, as a matter of fact, and looked askance to ensure their conversation was private. "You mean jasmine *tea*, surely."

"Do I?" Rathburn couldn't help it. He lifted his hand and plucked one of the blossoms from the spot just below her ear and lifted it to his nose.

Emma's lips parted and she looked every inch the innocent miss about to be embroiled in scandal. She went so far as to place her gloved hand over his forearm, forcing him to lower the flower. "That is hardly necessary."

He looked down at the way her slender fingers curled over the sleeve of his slate gray, superfine jacket. He even imagined he could feel the heat of her hand, and that she held on to him for a moment longer than was proper before she released him and clasped both hands in her lap. "Necessary?"

"Your flirtation ... this pretense ..." She gestured between them.

"Ah." He grinned, enjoying the way her teeth pulled on the corner of her mouth when she was flustered. Withdrawing a handkerchief from the inner pocket of his jacket, he carefully tucked the blossom into the folds. Then, simply to raise her ire, he pressed it to his lips and winked at her before he returned the handkerchief to his pocket. "You're mistaken."

On a huff, she turned forward and stared straight ahead at the musicians. "Hardly."

Yes, this was much better. After all, flirting came second nature to him. He felt more like himself. In fact, if he continued like this, he might even manage to convince himself that everything was the same between them.

Placing his hand on the cushion, he pressed down just

enough to cause her to lean toward him. Her shoulder brushed his. He lowered his head and drew in a breath, filling his nostrils with the warm, sweet scented air surrounding her. "The necessity of my actions is not for their benefit, but for mine. You see, it's taking every ounce of control I have not to kiss you. Right here. In front of everyone."

The truth of his words startled him. Yet, weren't all flirtations based on a semblance of truth? *Of course they were*, he convinced himself quite readily.

Still, he never knew how much he'd enjoy telling the truth until he met Emma Danvers. If he were honest with himself—a terrible occupation he'd begun recently—he'd been disguising his truth behind bold comments, and passing them off as mere flirtations for years.

She slid an inch away from him and he eased the pressure on the cushion so she wouldn't go too far. He liked feeling her pressed against him. Even though it was only her shoulder, he could easily imagine something far more intimate.

"Keep in mind that kissing me would not help your cause," she warned, though her words had gone breathless, likely revealing more than she intended.

He pondered her statement, and after a moment, he could find no downside. "How so?"

"Think of the scandal."

His gloved finger strayed to the fabric of her gown resting between them. "You mean that, should anyone seated in front of us turn around and discover us, we would be forced to wed."

She looked down, following the sweeping motion of his finger for a moment before she pulled the fabric away and smoothed it over her thighs. "Precisely."

His gaze lingered on the shape of her legs discernible beneath the creamy silk. They were long and slender. Just above her finely sloped knees, he could see the faint outline of the ribbons that tied her stockings. It seemed far too intimate a thing to notice of Danvers's sister—even for him. Yet, he felt his heart beat heavy and hard, trying to reclaim all the blood that was now pooling in his groin.

"Forced to wed in haste, no doubt." Forced to wed in truth, and with no hope of an annulment afterward without irreparably tarnishing her reputation. Something he'd vowed not to do. He kept his promises. Just like he'd promised his father that Hawthorne Manor would be a home again.

Oddly enough, the threat of a wedding—and an early one at that—didn't send icy shivers through him. Before now, he'd never given marriage much thought. His goals were set, after all. First, he needed the money to finish the manor and the hospital and then . . .

Well, he supposed he would marry eventually. After all, in order for Hawthorne Manor to become a home once again, presumably a family—or more specifically, *his* family—would live there. In that regard, marriage seemed the most likely outcome.

A thought blossomed suddenly, as if sprouting from a randomly planted seedling.

He looked at Emma again, watching the way her expression altered with the music as if she were seeing something within each note. He was seeing something, too. Only not in the music.

Rathbun knew from speaking with her parents the other day that she hadn't formed an attachment with another man.

He'd wanted to ensure his plan didn't interfere with any of hers. Last Season, he hadn't even seen her dance with a single gentleman. Of course, he might have had a hand in that. However, at the time, he'd felt it was his duty. After all, her brother had asked him to look after her.

Now, with Rafe away again, he was still looking after her. Only it was different now. Much different.

What if . . . he heard a voice say in the back of his mind as the seedling idea strained against the confines of its husk, stretching out with the solitary tendril of a root.

"I know what you're doing," she said quietly, refusing to look at him. "It won't work this time, so you might as well give up."

"What am I doing, Emma-*mine?*"

"Wooing me. Flirting with me to get your way—though I can't think of what else you could want in addition to my agreement to your scheme." She responded to his low chuckle by glaring at him. "You seem to think that I agreed to this because I imagined myself half in love with you. I know better. Only a fool would lose her head over you."

He studied her intently, hearing the truth of her words, which sparked a question within him. Why *had* she agreed to his scheme?

If there was some truth in flirting, then there might very well be truth in denial as well.

He grinned, at last beginning to understand why everything seemed so different this evening. Because it *was* different. "I don't want you to lose your head over me. I quite like it right where it is, blazing chocolate eyes, jasmine-laced lips, and all."

What if . . . the voice whispered again. *What if . . . she could be mine?*

The thought came unbidden to the forefront of his mind, causing him to draw in a startled breath. The scent of jasmine filled his nostrils, and suddenly he didn't know why he hadn't thought of this before.

CHAPTER SEVEN

Penelope pointed to a stone bench just off the park's walking path. "That looks like a fine place out of the sun. Perhaps I should have brought a parasol after all. No doubt Mr. Weatherstone will love that he was right."

"Surely, there's no need to tell him," Emma said with a sly grin. She'd left her parasol behind as well, not expecting the gray morning clouds to disappear so suddenly. On such a fine day, the park was fairly bursting with people enjoying the sunshine.

"If there's one thing about marriage you will soon learn," Penelope began with a secret smile of her own, "it's that one chooses the moments to allow one's spouse to be right. In such an instance, Mr. Weatherstone gains the pleasure of being right about my parasol, while I will gain the satisfaction of having him fuss over me later. He's positively obsessed with my freckles."

Emma tilted her head to the side and studied the wistful look on her friend's face. "You actually enjoy it when he fusses over you?" It sounded suffocating. She couldn't help but think of how annoying it had been when Rathburn's overbearing presence had chased away all of her suitors last year.

No, she most definitely would not like her future spouse, whoever he may be, to hover and bother her. As if in direct response to her thoughts of potential suitors, Lord Mabry and Lord Hutchings passed by, both lifting their hats and smiling in greeting as they passed. She couldn't recall having ever earned their attentions after being introduced during her debut, and so merely offered her own smile in return. *How odd.*

"Not always, I assure you," Penelope added with a small laugh that pulled Emma back to their conversation. "Let's just say there are certain perks to being married that I did not appreciate when it seemed Mr. Weatherstone and I were destined to remain friends and *only* friends."

Only friends. As in, not lovers. She felt spots of heat climb to her cheeks as she took in Penelope's meaning. "Marriage agrees with you. I've never seen you so happy."

"I never expected to be so happy. And to think, we'll have a child before Guy Fawkes Day." Briefly, she rested a hand over her still slender middle. "I can't wait for you to find your happiness with Rathburn."

Emma looked away, guilt gnawing at her over the deception. Another gentleman passed by, using the silver handle of his walking stick to tip his hat. Though she didn't recognize him, she offered the same smile as she had to the other two gentlemen before he walked on.

"And after last night, your betrothal is being touted as the grand romance of the Season."

She'd seen the mention of *Viscount R—* stealing a flower

from *Miss D—'s* hair in the gossip column this morning. Clearly, it had been a grievous error to make a single alteration to her usual appearance. Yet, receiving the flowers had thrilled her so much that she'd been inspired to wear them. Only Rathburn would dare such a bold flirtation. By sending a bouquet of jasmine flowers, not only did he remind her of their kiss, but he also admitted that he hadn't forgotten it either. He'd meant to unsettle her, she was certain. However, she'd been so pleased knowing their kiss had lingered with him that she'd suffered a romantic notion to weave those tiny white sprigs into her coiffure.

Now, she only hoped the dowager wouldn't think her too flamboyant. Of course, last night she'd seemed to approve, but with the mention in the paper, she might revise her original opinion.

"All because Rathburn is an outrageous flirt," she grumbled. Didn't he realize how his behavior might put his scheme in jeopardy? "I don't see how his actions caused any difference this year as opposed to any other year. He's always flouted propriety. I'm surprised he's allowed in society at all."

"There are a good many flaws the *ton* is willing to overlook when one has a title and one's uncle is a duke."

A fact she knew only too well. If her father had been the son of a duke instead of the third son of a baron, he might never have received the *cut direct*.

And she might already be married and therefore unable to aid Rathburn in his scheme.

Her heart sank as she thought about their deception. "Oh, Penelope, it isn't what you think," Emma said, suddenly unable to bear the burden of this lie any longer. "I know I'm not supposed to say anything, but I just have to tell someone."

Her friend smiled and squeezed her hand. "That you agreed to marry Rathburn so he could gain his inheritance?"

"Yes." She blinked and closed her mouth before her expression drew attention. "How did you know?" She drew out a folded piece of paper from her reticule and handed it to Emma. "I found this on Mr. Weatherstone's desk and forced him to explain it to me."

It was a carefully crafted list, labeling Rathburn's most pertinent problem and cataloging possible solutions. "It seems that he went over every possible option before making his decision to engage in a mock courtship with me. My name is at the very bottom of the page." Why that stung, she had no clue.

"My dear, you're looking at it all wrong. Don't you see how everything points to you?" When she shook her head, Penelope sighed. "Don't you see that yours is the *only* name on the page? Surely, that must tell you something quite profound."

"All it tells me is that he has a single-minded determination to gain his inheritance." Once he had it, he'd no longer see her as any sort of option. Not that it bothered her. It was just . . . she was beginning to wonder, and not for the first time, how she would manage to escape this mock betrothal unscathed. Because, while she professed to disapprove of Rathburn, that wasn't entirely accurate. In fact, the truth was far more complicated than she cared to think about.

Reputation notwithstanding, she was actually beginning to worry about her heart.

"Or perhaps the inheritance is simply an excuse, and his single-minded determination has everything to do with you."

"Penelope Weatherstone," Emma tsked. "It's quite obvious marriage has gone to your head."

She beamed, her eyes dancing. "Just wait. It will happen to you too."

A shadow crossed them, causing her to look up.

"What will happen to Miss Danvers?" Rathburn asked.

Emma started. How long had he been standing there? He nearly grinned at her as if he were savoring an amusing secret. The gold flecks in his green eyes seemed to capture the brightness of the sun, especially when he glanced down to her mouth. Perhaps it was her imagination, but his gaze lingered long enough for her to feel the warmth of it. He seemed quite determined to make Penelope and everyone in the park believe this mock courtship of theirs.

Thankfully, Penelope kept her wits. She surreptitiously plucked the paper out of Emma's grasp and refolded it before hiding in her reticule once again. "We were just speaking of felicitations in marriage."

He leaned forward and took Emma's hand, lifting it to his lips. "What a coincidence. My mind was similarly engaged."

Emma snapped out of her momentary sun blindness when her eyes threatened to roll to the back of her head. He was terribly good at pretending. She must remember that in the future. "There is no need to keep up pretenses in front of Penelope. She knows about our bargain."

Rathburn didn't blink an eye but kept his charm at full potency. He tugged her to her feet and chuckled when she was forced to place her hand against his solid chest or crash into him. "Your eagerness to end this pretense is admirable, darling," he teased, whispering low into her ear. Then he backed away before she had the chance to swat him. "However, I sought you out for a perfectly innocent proposal."

Innocent, Rathburn? Certainly not. "Dare I ask?"

Rathburn had never been so nervous in all his life. There was no accounting for it, really. He'd had workers here for two years. His two closest friends, Weatherstone and Danvers, had both stopped by on occasion. Even Gabriel, his fellow ne'er-do-well cousin had shown up, needing a place to hide out from his father, the austere Duke of Heathcoat. And yet, this was somehow different.

Now, Weatherstone's wife and Danvers's sister were about to see it. Or, more to the heart of the matter, this was the first time *Emma* would see the work he'd had done.

Her opinion mattered to him. So much so that his palms were slick with sweat beneath his driving gloves. He pulled them off with his teeth as he drove the curricle up the long driveway to Hawthorne Manor.

He blamed that kiss and those flowers. Ever since the Sumpters' musicale, he couldn't shake loose the seedling idea. The damned thing had taken root. *What if . . .* kept turning around in his mind, occupying his thoughts.

What if he married Emma Danvers?

With an actual marriage, at least his wayward thoughts would end in an honorable result. Surely, her brother could credit him for that and not slay him at dawn in a field of honor.

Marrying Emma Danvers would certainly be simpler

than plotting an end to their betrothal and fabricating a story to back it up while still remaining friends. Not to mention, much easier than getting an annulment after they were married. And . . .

She could be his.

The idea appealed to him.

Now, it was a matter of seeing if Emma felt the same.

He looked ahead, mulling over his options as the house came into view. Only the rear wing had been destroyed by fire, leaving the front much the same as it always was. The russet brick structure was three generous stories high, with rows of tall, mullioned windows topped with fanlights and trimmed in white stone. Gothic arched dormers jutted from the dark slate roof, matching the dramatic arch over the wide doorway. Single-story structures banked either side of the house. Encased with even more windows, they acted primarily as a conservatory and an orangery. Cobblestones lined the driveway and circled around the reflecting pond in front.

From this vantage point, the rear of the house wasn't visible. Even though the manor wasn't entirely finished, the main structure had been repaired, the brickwork done, the windows in place, the interior walls coated with smooth plaster.

"It's lovely," Penelope said quietly.

It was the first thing anyone had said since the house came into view. With his nerves so high, he hadn't noticed the still reverence that seemed to settle over them. Rathburn had been here nearly every day during the past three years, and so he'd grown used to seeing it. Used to remembering the awful night of the fire.

Occasionally, he still had nightmares.

Yet, for the most part, he'd come to terms with the loss of his father, knowing with every fiber of his being that his father would not want Hawthorne Manor to remain a shrine. Growing up, he'd had so many happy memories among these walls, he was certain they were lingering here, waiting to be rediscovered. His father had worked tirelessly to ensure Hawthorne Manor's longevity, and to bail the family title out of debt. Rathburn knew from the first that his father would want him to repair it, to live here with his own family and start again. Perhaps then, he could begin to make amends for the life he'd led.

"I've always thought it the finest of houses," Emma said as he slowed the horses to a stop and set the brake. When she turned her gaze from the house, he saw beneath the brim of her caramel-colored bonnet to the tender apprehension in her warm brown eyes.

"Then, perhaps, you'll help me make it that way again."

Startled, she lifted her face, her expression more alarmed than pleased. "Your wife will want that honor, I'm sure."

Before he could offer an outrageously bold comment about how she might want to get used to the idea, one of his footmen came out to assist Penelope to the ground. For now, Rathburn held his tongue and hopped down.

Not wanting to miss out on the opportunity to assist Emma, he took her hand. She looked over her shoulder to where Penelope was descending with the aid of Harrison and the step. However, Rathburn tugged Emma out of the seat and slipped his hands to her slender waist, lifting her cleanly out of the curricle to stand her before him.

"You are right, of course," he said with the pretense of responding to her comment. In actuality, he merely wanted the excuse to keep her near. A moment longer to keep his hands on her waist, just above the subtle flair of her hips.

Until this moment, he'd never had confirmation of her shape. They'd never danced. She wore the usual style of dress that young women preferred—high-waisted and made of muslin or silk or whatnot, conformed to fit the bosom.

In that regard, he'd admired Emma's figure on a multitude of occasions. Her breasts were quite perfect, round and supple, teasing him with the barest hint of her décolletage in her evening gowns. Now, beneath her dress and spencer, the luscious objects of his admiration were rising and falling with her quick breaths. Yet, Emma was modest to a fault, and she wore a frustratingly sturdy petticoat that kept errant breezes from outlining her form.

However, he kept his hands on her. His thumbs rested just inside the gentle slope of her hips. Unable and unwilling to help himself, he traced the top portion of the angled feminine bones, the likes of which he was quite familiar with on other women. On Emma, this was new territory, an adventure of pure pleasure, traversing over the flesh that was hidden beneath layers of fabric. He could feel the enticing heat of her body seep through his fingers.

It occurred to him that she'd made no move to retreat. She gave no indication of displeasure at being so near, of having his hands on her. Instead, her gaze traveled up from the buttons of his waistcoat, to the pin in his cravat, and then finally to his mouth.

She licked her lips. "You were saying?"

Her voice came out as a breath and the sweetness rose to

greet him, intoxicating him for a moment, and giving him the foolish thought of lowering his head, of kissing her in front of Penelope, Harrison, and the other members of his staff peering out the windows—and even that didn't deter him.

Yet, before he could, the horses snorted and whickered as if they were laughing at him for losing his head. And rightfully so.

Rathburn lowered his hands and took a step back. Clearing his throat, he forced himself to look anywhere but at Emma's tempting lips. "I would like your opinion, all the same."

"Of course," she said, albeit a little breathlessly. She looked marginally relieved, which didn't sit well with him. "You know me well enough to believe I wouldn't be able to withhold it regardless."

Her laugh sounded a bit forced, making him want to put her at ease again. He offered his arm. "True enough. Perhaps you would even grant your bold opinion on my garden."

This time, her laugh came easier, and he was glad for the pleasant sound humming through his ears. "I should love nothing more."

CHAPTER EIGHT

Since this was Penelope's first visit to Hawthorne Manor, Rathburn first led them through the old portion of the house that hadn't been touched by the fire. It was much unchanged since Emma had last seen it. The rooms were still elegantly furnished, with windows aplenty to fill each space with light.

Her mother would probably want to convert the entire first floor into a studio.

Never mind the beautiful oil paintings on the wall, the rosewood and marble tables, the luxuriant carpet and upholstered furniture, or the plaster moldings that lined the ceilings, doors, and windows. No, her mother would barge in one day, proclaiming that her muse must not be denied and then pile everything into a corner and drape a sheet over it.

Emma shuddered at the thought. She was actually worried about it, until she remembered that this wasn't going to be her home. She wasn't going to marry Rathburn, and therefore needn't be concerned.

She waited for relief to settle her sudden rise of nerves, but she felt a peculiar tightness in her chest instead. If she didn't know herself better, she'd almost believe it was disappointment.

Thankfully, she knew herself better. Most likely, the sensation came from indigestion from the roasted nuts she and Penelope had shared in the park.

"Are you unwell?" Rathburn asked, keeping his voice low as if not wanting to disturb Penelope, who was studying the woodland painting of Rathburn's hunting box in Scotland over the library's fireplace.

The tightness returned with another twinge as she looked up into his face and saw his friendly concern. "Perfectly well. I was just imagining how my mother would want to convert each of the front rooms into an artist's studio," she said with a forced laugh.

"Now I feel unwell." He made a show of shuddering, drawing out a genuine smile from her lips. "Do you think, perhaps, we could offer her a room on the second floor instead? I'm certain we could discover one that no one ever uses."

"Oh, it would all depend on the light," she added with a dramatic flip of her wrist. And actually, the light in here *was* perfect. Not to mention the view from the windows of the lush, rolling hills that led to the copse of trees bordering his property. She felt her hand twitch, suddenly feeling empty without a brush within it or a canvas before her.

Emma shook herself from the notion. She'd vowed years ago not to let those impulses rule her. After all, members of society must rise above them or risk the *cut direct*. "Thankfully, this won't ever be a problem we'll have."

"How so?"

She blinked. "Because we aren't actually getting married, Rathburn."

"Ah, yes," he added with a chuckle and reached out to brush the backs of his fingers against her cheek as if to tame an errant lock of hair. "I keep forgetting."

Every time he touched her, thoughts scattered like charcoal dust from a sketchbook. Her vision went hazy. All senses arrested on the place his flesh touched hers. The same way it had when his hands had lingered on her hips after he'd assisted her down from his curricle. It took a great deal of effort to remind herself that this was all a pretense for Rathburn, and that he was exceedingly skilled at flirtation.

She took a step apart from him and adjusted her glove. "Well . . . don't."

"I can't make any promises." He offered a rakish grin as he inclined his head. "Would you like to see the kitchens now? I've a sudden need to put something in my mouth."

Flustered, but not wanting to let on, she nodded and hoped her cheeks weren't as pink as they suddenly felt.

The three of them walked through the older portion of the house and into the new. It was a seamless transition. If she hadn't been here before, she wouldn't have noticed. The only difference was the walls. They were plastered, but not painted. Of course, there were no art or furnishings either. Yet, the floors were a perfect match in color and grain.

From the corner of her eye, she noted that Rathburn glanced over at her once they entered. She felt that tightness in her chest again and realized, quite unexpectedly, that it wasn't disappointment or indigestion at all. It was longing.

Oh dear. On one hand, she felt sad that he'd lost his father in the terrible fire. She also felt a mixture of sadness and pride at the fact that he'd done all this on his own for the past three years. But most of all, she longed to . . . undo the tragedy from his life. To return everything he'd lost. Every hope, dream, and most important, his family.

Her useless musings faded into the back of her mind as they entered the kitchen. The sweet fragrance of oranges filled the air. The room was immense, lined with polished wood countertops, a wide porcelain sink, a massive black oven with three chimney vents through the wall. Shiny copper pots and pans hung from hooks in the ceiling, and an enormous work-table, topped with rows of marmalade jars, filled the center of the room.

When one of the maids let out a chirrup at having spotted them, Rathburn took the opportunity to introduced Emma and Penelope to the cook and five kitchen maids before they returned to their tasks.

"The kitchen is further out from the house, compared to the original structure," he continued, leading them away from the kitchen and pointing to the hall that led to the house-keeper's and butler's offices. Since the fire had started there, it made perfect sense. "I wanted the main portion to be a single story, but still linked by those stairs to the main house, with the dining room nearby."

Emma glanced over her shoulder to where he was point-ing and all the breath left her body. She stared, stock still, at an endless row of red fire pails hanging along the wall. *Oh, Rathburn,* she sighed silently, her heart aching for him. Tears stung her eyes. It took every ounce of strength she possessed not to start crying.

She hid her face as he began to talk about the plumbing he'd installed in the house. Although she'd nodded at the appropriate times, she couldn't stop thinking about the fire pails. Looking at him, she saw how brave he was, how proud he was. Yet there was still a sharp sadness in his gaze as he talked about the new improvements and the safety precautions.

Her heart ached for him as they made their way upstairs to the family quarters, half of which had been destroyed by the fire. Rathburn must have sent Harrison to dismiss the crew working up here, because tools and pails were scattered over the floor. These rooms were more barren than those downstairs. Not all the plaster had been completed, or the moldings or trim; the floors hadn't yet been stained to match the rest of the house. They were just big, empty rooms, emphasizing the great loss even more. Yet, if it hadn't been for Oliver, his father, and Archie Smith—one of the footmen—the entire family as well as the servants would have perished.

The thought sliced through her veins like ice water. So, how could she not applaud Rathburn for his work and improvements? He'd done an outstanding job, turning Hawthorne Manor back into a home—or nearly so.

She wished she could get a sense of this new structure, feel the happy memories that used to reside here. They were near, she was sure, lurking in the breeze that came in through the open windows. Waiting for just the right moment to fill the emptiness once again.

Emma decided then and there that pretense or not, she was going to speak with Rathburn about furnishing and decorating the rooms when the time was right. Which wasn't now when she was so close to tears and the peculiar need to comfort him.

In the hall, Rathburn went to the wide panels that framed the doorway to the master bedchamber. "These hinged panels will all blend into the wall once the work is complete," he said as he opened one, revealing a vertical row of fire pails hanging in the hidden compartment.

Emma looked down the length of the hall and saw similar framing outside of each bedchamber. She exchanged a look with Penelope and saw sympathy for Rathburn in her friend's gaze. While he seemed pleased with the additions, he also looked lost—he'd done all this but was still unable to go back in time to save his father. It took all of her willpower not to reach out and take his hand, offering her support. And also to let him know that he would never have to suffer that kind of loss or pain again.

If only she could promise such a thing.

"This is the viscountess's suite," he said, gesturing through the open door for them to precede him. A tingle of awareness brushed down her flesh as she passed him. "My wife's chamber."

She swallowed. His voice, so low and deep, made her forget everything else she'd been thinking for the past hour. Even though the breeze was cool, she felt flushed and too warm. It sounded more like an invitation than a statement.

"Your wife, who will not be me," she clarified, needing to feel a sense of certainty.

Rathburn grinned. If she didn't know any better, she'd almost believe he meant it as a challenge. Or even more so, a dare.

She stepped past him, not allowing herself to be drawn in by his flirtations. They'd made a bargain. Had shaken hands on it. Had even sealed it with a kiss . . .

She let out a slow breath. No, she was not going to think about that kiss again.

As he passed, he ran the tip of his finger down the back of her arm. Through her sleeve, she could feel the heat of it. *Of him*. Her vision went hazy again. Convincing herself that he was merely flirting was getting more difficult, especially when she realized how much she wished he wasn't.

"Between the rooms," he said, returning to his tour master duties. "Just beyond the dressing rooms, is my favorite new addition."

They followed him, only to pause on the threshold. Both Penelope and Emma gasped, stunned. Creamy marbled tiles covered the expansive floor. In the center of the room sat an enormous claw-foot bathtub. A bathing chamber as large as her sitting room at home.

"Did you ever see such a thing?" Penelope was the first to respond, walking to the tub to trail her fingertips over the curved rim. She looked over her shoulder at Emma and laughed. "I'd never leave."

"You wouldn't have to," Rathburn said with pride as he demonstrated the faucet. "Cold water at your fingertips. A drain at the bottom that extends to the garden. A dumb-waiter for hot water. Every possible convenience."

"No more lugging the water up the stairs?" A job Emma had done for herself a time or two when she hadn't wanted to disturb the servants her parents were using as models.

Rathburn smiled again, pleased. "No."

A current seemed to pass between them, a level of expectation coursing through the air. It made her feel ... foreign. Not quite herself. Almost as if there were suddenly a separate person inside of her, trying to get out. The same person, she suspected, who had imagined him calling her his wife a moment ago.

The real Emma wanted to escape the sensation as soon as she could. "Was that a sitting room I spied across the hall?"

Both Rathburn and Penelope looked at her peculiarly. She didn't bother to explain. She just needed to get out of there.

It took Emma a few moments before she felt more like herself. It was easy enough for her to accept Rathburn's part, since he was forever teasing her merely to test her reaction. However, it was exceedingly difficult to tuck her own responses away into that part of her she'd cultivated for the sake of society's acceptance. She'd learned early on that acceptance was the key to the life she wanted.

She didn't want to be whispered about behind open fans, as her parents were. She didn't want her children to be looked at with pity and speculation. She didn't want to be judged and found wanting.

She wanted ... normal. Mastering the skills of decorum, polite conversation, dressing in a manner not to attract notice, and resisting less conventional urges kept one from being the object of scrutiny. Yet, Rathburn made her want to abandon decorum, dress in a manner to attract *his* notice, and give in ...

Emma felt it building within her more and more lately, seeking a way out. She was ashamed to admit that she hadn't resisted every unacceptable behavior. Beneath her gloves, she knew she still had a spot of crimson paint as proof, marking her.

Her greatest secret, and most detrimental flaw.

She took a breath and inhaled the fragrant cool air. Soon enough, this farce would end. This pretense of affection would cease testing her will. Rathburn would gain his inheritance, and she would return to seeking the well-grounded husband she required.

Emma knew he appreciated that she'd agreed to his bargain. Admittedly, she was actually pleased he'd come to her for help. Because she wanted to help him. That's what friends did, after all. Besides, the only reason he'd asked for her assistance was because he could trust her not to get carried away with the notion of marrying him.

In addition, if the friendly smiles from other gentlemen in the park were any indication, she would be able to make a true and solid match by the end of the Season. She must keep her mind on more prudent thoughts.

She curled her hands over the railing of the second-story balcony. From the sitting room, the view of the vast pleasure garden was similar to the one from the viscountess's suite across the hall. The fire had destroyed the tall row of boxwood hedges that lay near the crushed clay path. Yet, beyond the charred and barren stubs of branches, bright golden daffodils and red, orange, and violet tulips colored the landscape. New green shoots on trees and shrubs, along with even more-vibrant buds, were waiting to emerge. In a week or two, a full regalia of bright colors would beckon her.

Only now, in this quiet moment, with the soft breezes

toying with the ribbons of her bonnet, did she admit that she longed to return and witness the splendor for herself.

"It's beautiful," she said.

"I'm glad you like it," Rathburn said from over her shoulder.

This time, she didn't start at the sound of his voice. Instead, she felt her lips curve. Now that she managed to rationalize away the strange feelings she'd experienced earlier, she felt more at ease.

Once she had a moment to think about the afternoon, she even realized that his close proximity throughout the past hour's tour of Hawthorne Manor had been a comfort, instead of the irritant she thought it would be. She didn't know what had changed, but somehow their friendship seemed more . . . tangible than before.

He moved next to her, laying his hand on the rail beside hers. Even though an inch of space remained between them, it was as if there wasn't any separation at all. If she closed her eyes, she could feel the tip of his finger gliding over her flesh . . . She swallowed.

"Of everything that I've shown you today—all the rooms, the plumbing in the kitchen, the bathing chamber—you're most impressed by an overgrown garden."

"You're mistaken. The house is even lovelier than I remember. And as for the plumbing, I'm both amazed and astounded." However, at the time, she'd still been reeling from the amount of fire pails she'd seen. Her heart still ached for him. For all he'd suffered.

"You're frowning again," he said.

She shook her head, pulling herself away from those thoughts. "I was merely looking at the old boxwood."

"Once the house is finished, I'll be able to concentrate more on the garden. Most likely, I'll plant new boxwood in the row where the old is."

"Oh, don't. Another hedge would only hide the flowers. They're just beginning to bloom. It would be a shame not to give them a chance," she said, unable to keep her opinions to herself, just as he'd teasingly predicted. She lifted her gaze and saw they were of like mind, which caused her lips to curve again. "I can't help it."

His hand reached up to tug on the end of her bonnet ribbon, yet without the force to untie it. "What would you have me do instead?"

Caught off guard by his expression, she tilted her head and studied him for a moment, unable to form a response. Surely, she'd never seen him look at her with such tenderness before. Then again, surely, it must have been the way the wispy clouds flitted over the sun, because it altered in the next instant as his gaze dipped to her mouth.

Her lips tingled. Reflexively, her tongue darted out to soothe away the sensation. "Perhaps . . ."

He took a step closer. The cuff of his sleeve glided against her throat as his thumb brushed over her bottom lip. "Was it chocolate or jasmine tea today, Emma-*mine*?"

She must have forgotten how to breathe. Her chest constricted with the effort.

For a moment, she nearly forgot this was nothing more than a pretense and that Rathburn flirted with everyone.

For a moment, she very nearly imagined he saw her differently. As something more.

She very nearly imagined he was going to kiss her again,

even with Penelope only steps away. Perhaps he was merely waiting for her to ask. Her pulse quickened at the thought. And what's worse, she wanted to.

Foolish. Chiding herself, she took a step back. "It's getting late," she said, instead of answering him. "I'll want to rest before the ball tonight."

"Yes, of course," he said with wry half smile, as if he knew her to be a coward. "We can finish our *conversation* later."

CHAPTER NINE

Emma had once dreamed her debut would be like this. The hushed silence after her name was announced. The blatant looks of admiration. The smiles. The nods.

Now, she had the approval of the Dowager Duchess of Heathcoat, printed for all the world to see. It was as if she were reborn in society.

Normally, this wouldn't be cause for alarm. Yet, for the previous two Seasons, she'd come to depend on being looked through in the same manner one would a potted tree, and just as quickly forgotten. Unused to the attention, she momentarily forgot what response was required from her.

"My dear, it is customary to return a smile when given," the dowager said, not bothering to curve her lips. "Unless the person or persons smiling do so out of malice. Do you wish me to support you in your snobbery and give the Dorsets and their guests the *cut direct*? Or shall we continue on and enjoy the evening with all the niceties we can afford?"

Cringing inside at the reprimand, Emma produced a smile for the other guests. "I'm aware of no malice, just surprised to receive the greeting. Pleasantly so," she said without breaking her smile. Then as they turned toward the upper gallery that overlooked the Dorsets' ballroom, she added, "However, I am honored that you would support me if I found enemies here."

"Just as I am certain you will soon come to understand my sense of humor," the dowager said without missing a beat. "If nothing else, you have a sharp intellect."

Proceeding up the stairs at a regal pace beside the dowager, Emma felt her forced smile relax. A combination of relief and amusement eased the sudden tension when it occurred to her that the dowager was actually teasing her. In her own way.

"If intellect is what I have to recommend me, then I must confess to deception as well." She couldn't be too sharp witted. After all, she'd agreed to Rathburn's scheme.

"And modesty, no doubt."

Not wanting to lose the ground she'd gained, Emma pulled the corner of her mouth between her teeth to keep from laughing aloud. "Forgive me if I withhold agreement, for I do not want to add pride to the list."

Her efforts earned her a playful swat on the arm from the dowager's fan when they reached the top.

Having entered the ballroom ahead of them, Rathburn and his mother were already standing in the gallery, currently speaking with Merribeth and her aunt, Mrs. Leander, along with her friend, Lady Eve Sterling. Delaney and Bree were also there, standing on the far side with the dour-faced Miss Pursglove. With the collapse of her nerves only a disapproving look away, Emma was glad her friends were among their party of spectators.

Rathburn excused himself from the small group and

made his way to her, quirking a brow as he regarded first her and then the dowager. "Grandmamma, is that a smile on your lips?"

"What a notion." For his cheek, he received a swat of her fan as well. "Now, hurry along, I won't have you hovering over our Miss Danvers and scaring away all her partners again. Simply sign her dance card and be on your way."

He clenched his jaw and offered a tight smile. "With all the prettiest ladies holding court in the gallery, I wouldn't dream of leaving."

Even though he made the statement with his characteristic teasing air, the hardness in his gaze told her that he was serious. When he turned that look on her, she instantly recalled how Penelope had called that look *possessive*.

A secret thrill rushed through her, sending tingles beneath the surface of her skin, and causing gooseflesh to rise on her arms. However, she knew better than to let her imagination run wild.

"Miss Danvers," the dowager said, her voice abruptly dowsing the tingles. "Hand him your card so that we can be rid of him before he flatters us to distraction."

She swallowed. "I—I don't have a card."

Whatever ground she'd made with the dowager disappeared beneath furrowed scrutiny. "No card?"

Before Emma could shake her head, the dowager's censorious glower was cast to Rathburn.

"Obviously, this is your doing. After all, why would a young woman bother with a dance card if her escort behaves like a barbarian? If you're not careful, dear boy, you'll lose your place as my favorite grandson. Your cousin Gabriel is reforming quite well." By the time she was finished, all the reproach vanished from her tone. Reaching into her reticule, she produced an elegant card and handed it to Emma.

In turn, Emma handed it to Rathburn.

He frowned, staring at it with the same intensity he'd used on her, as if he were considering tucking it into his pocket and refusing to return it.

"*One* dance," his grandmother warned. "In such a crush, there can be only four sets before dinner, I'm sure. Since we will not stay much after dinner, you may choose only one."

"However, it is also perfectly acceptable if you choose not to dance with me," Emma added hastily, her heart suddenly pounding in her throat. "After all, I'm certain there will be other occasions . . . in the future."

The way his glance speared her, she knew her efforts were transparent. Unfortunately, he took her easy escape as a challenge and wrote his name in bold letters for the fourth set. The waltz.

Oh dear.

"Miss Danvers," he said with bow, returning her card in such a way as to dare her to accept it.

With his mother and grandmother watching—as well as half the *ton*, no doubt—she withdrew the card from his fingers and offered a curtsy. "Lord Rathburn."

Before he left the gallery, he passed by her slowly. "I look forward to seeing you on the dance floor."

His words were more of a promise than a threat, and yet, she wondered if he meant to suggest that he planned to watch her while she was with other partners. A way of keeping his eye on her.

"Then I shall do my best to procure the most elegant partners for you to admire," she answered just as quietly and smiled to herself when he stumbled a half-step, his grand exit thwarted.

He paused at the top of the stair and cast another hard look over his shoulder. *Possessive.* Another frisson raced through her, this time making the fine downy hairs at her nape stand on end. It was exhilarating as much as it caused her anxiety, and she wondered which sensation would win out in the end. Had he truly always looked at her this way?

"Allow me, Miss Danvers. After all, as your fiancé, it is my duty to guide the most elegant partners to you."

Before she could inform him that she could acquire her own partners, especially without a glowering brute standing over her, Rathburn turned and swept down the stairs.

"A valiant battle, my dear," the dowager said, clucking her tongue. "But I'm afraid my grandson bested you this time. Right now, he's below stairs finding you the dullest and most repellent partners in attendance."

She narrowed her eyes as she watched the top of his ash blond head weave his way through the crowd. It didn't matter if he did find her dimwitted or unattractive partners. So long as the gentlemen were eligible, she could still find a way to win the battle. After all, he needed a reminder that they were not actually engaged.

During the first set, she danced with Mr. Bastion, a distant cousin of the Dorsets'. He was exactly her height, with thinning brown hair, fleshy lips, and the unfortunate propensity to spit whenever he spoke. Although ashamed to admit it, she was actually thankful that he seemed too preoccupied with her bosom to offer up many topics of conversation.

Lord Mosley partnered with her for the second set. She managed to endure thirty minutes of his company without falling asleep. He was a gentle soul, but his conversation was limited to his mother and their home in Derbyshire. Even when she tried to interject a comment about the weather, he responded with the fact that his mother preferred cooler springs that were less sunny.

She hid a yawn behind her fan as he escorted her to the gallery stairs. If she weren't suddenly so exhausted, she could honestly murder Rathburn. If he thought for a moment that she hadn't noticed him smirking at her, he was mistaken.

Her partner for the third set, a widower who was not much younger than her father, was nowhere in sight. She breathed a sigh of relief.

"Pardon me," a stranger said from behind her. "I believe this dance is mine."

Closing her fan, she pasted on her best smile and turned to greet him. Only he wasn't the same gentlemen she'd been introduced to before. For starters, there wasn't a single gray hair on his head. Instead, it was black as midnight, even darker than Merribeth's. His eyes were a captivating pale gray that shimmered in the light of the chandeliers as if they were made of silver satin.

Entranced for an instant, she had a difficult time remembering he wasn't her partner for the third set. Then she felt his hand at the small of her back as he guided her to the dance floor. Before she could open her mouth to object, he already removed it, grinning down at her with a knowing air.

She paused on the fringes of two lines of dancers. "Sir, I don't believe we've been introduced."

Sure of himself, he smiled in a way that made her feel like the only woman in the room. "Of course we have."

"No," she said, somehow managing to stay clearheaded. "I would have remembered."

Apparently, this intrigued him because he studied her more closely. "Would you now? I can see Rathburn has his hands full with you."

"Rathburn has nothing of the sort. We are not married." Much to her surprise, the words came out like a challenge, as if she were flirting with him, bantering with a complete stranger the way she bantered with Rathburn. This was *wrong*, a voice inside whispered. Yet, it was the truth. She was *not* betrothed to Rathburn.

The stranger chuckled, the sound rich and alluring. Completely hedonistic. "Would it be too bold if I said I like you already, Miss Danvers?"

She tried not to blush as she took her place across the aisle from him for the quadrille. "Yes, far too bold."

He held her gaze as the music started and they began the motions of the dance, crossing in front of each other, circling, bowing. When he was near, he spoke again. "Good, because I do like you. Perhaps even more now that we have Rathburn's undivided attention."

The warning flared to life again. This stranger was far too bold. Far too familiar. She was about to walk away and leave him standing in line without a partner. But then she caught sight of Rathburn when she circled. He was livid. Murderous.

She felt her lips curl into a grin. After saddling her with those first two partners, it served him right. "I'm afraid I can neither chastise you nor return the sentiment without knowing your name."

"My friends call me Bane," he said with a bow that was perfectly timed with the dance. "Although, in more formal circumstances, I suppose it would be Lord Knightswold."

"Then while we are dancing, I'll refer to you as Lord Knightswold."

He grinned at her. "And when I deliver you to your betrothed?"

"I think we shall be fast friends." She couldn't help but smile in return, which drew his focus to her mouth.

"I've never been a jealous man, but for you I might make an exception." They were still for a moment, waiting for the other dancers to cross and turn and bow. "Wherever have you been all this time? Locked away in a convent? Hidden away in the country?"

"Lurking among the potted trees in ballrooms all over the city." She laughed. "Truly, this is my third Season."

Too bold, yet again, his gaze drifted over her in appraisal, renewing her blush. "I don't know whether to hate myself for not having discovered you first, or hate Rathburn for making the marriage noose so appealing. I must warn you, honor does not bind me to hate myself."

Unused to such glances from anyone other than Rathburn, she felt positively exposed. Where she always knew Rathburn was merely flirting, she was equally certain that Knightswold . . . wasn't.

"I'm afraid," she said as the dance ended and he escorted

her to the balcony doors where Rathburn stood, "honor does bind me."

With one last simmering satin look, he bowed. "I understand. A pleasure, Miss Danvers."

As if feigning jealousy, Rathburn settled his hand at her elbow and drew closer. A muscle in his jaw pulsed as he clenched his teeth. "The infamous Bane in attendance at the Dorsets' ball? I seem to recall a declaration, not long ago, to the effect of you never bowing to the whims of society."

"When societal trappings are so tempting, how could I resist?" A devious smirk toyed with the faint crease at the corner of his mouth.

Rathburn tensed and made a move toward him, but then stopped and lifted his gaze to the gallery. "Ah. I see your friend, Lady Eve Sterling, is watching our exchange with more than common interest. Up to your old sport?"

Knightswold lifted one shoulder in a half shrug. "Perhaps."

"Marking me as a jealous beau? I wonder what the odds were in the betting book at White's."

Bane inclined his head, his grin widening.

Instead of being angered by the confirmation that he'd been targeted for some sort of game, he chuckled. "Well played, even if I was an easy target for your scheme."

Bane turned his gaze to Emma, holding it for long enough to make her blush. "That was a poor attempt at a compliment to you, Miss Danvers. However, if you were mine—"

"*Now*, you've worn out your welcome," Rathburn growled, his good humor vanishing.

Without tempting fate or friendship any further, Lord

Knightswold bowed. "Perhaps I'll find your cousin in the card room. After all, Gabriel still has a sense humor."

He gave her a wink and then left without another word, leaving her feeling exposed by the incident. Of course, not every eye in the ballroom was glued to their tête-à-tête, just those around them, as well as a few in the gallery.

Not for the first time, Emma wished Rathburn wasn't so good at pretending. It might even have been nice if he actually were jealous. She held back a sigh for her foolish thoughts and made a move to step away.

"I believe the waltz is mine."

A tide of uncertainty washed over her. Penelope's promise that dancing changed everything resurfaced, and Emma was abruptly face to face with her greatest fear—to be judged and found wanting. What if dancing with Rathburn did change everything, only to fracture their friendship in the process? Then again, what if dancing with him changed nothing? At the moment, she couldn't decide which outcome frightened her the most.

"Yes, it is. However, I wonder . . ." She hesitated to find the right words, but decided a small lie would save her the embarrassment of revealing her fears. "I'm exhausted, Rathburn. I wonder if you might allow me a moment to catch my breath."

Concerned, Rathburn searched Emma's face. In her expression, he made no notice of exhaustion. Her chocolate eyes were bright as ever with no marring red lines. Her cheeks bloomed with a healthy glow. And yet, there was something guarded in the way she didn't hold his gaze and worried the corner of her mouth. "Of course. They have benches on the patio. Would you care for a breath of night air?"

Apparently believing he didn't plan to ask her about whatever she was hiding, she breathed a sigh of relief. "That sounds lovely."

They made their way past three other couples who shared the same idea of enjoying the cool midnight air. The sweet scent of evening dew drifted on the breeze. On the large stone patio, fragrant juniper topiary trees in large clay pots stood beside curved benches to allow for privacy without impropriety. Yet, even then, he couldn't stop himself from choosing the bench farthest from the door, farthest from the reach of moonlight reflecting off the fountain pond.

Emma had never been guarded with him before. Or at least when she'd tried, he'd been able to see through it. Not knowing why she was now bothered him more than he wanted to let on.

Then in an instant, epiphany dawned. Most likely, she was cross with him over the partners he'd chosen for her. "Did you enjoy dancing this evening?"

"Not until the last, but I think you know that," she said with a castigating look as she settled her skirts around her. "After all, you ensured my partners were the dullest in attendance. I imagine Lord Amberdeen would have been as well if not for his sudden absence."

"Yes," he growled low in his throat. That had been the plan, until Bane's unexpected arrival. "Peculiar. Even more so considering Lord Amberdeen is a particular enemy of Lady Sterling's. It wouldn't surprise me if she made sure Amberdeen was indisposed simply to allow Bane to sweep in, forcing me to make a spectacle of myself."

And he nearly had, right there in full view of his grandmother. The heated wave of jealously had been unexpected. For an instant, he'd pictured his fist connecting with Bane's jaw with enough force to knock him to the ground. And then, his imagination had produced him standing over Bane's prone body and boldly declaring that Emma was his. He'd never had such an urge before.

"Lady Eve and Knightswold are two bosom companions, after all," he murmured absently, but soon felt a fresh wave of jealousy assail him. "Which reminds me," he said with another growl, "I nearly murdered two men this evening for ogling yours."

She blinked. "My . . . companions?"

"If that's what you call them." He lowered his gaze, letting it slide over the exposed swells of her flesh in a way to make it very clear to which he was referring.

She blushed and opened her mouth to speak—to change the subject, no doubt—but no sound came forth. Which left him with the perfect opportunity to admire her mouth. The memory of their kiss tormented him day and night. Here, on their partially secluded bench, he could easily imagine leaning in a fraction more, feeling her breath against his lips, teasing her flesh apart, tasting the flavor on her tongue—

Emma turned away, her shallow, rapid breaths betraying her thoughts.

He grinned, knowing that they were of like mind. "The only thing that saved them was your response."

Returning her gaze to his, a worried frown puckered the flesh above her nose. "Did I appear cross with my partners?"

"Your expression, at least to everyone else, was perfectly pleasant and very pretty. You move gracefully, as well. No one could find fault in your dancing or demeanor." He wished she wasn't so concerned about what people thought of her. They were too alike in that regard, both fearing that a single scathing remark could ruin their futures. For now, they must keep up appearances.

"No one other than you."

"It isn't that I found fault, darling," he chided softly. To him, she needed no improvement. "It's merely that I know when you're pretending to enjoy yourself for the sake of your partner. And I also know when you are truly content."

She blew out a breath. "You're teasing me again."

"There's a particular way you tilt your head when you're deeply enthralled." He lifted a finger to trace the edge of her jawline to reveal the subtle tilt of her head toward him. "And your cheeks flush to a becoming rosy hue."

Emma reached up to swat him away, but he took hold of her hand instead and held it. She started, studying him closely as if trying to take his measure. "What are you about? That sounded suspiciously like a compliment. Yet, there is no one near enough to admire your pretense of flattery."

"If you haven't noticed, I always compliment you." And he realized with sudden truth, that it wasn't merely about flirting either. It was different with Emma. Perhaps it had been different from the very beginning. After all, he'd gone to her with his scheme, knowing that—if nothing else—she wouldn't judge him for it. Judge him and find him wanting. No, not Emma.

"But you've always been teasing."

How could she still believe that, especially now when he felt she must surely see the truth in his gaze? "Perhaps you merely wished me teasing so that you wouldn't risk your heart," he whispered, hoping to draw her out.

"Rathburn, I—"

"Oliver," he said with a grin, pleased to see that she wasn't as good at hiding from him as she thought. He wasn't wrong, after all. The tenderness in her gaze told him everything he needed to know. He could see it plainly, as if it had been there all the while. "I told you, I only like it when *you* say my name. The sound of it from your lips is the only way I'll ever get used to it."

Her eyes widened in panic for a moment. "I . . . don't think the night air agrees with me."

"Coward," he murmured, his amusement humming in his throat. "What of our waltz?"

"I don't think that would be a good idea."

"Why not?"

The moment she opened her mouth and her gaze shied away from his, he knew she was going to attempt to veil her response.

Tucking his finger beneath her chin once more, he brought her focus back to him and arched a brow. "There is nothing you ever need hide from me, Emma. We've come too far for any more pretense."

She held his gaze and then let out a breath, as if resigned. "It will sound silly, I'm sure."

He waited, his attention fixed on her.

"It all started when Penelope said that dancing changes everything. From that moment on, I've been dreading the

Dorset ball. I knew that you"—she pointed at him and glared without malice—"would request the waltz."

"Which I did," he said, tugging on her gloved finger and closing his hand around hers. A pleasant warmth enveloped him at the simple touch. The whispered *What if . . .* returned, stirring a fragile longing within him.

"Yes, and even before tonight, I've thought about it."

"An obsessive preoccupation, to be sure."

She nodded, but her attention was diverted to the lazy sweep of his thumb across the area between her thumb and forefinger. However, she shook her head and shifted slightly—though not enough to dislodge him—and refocused on his face. "I imagine, you can understand how much is at stake if we should waltz?"

"Completely." He turned her hand, moving his attention to the center of her palm and noted, with pleasure, how her eyes darkened and her lips parted. "I've had a similar preoccupation of late. It keeps me awake at night. I'm a fairly useless creature during the day. I can't even go more than five minutes without thinking about it."

She breathed a sigh of relief, as if believing they were of like mind. "Then it was a good thing we avoided the waltz."

"Oh, I wasn't speaking of the waltz."

"You weren't?"

He leaned close to whisper. "No, Emma-*mine*. I was thinking about our kiss."

"Which only happened to seal our bargain. Perhaps it would be better if we forgot . . ." Her words trailed off when he shook his head.

"Our *next* kiss," he clarified with a slow, promising grin.

She glanced down to his mouth, her head tilting in such an inviting way. It took all of his control to keep what little distance remained between them. He wanted her. Ached for her. He could easily imagine slipping his hand beneath her skirts and touching her most tender flesh with the same unhurried strokes his thumb was now circling into the center of her palm.

She shifted slightly, pressing her knees together as if he'd spoken the desire aloud. The rake in him plotted an escape from scrutiny, calculated the number of dark alcoves, practiced excuses that would allow him to escort her home early—

"Oliver . . ." His name slipped past her lips and he nearly convulsed at the breathless, throaty sound.

She wanted him, perhaps even as much as he wanted her. Yet, no matter how much he wanted to pleasure her and then take his own, he couldn't do that to her. He couldn't rob her of the right to choose her fate. He'd given his word that she would come away from this mock betrothal unscathed. Already, the kiss had pushed some boundaries. He couldn't risk another, not until she knew the risks and realized she was making a permanent choice to be his.

After a moment, Emma shook her head, opened her eyes, and slowly pulled free of his grasp. "Rathburn, you could tempt a saint into ruin, I'm sure. Every breath you expel is a flirtation meant to entice and seduce. I have only recently discovered just how far from sainthood I am."

His eyes widened at her confession and a breath holding the last shreds of his control staggered through him. "Emma . . ."

She held up her hand. "Please remember that part of our

bargain was to keep my reputation intact, so that I may find a suitable husband when this has finished."

He flinched, feeling as if she'd struck him with a block of ice. His ardor cooled in an instant.

A suitable husband. Never before had an admonishment stung so much. From anyone else, it wouldn't have. Any hope he'd had that she'd never judge him and find him wanting vanished like a pickpocket in St. Giles.

A suitable husband, indeed. If nothing else, she deserved one of those.

Before he gave himself away, he schooled his features. "Of course," he said pleasantly as he stood and offered his hand to assist her. "We should return before anyone *else* gets the wrong impression of my intentions."

CHAPTER TEN

Twenty-one days, Emma thought. *Twenty-one days of no mistakes. Twenty-one days for Rathburn to gain his inheritance. Twenty-one days to break the betrothal.*

She stood on a pedestal in the blue room at Rathburn's townhouse, staring at her guilt-ridden reflection. It was a shame the dowager was wasting all this money on a gown she would never have the chance to wear. It was such a lovely gown, too. Wearing it, she felt regal. Not at all like the twin to a potted tree.

Lady Valmont's modiste fitted the under portion of her dress, pinning it beneath the gathers covering her breasts, and nipping it in at the curve of her waist. "This satin will embrace your form," the woman said with a nod. Even through a mouthful of pins, her French accent was thick. "The outer robe will drape nicely from the line of your shoulders to the floor. Elegant, no?"

"*Oui,*" she said, nodding, feeling conflicted.

Yet there were a few moments, when she'd been ordered to stand very still, that she'd let her mind drift off in a dream.

She imagined Rathburn dressed in his finery, standing at the end of a long aisle, his eyes focused solely on her, his gaze filled with the blatant desire she'd witnessed at the Dorset ball. Or at least until she'd opened her mouth and those foolish words tumbled out. Oh, how she hated herself for saying them.

However, at the time, she'd felt a jolt of fear overtake her that let loose her insecurities. With the way he'd been looking at her and touching her, it had been so easy to forget for a moment that Rathburn could have chosen anyone to help with his deception. He may have only chosen her because some part of him acknowledged that she could never deny him. As he'd proven time and again, he was far too perceptive for her comfort.

She couldn't risk being lured in by him again. Already, she'd grown far too fond of him. She even enjoyed his rakish flirting. Each time he spoke, he drew her closer to wanting more. More of this closeness. More of Rathburn.

However, that could never be. She needed a well-grounded husband, not one who made her forget herself. So much so that she feared her carefully crafted façade might slip. That everyone would learn her secret.

Though she tried hard to hide it, to fight it, she was too much her parents' daughter to deny it any longer. At least to herself. She still wouldn't risk telling a soul of the unfettered urges that came over her, ones that only a brush in her hand and a canvas before her could begin to soothe.

The shame of her weakness brought her back to reality and the impossibility of her fantasy. Not that it was a fantasy, because she would never be foolish enough to imagine that she and Rathburn could ever marry. Well . . . *nearly* never.

However, there was no way the dowager would approve of her and release Rathburn's inheritance if she knew the truth about their mock betrothal.

"I do think the pearls are a bit tasteless," her mother said, pulling Emma away from her conflicted thoughts. "I wish you'd consulted me. I am, after all, the mother of the bride." She picked up the sketch of the wedding dress and turned it this way and that, her brow furrowed.

Lady Rathburn should have known better than to have left Emma's mother *and* the dowager in the same room without a chaperone to keep them on their most genial behavior. There weren't two more opposing women with stronger personalities in all of England, she was sure.

Emma only hoped that the dowager would still hand over Rathburn's inheritance once she realized an alliance between their two families would never work. After all, their incompatibility wasn't his fault.

"*Tasteless* is a rather ironic word coming from the woman wearing the turquoise beads with the apricot-colored gown, my dear," the dowager said with a snort. "Perhaps you'd better leave the fashion decisions to me."

Much to her credit, Celestine Danvers smiled. "I'd rather not see her look like a mourning dove on her wedding day, if it's all the same to you."

"Her gown is white with a robe of the palest pink."

"And weighted with a thousand pearls or more."

"No doubt, working with clay addles one's perception over time. There are hardly more than a dozen. I do hope your daughter never suffers the ill effects from any peculiar artistic traits."

Emma sucked in a panicked breath. "Mother—*oh!*" She winced when one of the pins pricked her flesh.

The modiste gave her a disapproving glance. "Hold still, if you please. We cannot have a lopsided bride."

"It's fine, dear. I'm sure Her Grace cannot fault you for having your own talent. You see, when Emma was younger, she had quite a hand for drawing and painting—"

"Much, much younger. A child, really," Emma said quickly, trying not to move or breathe. When the dowager frowned, Emma added, "I lost interest years ago."

"As any girl would once she realized how cruel those who rule the *ton* can be."

"Mother," Emma warned, knowing by the lift of the dowager's penciled brow that her accusation had hit the target, as intended.

Celestine flipped her wrist. "Oh, Emma. Her Grace and I were just challenging each other's fortitude."

"Your mother is quite right, my dear," the dowager offered, though her mouth was severely pursed in disapproval. "I detest simpering fools more than anything, so she's bound to be an improvement. At least, one can hope."

Her mother cast her a wink and hid her smile behind her fingertips as she pretended to study the modiste's sketch again.

Emma would have liked to breathe a sigh of relief, but she was afraid of the seamstress drawing blood next. Not only that, but she was sure this tête-à-tête was far from over.

"**M**other, what were you thinking to leave them alone with each other?" Rathburn stood up from the settee and paced the length of the sitting room. Supposedly, Emma was across the hall, being fitted for her wedding gown. However, he had his doubts it was that simple.

"Relax," Victoria Goswick said before she sipped her tea. "I have complete faith in Celestine Danvers. She knows how to hold her own."

He stopped at the door and rubbed his temples with the tips of his fingers. This was a disaster. "Don't you see? That's exactly what I'm afraid of. The Danverses are a different breed of people. They hide their strong wills behind an artistic façade. They don't know the first thing about cowering to a societal beast like Grandmamma."

His mother grinned. "I know."

He pressed a fist to the center of his chest and rubbed against the tightness he felt. "Don't you see? She could easily remove her approval."

There would be no inheritance. No Dr. Kohn for the hospital. No wedding to Emma. The strange thing was, he was no longer sure which thought bothered him most of all. He'd already gained Collingsford's agreement to continue paying the laborers, with the promise that he would have the rest of his money as soon as he was wed. There were people counting on him.

Yet, there was also this seedling idea of marrying Emma Danvers. It had already sprouted. And he found he wasn't ready to pluck it from its root—even if she didn't see him as a *suitable* husband.

He frowned at the reminder. Obviously, he would have to convince her otherwise. What was she looking for, exactly? A sedate gentleman who was all polish and no substance, or perhaps the other way around.

"You don't give your grandmother enough credit. She happens to like strong-willed people. She's fond of you, isn't she?"

"Only after I resigned my will to hers," he grumbled.

After his father had died, gambling hadn't been an issue. Yet now he refrained from playing a simple round of whist at a party. He'd stopped drinking, as well, though he'd rarely done so to excess. He had a reputation of being a rake, and . . . well, that one was earned. Yet, once he realized that his grandmother refused to release his inheritance because he wasn't settled, he'd even given up his mistress.

Then again, if he were honest with himself, even that wasn't as difficult as it should have been. Lily was beautiful and passionate, every dream a man could want. Yet, he'd wanted more. At the time, he hadn't known what the *more* entailed. He hadn't known that Lily was missing a key component that meshed well with his character. He hadn't known exactly what he was looking for . . . Not until he'd tasted sweet jasmine tea on Emma Danvers's lips.

Now, he knew exactly what he wanted and was astounded by the fact that he hadn't seen it all along.

The trouble was, he needed to make her see it as well. He needed to become . . . *suitable*.

"Sometimes all that's needed is a nudge in the right direction."

Rathbun nodded absently, distracted by his new plight. He wondered, and not for the first time, what he would be doing now if not for his grandmother's interfering clause in his inheritance contract.

It went without saying that he would have settled down at some point. After all, he wasn't as far gone of a rake as some might have thought. In fact, for the most part, he'd used that first year after his father's death as a diversion from his true purpose. He hadn't wanted anyone to know what he was actually doing with his time. Being a ne'er-do-well was the perfect excuse for traveling the continent in search of the ideal surgeon for the hospital without anyone the wiser.

"I'm sure you would have gotten around to proposing to Miss Danvers eventually."

He started to nod again in response until his mother's words filtered in through his thoughts. Stopping mid-stride, he looked at his mother in surprise. It was almost as if she were privy to his thoughts.

"It's been clear for ages," she said, smiling, her eyes luminous with unshed tears. "Ever since she waited a year for her debut out of respect for your father."

He'd forgotten that. No, that wasn't entirely the truth. The truth was, that might have been the reason he was so drawn to her. At least at first. Now it was more.

"And when you spent most of your free time with the Danvers family, your grandmother and I both thought you'd had an understanding, and that you were waiting for an appropriate amount of time before you announced your engagement." She sighed in disappointment, blotting the moisture from her eyes with a handkerchief. "Then one year turned into two, threatening a third. Last year, when you kept any possible suitor away from Emma, we were certain of an announcement."

He frowned, shaking his head. "I wasn't. I was merely doing the job her brother assigned me. If I saw someone unworthy of her, then I easily warned him off. Which says more about *their* level of commitment to her than my behavior."

"If that's what you choose to believe."

Ignoring the pointed look his mother gave him, he turned to the open the door. At that same moment, a flustered-looking maid emerged from across the hall. She closed the door and bit down on the knuckle of her forefinger. The instant she saw him, she bobbed a curtsy.

"Begging your pardon, your lord and ladyship. But Her Grace asked for a tray of tea to be brought up."

"I don't see why that should be a problem."

"It was Her Grace's request for arsenic in the sugar that makes me fret, if you'll excuse me, your ladyship."

Rathburn cast an alarmed look over his shoulder.

His mother pressed her lips together to hide the grin that was wrinkling the corners of her eyes. "I'm sure the dowager was merely teasing. You may retrieve the tea tray, without the arsenic."

"Yes, ma'am." The maid curtsied again and left in a rush.

"I don't know about you," she said with a shake of her head, "but I won't be having tea in the blue room today."

"Mother . . ." This wasn't the least bit amusing.

"Perhaps I should check on them, after all."

CHAPTER ELEVEN

Delaney blew into the Weatherstones' parlor like a hurricane. She closed the door behind her and sagged against it as if the storm threatened to follow her in. "I'm sorry to be late," she said, flushed and out of breath. Wild copper tendrils snaked out from beneath her sea green bonnet. "I've just learned some news . . . and before Bree, I might add. Though this particular time, I cannot crow about it."

"Whatever it is, it certainly isn't more important than Emma telling us about how the dowager tried to poison her mother," Merribeth interjected, leaning forward to pour Delaney a cup of tea.

"Well, I don't—" Delaney stopped, the ribbons of her bonnet hanging limply in her hand. "It's true, then?"

Emma shook her head, holding back a sigh. The words *news* and *rumor* were essentially interchangeable within their group. "She didn't even try. The dowager merely made a comment to my mother, suggesting that arsenic was a good way to get rid of unwanted relatives. To which my mother responded that she wouldn't dream of taking tea with Her Grace, for surely the poison would be mixed in with the sugar. Then Her Grace said it was a splendid idea, and ordered a tea tray, heavy on the arsenic." She bit down on the inside of her lip to keep from laughing. "The maid took her quite too literally."

"Oh dear," Merribeth giggled.

Delaney snorted as she sank down onto the settee.

Penelope tried to hide her smile behind her handkerchief, but her eyes were brimming with laughter. "It sounds like quite the eventful afternoon."

Giving in to the absurdity of it all, she grinned. "Yes, and what's worse is that I'll have to return next week to endure it all over again. My mother said she wouldn't miss it, no matter how fine the sun was shining through the windows."

"The parlor?" Penelope asked.

"Yes," Emma sighed. "Her muse is still holding the parlor hostage."

Placing two macaroons on her plate, Merribeth grinned. "I hope the dress is worth it."

"Oh, it is," she assured them, wishing that they'd all have a chance to see it, but knowing they wouldn't.

"What of Lord Rathburn? Bree was told he nearly burst through the doors to ensure you were not being tortured . . ." Delaney said, her own story apparently forgotten.

"Or poisoned," Merribeth added.

"Another exaggeration," she said, hoping the twinge of disappointment she felt didn't come out in her tone. "He was in the house and was kind enough to escort my mother and me to our carriage. That is all."

Penelope clucked her tongue and let out a breath, not hiding her annoyance. However, Emma refused to entertain her friend's notions of how Rathburn held a secret *tendre* for her. That was merely wishful thinking on both their parts, though more so on hers than on Penelope's, she'd guess.

She'd spent far too much time wishing lately, and unfortunately, it came out in her painting, which was getting harder and harder to hide.

"It was then that he asked you to the theater, right?" Delaney asked, her cautious tone instantly drawing her attention, as well as everyone else's. Delaney McFarland was never one to beat around the bush.

Feeling a strange chill of foreboding settle around her, Emma lowered her needlework to her lap. "No, he never asked. It was arranged by his mother. We'll be watching *Othello* from the duke's box."

Merribeth beamed. "Oh, how lovely. I've heard wonderful things about the production."

Delaney's expression remained unchanged. "What was Rathburn's reaction to this?"

Emma thought back for a moment and then frowned. Actually, he had seemed a trifle pale. Then again, she'd attributed that to the mention of the wedding being less than three weeks away. They were running out of time to gain his inheritance *and* call off the wedding.

However, her friend was acting peculiar and no longer meeting her eyes. "Delaney, is there something you wanted to tell me?"

Delaney sipped her tea and shrugged. "It's only a rumor."

Strange. Before, it had been *news*. Now, that peculiar chill wrapped around her like a tightly cinched corset.

"I overheard it from Elena Mallory outside of Haversham's." They all frequented Mr. Haversham's draper shop. In fact, a mix up in their embroidery orders—for they all lived on Danbury Lane—was how they'd come to know one another in the first place. Setting their orders to rights had brought them an instant bond of friendship and had started their needlework circle.

Elena Mallory also frequented Haversham's. However, she never shared rumors of pleasant occurrences.

Emma braced herself.

"If you keep us waiting any longer, we're going to send for your sister," Merribeth scolded. "She would have told us before she had the chance to draw a breath."

"You told me to wait," Delaney blinked innocently, as if she were suddenly possessed by a heavenly host. They all knew better. "So, I waited."

Penelope cleared her throat and tapped her foot on the soft carpet. "And now we're waiting . . ."

"So testy. Did it ever occur to you that the rumor might be of a delicate nature?"

Oh dear. This couldn't be good. Nonetheless, they all leaned forward marginally and held their collective breaths.

Delaney set down her cup and smoothed her skirts. "Once your outing to the theater became common knowledge, so did talk of Lord Rathburn's previous . . ." She cleared her throat and glanced over her shoulder to the door. "Previous . . . *activities* with the actress who plays Desdemona."

Emma inhaled sharply. Lances of heat pricked every inch of her skin as if she'd fallen into a bed of thistles. All at once, anger spiked within her. The sensation felt hot and uncomfortable . . . and she absolutely *refused* to identify it as jealousy.

After all, the feeling was completely unfounded. She knew the real reason for their sham courtship. She knew Rathburn saw her only as a means to an end. And she shouldn't allow herself to forget it for a single moment.

"The theater will be packed to the gills and every eye on you, Rathburn, *and* . . . Lily Lovetree, whom it is said still pines for him."

"Delaney, really," Penelope chided, and placed her hand on Emma's back, patting her as if she were a child. "Did you feel it necessary to add the last bit?"

Merribeth reached over to pat Emma's other shoulder. "The first bit was bad enough."

Emma sat up straight, nodded to both Penelope and Merribeth in reassurance, but politely shrugged them off. She didn't want their pity. "I know of Rathburn's reputation. It's hardly a secret that he kept a mistress."

Although why it bothered her to hear confirmation, not to mention the woman's name, she didn't know. Yet, against her better sense, a terrible, yearning twinge stole into her heart. If Lily Lovetree pined for him, then did he feel the same way?

Penelope sighed and shook her head. "I hope you realize that the only reason people are saying such cruel things is because the entire *ton* is green with envy over your love match. Elena Mallory most of all."

It *was* bad news. The worst sort of news, though her friends had no idea how detrimental it was for Rathburn. If the *ton* was abuzz about his prior involvement—at least she hoped it was prior—then it could spoil his chance to win the dowager's approval. If that happened, then he'd no longer need Emma's help. And if *that* happened, then he might very well seek an heiress to marry after all. The thought gave her a terrible headache. Her stomach twisted in knots at the emptiness she suddenly felt inside.

"Of course," she said, trying to sound like she believed it, at least to the others who didn't know about her bargain.

"I shouldn't have said anything." Delaney looked crestfallen.

"How could you not have?" This time it was Emma who reached across the table to comfort her friend, taking her hand. "For the first time in an age, you were the proprietor of gossip concerning your friend, and all before Bree caught wind of it. I don't blame you. In fact, I'm grateful to know why everyone will be staring at me tonight."

Even so, the displeasure she felt at being the object of pity and curiosity paled in comparison to the burning jealousy that erupted at the thought of being in the presence of a woman who'd spent time in Rathburn's arms and tasting the pleasure of his kiss.

"Never fear," Delaney offered, squeezing her hand in return. "Rathburn couldn't care a fig for a harlot like her."

"I'm certain he won't even look her way this evening," Merribeth promised, placing her hand on top as if they were the Knights of Camelot. Penelope was the next to proclaim her fealty.

However, the chorus of "never fears" and "I'm certains" failed to ease her mind. She didn't want to see the woman who'd possessed every bit of Rathburn. The woman who didn't fear losing the dowager's approval. The woman who didn't hide what she was for the sake of blending into society.

It wasn't fair. Emma was only now beginning to realize

how much she stood to lose, and how much she wanted to believe Rathburn could be hers to keep.

Persevering in the face of misery, she smiled at them all. "You're right, I'm certain."

"So, tell us about the dress," Merribeth said, the first to resettle herself in her seat and resume her embroidery. "I've heard there are over a hundred pounds of pearls to be sewn on."

"I heard it was two hundred," Delaney said with a needle between her teeth.

Not to be outdone, Penelope interjected, "I heard three."

"And I heard," Emma added cheekily, "that it will take a coach and four to drag me down the aisle."

Chapter Twelve

Rathburn adjusted the tails of his evening coat as he fought for a comfortable position in the theater box chair. In front of him, his mother and grandmother hadn't so much as fanned themselves or fidgeted. Other than his grandmother's occasional lifting of her lorgnette, he wouldn't even know if she'd turned into a statue.

Beside him, Emma hadn't moved either. She sat rail-straight and stared toward the stage, her expression filled with the unease of one approaching a great abyss.

She hadn't said more than a half dozen words to him the entire evening. Although, he wasn't a font of conversation either. In fact, everything out of his mouth seemed stilted and forced. He'd felt this way ever since yesterday, when his mother had said they were attending the theater.

The theater. He'd known Lily was in this particular production. She'd been rehearsing for the role when he'd ended their yearlong . . . *arrangement*. At the time, she'd taken the news rather dramatically, as expected. After all, that was who she was. She was used to playing a part every day. There had even been times when he didn't know what to expect from her. She was very unpredictable. For the first few months, that quality had been exciting. In addition, she'd demonstrated things he'd only read about in Arabian fiction.

Yet, there were times when he didn't want a performance. He'd tried to get to know her, learn about her life and whatever dreams she had. He'd wanted to be her friend. She went along with it, of course. However, after her story changed time and again, he found his excitement waning. Apparently, for her, answering his questions had been nothing more than an acting exercise.

So, when his grandmother refused his request for his inheritance a few months ago, citing the fact that he was still causing rumors to run amok, it was quite easy to break it off with Lily. He'd even introduced her to a very appreciative sycophant—a widower with more money than he knew what to do with. In the end, they'd both gotten what they wanted, no matter what the current rumors throughout the *ton* were.

Rathburn glanced over at Emma. Tonight, she wore her hair up off the nape of her neck, with a fall of mahogany curls sweeping forward. This time, she didn't wear the flowers he'd sent. Instead, she wore a white silk ribbon in her hair, fastened with a bronze brooch that matched the hue of the sash tied at the waist of her snow-white gown. However, she had brought the flowers along—in a small bouquet of tiny white blossoms that she held in her lap.

She glanced at him and then went back to watching the play. There was a distinct coldness in her usually warm, brown eyes.

Suspicion entered his mind. He felt a chill rush through

him and wondered if she might know the reason for *his* discomfort this evening. Had she heard the recent rumors?

He shook his head. Knowing Emma as well as he did, he knew that she wouldn't have been able to hold her tongue for this long if she knew. She would have called him out from the start.

"She's very beautiful," she whispered.

Rathburn stilled. There was a razor-sharp edge in her tone he'd never heard before. He turned to look at her again, wondering. She speared him with a glacial stare.

Oh yes, she'd heard.

He cleared his throat and kept his voice low so that his mother and grandmother wouldn't overhear. "I'm sorry, what did you say?"

"I said, the actress who plays Desdemona is very beautiful." She pinned him to the spot with that look. Then, for an instant, he imagined a swift bolt of lightning flashed in those chocolate depths. "Wouldn't you agree?"

He cursed silently. Swallowed. "She pales in comparison to you."

"Pale? Yes, her hair is quite pale." She glanced down to the stage again. "Perhaps you prefer pale hair. Truly, she's quite stunning and vibrant. I imagine she has a great many admirers."

This time, when she returned her gaze to his, he saw that he'd been mistaken. She wasn't angry. She was hurt, wounded. Perhaps even jealous? The last thought shot a jolt of warmth through him. If she was jealous, then perhaps she saw him as more than an *unsuitable* husband. Not that he could ask her now, or continue this whispered conversation in full display of the *ton*. Many lorgnettes had been trained on their box for the first two acts.

However, he knew he must stop Emma from believing he cared anything for Lily now.

The stage lights dimmed. Intermission. Rathburn hadn't been paying attention. Now, he took it as an opportunity to speak with Emma alone.

In the hall, he heard the voices of the Hastings leaving their box for refreshments below. He stood. "Miss Danvers, would you care for a glass of punch this evening?"

"That would be lovely," his grandmother answered instead. "Bring enough for all of us, if you will."

"I'm afraid he'll need an extra set of hands for that," his mother chimed in. "Emma, why don't you go with him?"

Emma nodded stiffly and rose from her seat. Out in the hall, he took her by the hand and pulled her into the curtained vestibule past the Hastings' box.

"Rathburn, really, I'm in no mood for games," she whispered and tugged her hand free.

Before she could walk past him, he placed his hands on her shoulders, imploring her to stay with a look. He leaned in so their conversation would not be overheard.

"My parents were not typical among the peerage," he said, hoping to get his point across quickly. They didn't have much time. "When they married . . . they were true to each other."

She tried to shrug him off. "I don't see why you felt the need to tell me that."

He tried again. "Emma, I cannot change my past, but if we were to marry—"

"We would get an annulment." She lifted her chin, pressing her lips into a firm line.

However, her action had the opposite effect she'd intended, he was sure. It brought their faces closer. Their mouths mere inches apart. He saw the moment she realized it too, noting with pleasure the widening of her pupils.

"If we were to marry, and if an annulment were *not* possible," he added, speaking softly, holding her gaze, "I would be true."

Her lips parted on a soft gasp at his declaration. "You cannot promise such a thing. You enjoy your life the way it is, free and unhindered. You're only saying this because—"

"In all the years you've known me, have I ever made a declaration I didn't stand behind?"

He licked his lips, tasting her sweet breath. Her lashes lowered, her gaze dipping to his mouth. Adjusting his hold, he slipped his thumbs beneath the cuffs of her cap sleeves and stroked her flesh. He only wished he wasn't wearing gloves and could feel her skin against his, *free and unhindered*. At least she was right about one thing. As for the rest . . .

The air felt alive in this small space, flaring around them like sparks shooting from a fire. Tiny embers cascaded down his skin, making him long to do more than caress her shoulders. He wanted to feel her against him. Feel his body pressing into hers. Watch her eyes as they darkened with desire . . .

The inches between them were dwindling like the last remnants of his control. Only he wasn't the one closing the distance.

Much to his surprise, Emma took a step closer. Her slippers brushed the inside of his boots. Her thighs lightly grazed his with barely enough pressure for him to notice. But he did. The surge of blood to the heated space between them made him hard as forged iron.

He wasn't the only one affected by their nearness. Her eyes were back to being the color of steaming chocolate. He ached with thirst.

Boldly, she brushed her lips across his, not in a kiss, but in something elementally more substantial. "Then if we were to marry—"

"And an annulment were impossible," he added, feeling his breath slide into her mouth and tasting her response in return. If she kept looking at him that way, then an annulment would definitely be impossible. In fact, he would need a special license in an embarrassingly short amount of time.

She trembled, but held his gaze. "I would be true, as well."

Rathburn wanted to kiss her, to plunder the depths of her sweet mouth—

Voices nearby put a halt to his desires. Disappointed, and yet filled with a strangely potent satisfaction, he took her hand and pulled her out into the hall.

Thankfully, the Hastings had their backs turned, carrying on a conversation with his grandmother. Intermission was nearly over, and so he slipped past the Hastings, ducking his head a little so his grandmother and mother wouldn't see them coming from the opposite direction of the lobby. Then, he headed through the rotunda and down the staircase.

At the bottom, Emma pulled her hand free. "As much as I love being dragged behind you . . ."

He turned with a ready apology, but stopped when he caught her grinning at him. Then, just because it suited him, he snatched her hand again and brought it to his lips. "I'll be sure to remember that."

She tried to slip her fingers free again, but this time he wouldn't let her. "You are too bold, Rathburn."

"We are betrothed. A press of the hand is perfectly acceptable behavior," he said as he tucked it into the crook of his arm. Then he turned and bent to her ear. "Besides, it's far more acceptable than what we would have been doing if the Hastings hadn't returned."

She shushed him, her face a mask of disapproval. However, the blush on her cheeks gave her away. "You know nothing of the sort."

The rake in him grinned at her, but he held his tongue.

"Oh, Miss Danvers," someone called from behind them.

Rathburn and Emma turned as one and saw not one, but two of her friends rushing to greet them. The one with the vivid red hair spoke first and linked with Emma's free arm. "Pray, forgive me," she said, her voice louder than necessary. "Our conversation was cut short when I spotted Miss Wakefield on the stair."

Rathburn furrowed his brow and saw that Emma looked equally confused by this greeting.

Then Emma laughed and leaned in to whisper, "Delaney, since when do you use a phrase like 'Pray, forgive me'? Is the dour Miss Pursglove, nearby?"

"Heaven forbid!"

Her friend with the dark hair subtly motioned for them to step out of the refreshment line. The soft strains of music began, signaling the end of intermission. They had only a moment.

Compelled by the unknown mystery that caused her friends to worry, Rathburn motioned to the server to set aside four cups of punch before they walked near the alcove beneath the stairs.

"Emma, I had to find you right away," Miss McFarland said. "Merribeth and I were seated directly below the Earl of Marlbrook's box, where Elena Mallory was seated."

He felt Emma stiffen, her fingers curling around his forearm. Apparently, this wasn't good news.

Miss Wakefield spoke next. "She made a terrible fuss about seeing you and Lord Rathburn leave the box, but even more when you didn't emerge from the stairway."

Emma swallowed. "How terrible?"

"She said that she wouldn't be surprised if the *Post* mentioned how *Miss D—*'s coiffure was mussed after the first intermission, proving once and for all that *Lord R—* was a true fan of the theater." Miss McFarland gave her a thorough once-over. "Thank goodness. Not a thing out of place."

"That's because," Miss Wakefield added, "Miss Danvers and Lord Rathburn were merrily conversing with us the entire time."

Emma relaxed for an instant, but then went rigid again. "But what if someone spied the two of you where you professed not to be?"

The redhead shrugged. "Then they were mistaken."

"And we are just about to return to our seats, speaking very loudly about our amusing conversation," Miss Wakefield said, but arched a wickedly intimidating brow at him, no doubt chastising him for getting her friend into a sticky situation.

He took it on the chin like a man and inclined his head. "Don't forget how you were both delighted to receive an invitation to a spring picnic at Hawthorne Manor."

Both of her friends lit up at the invitation. Emma herself lifted her gaze, awarding him with a smile so true it nearly stole his breath. He felt redeemed.

"Pray, forgive me, Lord Rathburn," Miss McFarland said with a wink to Emma. "But I seem to have forgotten the date already."

"A week from today," he offered, hoping he could achieve a great deal in the next few days.

"Splendid!" Miss Wakefield added before they said their goodbyes to Emma and returned to their seats.

A servant came up to them, carrying a tray of punch-filled cups. Rathburn asked that they be taken up to the Duke of Heathcoat's box, then made sure to follow closely so that he wouldn't put Emma in the path of scandal again.

She blew out a breath. "That was a close call."

"Yes. Apparently, Miss Mallory is no friend of yours."

Emma shook her head. "And all because of a simple conversation."

He frowned and slowed his steps, as they were nearing the top. "Was it merely a *simple* conversation?"

"How can it be otherwise? Everything that was said, every promise made, was surrounded by a very large *if*."

"*If* we marry in twenty days, you mean," he said, though he was having difficulty believing what he was hearing. Surely, she couldn't still . . . "You still believe nothing has changed."

How could that be, when everything was patently different for him? What would it take for her to see things as they truly were? How he'd changed? How he was serious?

He was tempted to march straight up to the box and confess the entire mock betrothal to his grandmother, solely so he could propose to Emma earnestly. However, her next words stopped him from doing just that and made him realize he might have to resort to other tactics.

"That was our bargain, after all," she said solemnly, slipping her hand free to stand apart from him, and leaving him cold in more ways than one. "This pretense was the first of our promises to each other. If we cannot keep that, then there is no reason to believe in the others we've made."

CHAPTER THIRTEEN

The following morning, the *Post* made no mention of an encounter between *Miss D—* and *Lord R—* scandalous or otherwise.

Rathbun searched the copy again and again to be sure. He even asked Stewart if he was certain this was the entire paper. When the head butler looked at him peculiarly, he realized that he sounded like a crazed buffoon.

He probably was. In fact, he'd lain awake all night, practicing the speeches he'd prepared for his grandmother and the Archbishop of Canterbury, listing the reasons why he required a special license. Why he *must* marry Emma Danvers.

Yet, in the morning, when it was clear he didn't need to deliver any speech at all, a rise of unspent energy churned inside him.

While he kept himself busier than usual of late—primarily to abstain from compiling a list of ways he could get Emma Danvers alone in order to prove to her that his intentions were serious—he gave himself another occupation.

Restless, he left the townhouse and drove to Hawthorne

Manor. It wasn't uncommon for him to remove his morning coat and roll up his shirtsleeves to assist the laborers. So, when he came prepared to expend more than his share of energy, the workmen kindly let him apply himself to constructing the massive four-poster bed in the viscountess's bedchamber.

The servants now referred to it as Miss Danvers's room, and he'd never bothered to correct them. Referring to it as *Emma's chamber* in his own mind was probably the reason why he'd had the plaster workers add sprays of jasmine to the corner molding in the room and over the doors. The finest silk wallpaper decorated the space in a beautiful pearlescent cream color, with ribbons of pink adorning thin stripes of chocolate brown. The colors worked perfectly together, creating a space that was simple and yet elegant, just like the woman who'd inspired his choice.

This is all for her, a voice whispered inside him. Not just this chamber, the sitting room, or even the bathing chamber, but the whole house and the view from each window. Each day, he found himself wondering about her opinion on everything from the colors of the draperies to the buds sprouting from the earth outside. "*They're just beginning to bloom,*" she'd said to him that day he'd given her a tour. "*It would be a shame not to give them a chance.*"

A profound realization coursed through him as sudden and as exhilarating as a summer storm. They were the blooms, fragile, fresh and new, waiting to blossom. Waiting for a reason to end the pretense in favor of a true betrothal.

Rathburn could no longer deny it. He wasn't pretending any longer, or acting according to his grandmother's expectations. In fact, he doubted he ever was.

He *wanted* to marry Emma Danvers.

She'd told him how only a fool would lose her heart to him. Yet, that's exactly what he wanted from her. He wanted her to lose her heart, or more to the point, to give it to him of her own free will.

Now, the only problem was convincing her that he would take proper care of it once she did. He needed to convince her that he was a suitable—

A gasp at the door broke his concentration and he dropped the corner post on top of his foot. However, seeing that it was his grandmother doing the gasping, he bit back the curse on the tip of his tongue. Gingerly, he eased his boot out from under the bruising weight.

"When the servants said I'd find you working in the viscountess's bedchamber, I didn't actually imagine I'd find you ... *laboring*." The last word held the same censure as if she'd learned he had leprosy and didn't want to catch it. "Surely, you should be overseeing the laborers, not doing their work for them."

"Good morning, Grandmamma," he said as pleasantly as he could with his foot throbbing. "Did you come all this way to ensure I wasn't holed up in a den of debauchery?"

"It is the *afternoon*, and don't be cheeky with me," she scolded as she walked into the room. Once she finished leveling him with her glare, she surveyed the room, pursing her lips, occasionally nodding. She pointed the tip of her cane to the corner molding. "Inspired by Miss Danvers, I presume?"

He half shrugged. "I don't know what you mean."

That earned him another glare as she lowered her cane and tapped it against the freshly varnished floors, the sound echoing around them. Yet, for some reason, he had the suspicion her crossness was merely a façade. Was that a trace of a smile he spied? Surely not.

"There is a rumor flitting about of a picnic to be held here in a week's time," she began, but turned away to examine the view from the windows, effectively telling him that she didn't want or expect his response. "A week is hardly enough time to make the garden acceptable. Unless, of course, you remove the old boxwood and put in a temporary screen of sorts. That way, the guests can still dine on the patio and their view won't be an unpleasant reminder of this home's tragic past."

Her words hit him harder than they should, the wound still too tender for him to respond. Yet, it was her use of *home* that gave him a sense that she wasn't as unfeeling as she'd usually appeared.

She continued her perusal of the room, her steps and the tip of her cane marking her slow journey. She usually walked with purpose, so her change in pace left him to wonder about the reason.

"I don't regret much in my life," she remarked after a short while. "However, I do regret never telling your father how much I admired him for making my only daughter happy. And for bringing up a fine grandson for me." At that, she offered a crinkly smile before she quickly cleared her throat and resumed her usual severe expression. "It is because of that, I've come here with this letter."

She withdrew a thick packet of papers from her reticule and held it out. Curious, he moved forward to take it, but found her grip stayed firm.

"Before you read it," she said with a slight shrug, the un-

characteristic action making her look softer and approach-
able. Heaven forbid if he told her such a thing. "I'll simply
tell you that I've released your inheritance to you, without
condition. You've done a remarkable amount of work here
and all on your own. I thought it high time—before time
gets away from me—to tell you, I find that an admirable
quality."

Rathburn stood there, speechless. It took him a moment
to recover and realize that she'd released the letter. The bulky
packet felt heavy in his hand, as if weighted by the responsi-
bility that went with it. "Without condition?"

"While you may have believed that I wanted you to prove
yourself worthy, the actual reason I withheld your inheritance
was for you to come to terms with the demons of your past.
After your father died, you closed yourself off from the world
for a time. Your behavior worried me and I feared you would
end up traveling the same path as so many of your predeces-
sors. As long as I limited your funds and kept you thinking
about your true goals, instead of getting lost, I felt you had
a chance." She flipped her hand in a gesture as if to say that
was over now. "You needn't marry, if you aren't so inclined—
though I say that with reservations, because it would be nice
to enjoy the sight of a great-grandchild before I'm bedridden
and half blind."

"I don't know what to say."

A sigh escaped her pursed lips as if she were perturbed,
yet there was a gleam of amusement in her gaze. "Under these
circumstances, it's appropriate to kiss your grandmother on
the cheek and thank her, I'm sure."

He did just that, and then hugged her for good measure,

startling a laugh out of her as she swatted him away. "You are coming to the picnic, aren't you?"

"Is that my invitation?"

He bowed. "Grandmamma, I would be honored if you would attend a picnic here at Hawthorne Manor in six days' time."

She turned away and walked at a fine clip to the door. "I'll check my schedule."

Normally Emma dragged Maudette with her on her weekly errand to the shop in St. Giles, but today she was in too much of a hurry. After paying the hack, she walked across the sidewalk, ignoring the filth beneath her feet, and stepped through the door with a basket in one hand and a bundle of clothes in the other.

A cheerful bell chimed as the door closed and a fresh-faced young woman in a ruffled cap came out of the back room, wiping her hands on her apron. "Miss Danvers!" she greeted with a broad and genuine smile, rushing forward to help with the burden. "Why, today isn't your day, at all. You usually come here on Thursdays."

Emma gratefully handed over the clothes so she could use both hands to hold on to the heavy basket. "You're right, Penny, but this Thursday I have another engagement. So, I thought I'd come early."

Penny and Archie Smith, owners of the shop, had once worked at Hawthorne Manor. Married less than a month before the night of the fire, Penny had been a parlor maid and Archie a footman. However, that night, everything changed.

Neither Penny nor Archie managed to escape the fire unscathed, Archie worst of all.

"Gracious," Penny said as she set the bundle down on the long chest of drawers near the back of the room. "What if his lordship decides to come early today?"

"Then you'll have to stuff me in the wardrobe," Emma said with a grin as she lifted the basket.

She'd been coming to High Street once a week for the past three years. Initially, she'd asked Penny to keep her visits a secret, though over the years, she'd become less concerned about it. Even so, neither she nor Rathbun brought it up in conversation. However, today, because she was here without a chaperone, she would hate for him to discover her, especially after she was always making a big fuss about propriety. If he caught her, and if—*heaven forbid*—his grandmother were with him, she would never hear the end of it. Not only that, but the consequences could be disastrous for Rathbun gaining his inheritance.

Penny untied the string around the bundle, fumbling a bit with the knot due to the gloves she always wore. While her natural beauty had been saved due to the wet blanket over her head as she'd rushed from the house, the hands clutching the blanket hadn't been as lucky. Terribly burned, scarred flesh covered her hands and her lower arms.

Archie wouldn't have suffered such an awful fate if he hadn't been the one who rushed back into the burning house with Oliver to search for the late Lord Rathbun. When Oliver emerged from the fire, carrying Archie over his shoulders, he'd told the story of how the brave footman had pushed him out of the way of a falling beam.

Archie had saved his life. A miracle that Emma was grateful for every single day. A world without Rathburn would seem far too empty and lackluster—or at least her world, her life would be. A fact that had occurred to her the night of the play, when she'd found herself wishing his bold declaration could be true.

For an instant, she'd forgotten their engagement was only a pretense, and she found herself wishing she could have him in her life forever.

That wish had made her speak from her heart and very nearly kiss him without thought of consequence. And then she'd heard voices in corridor and remembered where she was. Her insecurities had resurfaced as she thought of the beautiful, ethereal Lily Lovetree, and how Rathburn might still have her as his mistress if not for his need to prove himself to his grandmother. And the realization that he would never have considered Emma for his bride out of his own desire.

"These are too fine," Penny said, looking at the gowns Emma had collected from her own wardrobe and her mother's. "Surely you can't part with these."

"My mother wears only bright fabrics now, with garish flower prints. You would shudder to look at her," she exaggerated with a laugh and earned one in return. There was even a dress her mother had wanted Emma to wear this Season, but the peacock blue was far too flamboyant and wouldn't have suited Rathburn's quest. Although, she did wonder if he'd have remarked on the color should she have worn it. Would he have found her pretty, perhaps?

Penny knew better than to argue with her and accepted

the clothes with a gracious smile. There were also a few of her
father's more sedate shirts and waistcoats, along with little
odds and ends for the shop that Penny's parents had owned.
Inside the basket were a few essentials: cakes of fragrant soap,
hair ribbons, handkerchiefs, and ruffled caps. She'd also
brought a crock of soup, a loaf of bread, and a small ham that
the cook had prepared special for the Smiths. It was the least
she could do to repay the Smiths for all they'd sacrificed.

"You are too kind." Penny fought back tears this time.
"When I think of the generosity your family and Lord Rathburn's family have bestowed on us, it makes my heart burst
for how much it swells."

Emma leaned in and hugged her, though she wished she
could do so much more. "Both you and Mr. Smith are the
kindest—"

"Gracious me!" Penny said with a start. "His lordship. Oh
dear! I just knew it would happen."

Emma jerked her gaze toward the storefront window.
Sure enough, Rathburn's curricle was directly outside. *Oh
dear, indeed!* "Is he alone?"

"I'm not sure, Miss Danvers." Penny fretted, pressing her
knuckles to her lips. "Though he would hate to know you
were here without a chaperone."

Surely, he wouldn't bring his grandmother here. Nonetheless, she couldn't risk being seen unless she were absolutely
certain. "Is there a back entrance to your shop?"

"No. Only the front," Penny said in a rush, dashing
through the door that led to the back room, gesturing madly.
"Quick. Through here. There's a curtained pantry between
the kitchen and the parlor."

Emma didn't hesitate. "Thank you, Penny," she whispered as she dashed to the room.

She found the heavily draped pantry and slipped into the darkened alcove just as she heard the jingle of the bell. The familiar rumble of his voice made her heart quicken. She needed to calm herself, and her audible breathing, or else he'd discover her the moment he passed by on his way to the parlor, where Archie spent most of his time.

Having lost his leg in addition to having severe burns on the same half of his body, Archie had trouble getting around. Yet, his mind was still as sharp as ever, and he had the use of his dominant hand to help him earn income by fixing clocks. Rathburn seemed to find a clock or personal timepiece each week for Archie to fix.

When the thud of his footfalls came near, she held her breath, waiting for him to pass by.

He opened the parlor door, but didn't bother to close it behind him, which kept her prisoner in the pantry.

"Just the man I wanted to see," Rathburn said, his voice cheerful. "No, don't you dare try to get up. It's only me, after all. Besides, I'll only be here for a minute."

Lighter footsteps crossed in front of the pantry and soon Penny peeked through the curtain, her face pale and anxious. Emma nodded, letting her know that all would be well.

"It's good to see you, Lord Rathburn," Archie said, his voice raspy but strong. "Unfortunately, I haven't finished the clock . . . as you can see by the state of the workings strewn over this table."

Rathburn chuckled. "There is no rush. Of late, I need no clock to remind me of the passage of time."

Hearing this, Emma felt a pang of remorse. The date of their wedding was fast approaching. Fifteen days. It must be weighing on his mind as much as hers. Strange, she hadn't realized until now how difficult the situation must be for Rathburn. The more that time passed, the more strained and fragile their bargain became, and their options for severing it even fewer. And the less she wanted to.

"However, I bring good news," he continued. "Mrs. Smith, come into the room, for you will want to hear this, too. I have just received word from Dr. Kohn, the great surgeon from Germany, whom I mentioned to you before."

He waited a beat, leaving Emma enough time to wonder what this could be about. Rathburn had never mentioned correspondence with a surgeon from Germany before.

"The good gentleman has accepted my offer. In two months' time, he will be here in London, and it is my greatest hope that he will find Goswick Hospital to his liking."

Emma heard Penny's cry of joy. Her own hand came up to cover her mouth, even though she wasn't entirely sure what was being said. *Goswick Hospital?* As far as she knew, there was no such hospital near London.

"Don't get your hopes up, Penny," Archie said, even though his voice had gone softer, as if he were holding back emotion. "It's been years since the fire, and there might not be anything he can do for me."

"It's true, my friend," Rathburn said. "He stated the same to me in his letter. However, that is not to say he doesn't know a thing or two about making you more comfortable. So, he leaves us to hope for small things."

Emma listened carefully as they continued to speak about

the hospital and how long the project had taken, from the first brick to the last. Apparently, Rathburn had decided soon after his father's death that he wanted to leave a legacy in his father's name.

Hot tears streamed down her cheeks, her heart breaking for him. A lesser man would have allowed the loss of a parent to excuse poor decisions. Yet, Rathburn had chosen to rebuild Hawthorne Manor *and* a hospital to honor the memory of his beloved father instead.

She'd known all along that Rathburn was a good man at his core. Now, she had proof.

No wonder he'd been desperate to gain his inheritance.

A small sob escaped her. Covering her mouth, she finally admitted to herself the traumatic truth—she loved him. Some part of her always had.

The painful realization struck a mighty blow that wrenched her heart: She could never marry him.

After all, how could she, in good conscience, jeopardize his inheritance? He needed to marry someone of whom his grandmother approved. If the dowager ever discovered how similar Emma was to her father . . . all would be lost. Society had shunned him, just as surely as they would shun her if her secret were revealed. Therefore, Rathburn would be ruined by association in the eyes of his grandmother and the funds he needed to finish Hawthorne Manor and Goswick Hospital would be forever out of his reach.

Not only had she lost her heart to him, but her head as well.

Oh, Emma. How could you have been so foolish?

Feeling brokenhearted and bereft, she needed to leave

and figure out her next course of action. However, before she could make her escape, the curtain jerked to the side. Emma started. The sound of the rings sliding over the pole reverberated in the small pantry.

Rathburn stood there, staring at her in stunned disbelief. "Emma, what are you doing in here?"

"I—" Guilty, she swiped the tears from her cheeks. As his expression altered, she realized there was no use pretending she hadn't heard everything. He'd already figured that out. "Why didn't you tell me about the hospital?"

His shoulders lifted in a shrug and his gaze disconnected from hers for a moment as if he were embarrassed. "For the same reason, I suspect, that you never speak of coming here each week. Although, I would prefer it if you would allow me to chaperone you in the future. After all, Maudette certainly isn't"—he stopped and his gaze collided with hers again—"Where exactly *is* Maudette? And I don't believe I saw your father's carriage . . ."

Now it was her turn to look away.

"You came here alone? Without any chaperone, or any protection at all?" His tone was deadly quiet. Reaching out, he took her chin in a gentle but firm grasp, commanding her to look at him. "Promise me you will never . . . *ever* . . . do that again."

Mutely, she nodded. His eyes blazed with a mixture of anger and fear. Was he actually worried about her?

He lowered his hand, but instead of stepping back, he reached for hers. His mouth hitched up on one side in a smug grin. "Good. I see no reason why we cannot combine our visits from this point forward."

She would argue with him, but this was not the time or place. In fact, she was starting to believe all this talk about her venturing out without a chaperone, when it had never concerned him before, was nothing more than a way to distract her.

"Goswick Hospital," she said softly, steering the conversation back to the issue at hand. The real reason behind his desperation for his inheritance. "I think it's a very noble endeavor. Your father"—her voice cracked, threatening to break—"he would have been so proud."

Rathburn squeezed her hand. With a slow shake of his head, a dark shadow of overwhelming sadness snuffed out the golden specks of light in his eyes. "I couldn't save him, Em," he whispered as if this was a secret he could share only with her. "I tried, but I couldn't . . ."

And in that quiet moment, standing in the pantry, she fell in love with him even more.

CHAPTER FOURTEEN

Now that she knew about the hospital, Emma had to tell Rathburn the truth before it was too late. Her terrible secret would surely end their pretend betrothal, just as it would ruin any chance for her to marry at all.

But she couldn't risk waiting any longer. It had to be today. The wedding was less than two weeks away.

"I felt this way, too," her mother said on their way to Hawthorne Manor for the picnic. She reached across the carriage and squeezed Emma's hand. "In the weeks leading up to marrying your father."

Emma drew in a breath, refusing to mention how it wasn't the same at all. They all knew the truth. Rathburn needed the money. She made a show of peering up at the sky, instead of staring aimlessly at the passing landscape. "I don't feel any way in particular. I was only worried that it might rain and spoil the picnic."

Her father bit down on the end of his unlit pipe and peered up to the sky as well. "It has been an uncharacteristically sunny spring, though that is not to say we haven't had our share of drizzles. Unlikely though it may be, I suppose those ebullient clouds could suddenly squeeze out a few drops."

The view through the window drew her attention again. Yet, instead of the grove of trees that flanked either side of the park surrounding Hawthorne Manor, she only saw Rathburn's face, and heard his unexpected declaration at the theater. The more she thought about it, the more it confused her. Especially after learning about the hospital and truth behind his need for his inheritance.

Why did he pretend to care more than he did? Only one conclusion made sense to her. Rathburn must have realized she'd found out about his mistress and had sought to pacify her. In the heat of the moment, he'd made an outrageous vow.

Yet, she couldn't disguise the fact that she'd been ensnared by his demeanor. He'd seemed uncharacteristically serious. There hadn't been even a shred of his usual teasing manner. In fact, for days, her foolish heart wouldn't allow her head to drop the matter. She'd even started to wish that the declaration they'd both made at the theater a week ago had been true. Or could be true.

If only.

That enormous *IF* hung over her head like the clouds dotting the sky today, only hers were much darker and threatened to spoil what could have been a perfect afternoon, and a dream that had only started to blossom.

Her mother smiled at her in the mysterious way she often did. "Be careful, my dear. If you spend too much time looking for rain, you'll likely find it."

Instead of making an argument against her mother's as-

sertion, this time Emma took note and nodded. She didn't
need to look for the dark cloud, because she carried it with her.

The carriage came to a halt in front of Rathburn's grand
estate. Her heart started to flutter in opposition to her twist-
ing stomach. The first footman assisted both her and her
mother from the carriage. Rathburn was detained further
down, assisting the dowager duchess, as well as his mother
from their carriage.

The Weatherstones were directly behind them. She'd
known in advance that Merribeth and Delaney were planning to ride with the newlyweds, so it came as no surprise
when her friends came rushing forward to pull her away from
her parents.

"Elena Mallory is positively chartreuse with envy. She
even tried to cajole an invitation from me, if you can believe
it," Delaney said with no small amount of delight brightening
her broad grin. "She went so far as to suggest that I should
explain to Lord Rathburn how she and I are cousins."

Only the tail end surprised Emma. "*Are* you cousins?"

She gave an offhanded shrug. "Distantly, through my
mother's side. Although, after last year," she said, her mouth
tight, her voice lowered, "it's no wonder she hasn't acknowledged the association until now."

"I for one am glad she's a horrid green. I've been pinching
myself all morning thinking about my first visit to the famed
Hawthorne Manor. The balls once held here are still talked
about," Merribeth said, gazing starry-eyed at the house.
Some of the most legendary parties were from the era before
the Rathburn title had reformed. "I don't know if I'm more
excited about seeing the house or the gardens."

"You'll be pleased with both," Penelope said, walking up to the group on the arm of Mr. Weatherstone, who inclined his head.

"Miss Danvers. A fine day for a picnic."

Embarrassed that both Ethan and Penelope knew about the mock courtship, a rush of heat rose to her cheeks. "Rathburn would have it no other way, I'm sure."

Her friend's husband broke free of his usual stoicism and surprised her with a chuckle, before his gaze shifted to a spot over her shoulder. "My thoughts exactly."

Emma didn't need to hear the sound of the gravel crunching beneath his boots to know that Rathburn stood behind her. She could feel it through every pore on her body.

"My lady has arrived," Rathburn said, settling his hand into the small of her back as if the gesture were familiar to them both. It wasn't, and yet it felt . . . right. "And Weatherstone in tow with his beautiful entourage."

Penelope and Delaney both beamed, their gazes missing nothing. Merribeth would have, too, but her attention was still diverted to the towering brick and windowed façade.

Charming as ever, Rathburn greeted them each in turn and finally gained Merribeth's attention. "Where is Mr. Clairmore? I thought surely he would be in town by now."

"It was so kind of you to extend the invitation to him," she answered, her eyes brightening at the mention of her nearly betrothed. "I wrote to Mr. Clairmore about the picnic and suggested that he might want to travel up from Fernbough to get to know the wedding party before the happy day. Unfortunately, pressing matters keep him away. However, the wording in his letter leads me to believe I should expect a visit from him soon. I'm anticipating a grand romantic gesture any day."

Emma had always admired Merribeth's unshakable faith in Mr. Clairmore's affection. She felt a pang of envy, wishing she could have the same certainty.

"When he is next in town, I shall arrange a dinner for us all," Rathburn said, and then turned to address the group at large while keeping Emma at his side. Each time his fingers moved slightly, it sent a riot of tingles beneath her skin, which made it all the more difficult to remind herself that they were only playing a part. "I thought a tour of the main level would enhance our appetites."

The small party agreed. However, when he proceeded to walk toward the wide entrance of the manor, she hesitated and turned her head to whisper. "Perhaps it would be best if you were to escort your mother. This must be difficult for her."

Rathburn smiled down at her. "Your concern does you credit, and reminds me that we have much to talk about. Later," he promised. "As for my mother, we spent yesterday together, here. As you might expect, there was some sadness, but overall she is happy that Hawthorne Manor will be a home once again."

Confused, she frowned. Surely, he wouldn't allow his mother to believe their pretense and had explained everything to her. "But—"

"*After* the picnic," he said, his gaze locking with hers as if to speak through thought alone. However, it was a language she'd yet to learn. He must have noted her frustration, because he dropped his arm from her and drew in a breath. "Patience, Emma-*mine*. Until then, I must remember to keep my distance, for the sake of propriety."

Emma stared after him as he walked to the door.

The tour was much the same as it had been before. Yet this time, Rathburn didn't want anyone to go upstairs. Instead, he guided them through the main floor and kitchen.

He also made a point of not looking at her again for a while, which left her oddly bereft. Not only that, but since she'd overheard his conversation with the Smiths, she felt unworthy of him. How could she ever have thought he was an irredeemable rake? How could she have been blind to the truth all this time?

Her musings left her unable to enjoy the banquet of fruits, cheeses, and breads. Instead, she stared out at the garden. The old hedgerow had been removed. In its place were polished, dark wood poles draped in white canvas and silk, looking very much like corsair pirate sails as they caught the breeze and undulated with it. The canvas and silk sails were used on every other space, showing a glimpse of the garden through one, just enough for a hint of what lay beyond.

"What do you think, Miss Danvers?" Rathburn asked, coming near to her for the first time in what seemed like hours. "Of course, it isn't permanent, but for an afternoon picnic, I thought it was enough to see the blooming flowers beyond. After all, they are timid little blossoms," he added with a grin that he mostly kept to himself.

She tamped down a sudden rush of longing when she lifted her gaze to his. How much longer would she be able to look at him like this before their mock betrothal ended? "I feel like I'm staring out at an exotic land, with the hint of color waiting to be explored."

"Perhaps you'd like to join me for a walk?"

Her parents overheard the request and gave their consent. There was no harm in walking in full view—or nearly—during a picnic. However, she didn't want to risk anyone overhearing what she had to tell him. Besides that, she'd brought something with her that would finally reveal her secret.

"If it wouldn't be too much trouble, I wonder if you might have a book on . . ." —she hesitated— "flowering perennials I could borrow?"

He frowned in confusion. However, curiosity lifted his brows and he offered a slight nod. "I have several. Would it be acceptable for me to escort your daughter to the library?" Apparently, he was far more adept at understanding the language of her unspoken thoughts.

Her mother hid a sly grin behind her napkin, obviously having the wrong idea. If Emma hadn't been so nervous, she would have said outright that Rathburn didn't see her in that manner. Then again, she hardly ever said what was on her mind. Instead, she held it inside until it rushed out in the only way she knew how to truly express herself.

Her fingers twitched. She looked from one parent to the other and then to the faces of those gathered, her nerves raw and frayed. She suddenly realized she couldn't do this any longer. She couldn't pretend to be practical, sensible Emma. She couldn't keep lying to them about—

"Certainly," her father said. "She's spent a great deal of time studying horticulture recently. I would never deter my daughter from her pursuit of knowledge."

Once Rathburn led her away through the ballroom doors, he arched an enquiring brow at her. "Horticulture?"

"Merely expanding my Latin vocabulary," she lied. Her determination to tell Rathburn her secret wavered, vacillating between two schools of thought. The first school being the *It's Too Late*, whereas the second one was the *It's Now or Never*.

"You have been very busy with the manor of late," she said, in an effort to ease her way into their inevitable conversation.

"Have you missed me?" he teased, but looked pleased by the notion.

She had, only she wouldn't admit it. "I know you have obligations to oversee the labor."

"Perhaps I've been waiting for you to flatter me with demands for my time."

He was the last person who required more flattery, as her adoring gaze must surely be showing him. "I'm not the demanding sort."

"No, you're not, though I wouldn't mind if you were."

Her heart issued a tremulous flutter at the way his words drifted off to a whisper. Almost as if he hadn't planned to tell her, which made her want to believe it all the more. "Demand that you attend the Binghams' dinner tomorrow evening? A tour of the art exhibit in the afternoon. A carriage ride through the park each morning. Lord and Lady Finch's ball next week . . ." She let her schedule drift off into oblivion.

"I will concede to each one, except for the tour of the exhibit."

Of course. The only one she'd been looking forward too. "Why ever not?"

"Because the instant you mentioned it, I could only think of all the different dark corners and hidden alcoves I could lure you into," he said, his gaze holding her captive. "Alone with you, I cannot be trusted."

Her heart gave a sudden jolt. She tried to ignore it and tore her gaze from his. That's when she realized they were already standing in the library. On the opposite wall, a tower of books stood from floor to ceiling, with a steep wooden ladder attached to a brass rail near the top. Twin sets of hunter green brocade curtains were pulled back to bathe the room in sunlight, allowing her to see the corner desk clearly. Earlier, she'd secretly asked Tom, her parents' driver, to leave the leather case in the library when all the guests were on the patio. And now, here it sat, waiting for her courage to make an appearance.

"We are alone now," she said without thinking.

Rathburn went stock-still and captured her gaze again. That hard, possessive look flashed in his dark pupils, and suddenly the air between them became thick and heavy. She went still, too, not realizing how swiftly the mood could change from companionable conversation to something more palpable.

For a solitary moment, she forgot why they were there. Unlike earlier, the room was now warm and humid, which seemed unlikely on such a fine spring day. Beneath her gloves, her palms grew damp, and she pressed them together to ease her discomfort. At her wrists, her pulse beat rapidly.

"You wanted a book on flowering perennials," he said, though his words were more like a question.

No. She wanted to close the distance between them. She wanted to wrap her arms around his neck. She wanted to kiss him. A book was the farthest thing from her mind—

The shock of her bold thoughts abruptly drew her back to her purpose. She remembered why it was necessary to have him alone in the library, even though this more recent option kept her titillated. "Actually, I wanted to have a moment with you. In private. I wanted you to know . . ." Her voice suddenly gave out, forcing her to clear her throat to reclaim it.

He studied her closely and shifted his stance as if he couldn't make up his mind whether to stay still or move toward her. Beneath the hard line of his jaw and above his cravat, his pulse matched hers. He swallowed and tore his gaze away before he shook his head as if convincing himself he was wrong about whatever he was thinking.

"If this is about our discussion, I'd rather wait until we have a bit more time," he said, moving past her and walking toward the desk.

She took a deep breath. "It isn't. Actually, it has to do with the case on your desk and what's inside."

He looked down, confusion furrowing his brow as he lifted the case. "You wished me to see this?"

"What's inside . . . yes," she answered. Overcome by uncertainty, she stepped forward, too.

Since ignoring her tumultuous feelings regarding Rathburn had been a Sisyphean task, she'd found another occupation—or rather another occupation had found her once more. Unable to contain the emotions roiling within her, she'd begun to paint again.

Oh, she knew how such an act would be perceived by the *ton*. If anyone discovered her secret, she'd become the pariah her parents were. She knew the risk.

So, when her father had approached her, years ago, with

the idea of applying to the Royale Academy, she'd had to make a very difficult decision. She knew that if she ever wanted to marry and have a family of her own, she had to cease her own pursuits.

Of course, sketching and painting with watercolors were acceptable—even expected—hobbies for the well-rounded debutante. However, for an unmarried young woman, painting with oil was seen as wanton and ill bred, beyond the pale even more than gaming or reading romances. A *lady* simply did not paint with oils. Add her parents' reputations to her own tendency to allow her emotions to run through each stroke of the brush, and she knew she couldn't display an inkling of artistic tendencies without drawing unwanted attention. Therefore, she'd told her parents that she'd lost interest in painting.

However, lately, the part of her nature she'd kept buried for years in order to fit in refused to stay hidden. There were moments when no amount of needlework would occupy her hands. But she'd needed to express herself, to say everything she kept bottled inside her without risking too much of herself.

Yet, pages of charcoal sketches didn't help. Nor did another foray with watercolors capture the torturous depths of these feelings. Only oil could do that for her. And she kept her shameful secret hidden beneath a false bottom of her wardrobe.

Earlier today, she'd slipped the canvas inside one of the carrying cases her father used and asked the driver to conceal it for her. After all, she couldn't risk being seen with it. She didn't want to explain to her parents what was inside.

And now, Rathburn turned the clasp.

The case fell open over his desk. The painting lay there for all the world to see . . . or at least for Rathburn to see.

She found herself struggling between wanting to hurl her body over the painting to conceal it, and wanting to hear his opinion.

"You brought me a painting of a garden. It's quite lovely, though I cannot imagine—*Oh*. This is a painting of the garden here, or at least what it could be." He glanced up at her, a true smile on his face. Nothing hidden this time. Nothing he kept for himself. Instead, he gave her all of it.

She steeled herself for what she must say.

Beside her, Rathburn lowered his gaze to the oil landscape. "Wherever did you find it? The artist's talent is remarkable. And the garden is laid out in a way that mimics the one here."

"I—" She broke off abruptly as his words seeped in. A newfound pleasure washed over her at hearing his praise. Knowing that he mistakenly thought he was paying compliments to an anonymous artist didn't stop a light airy sensation from filling her. "You think it's remarkable?"

"There is a depth to every stroke that makes me see the garden in an entirely different light. The flowers are alive. If I didn't know better, I'd almost believe their fragrance filled the room."

Though he may not know it, he was seeing part of her, a part she kept hidden from the rest of the world, even from herself. In his expression and comments, she found a kind of acceptance.

"Do you like how the walkway is lined with a combination of pruned topiaries and hydrangeas instead of boxwood?"

"I do. They remind me of . . ." His gaze held hers as if he could see the inner workings of her mind, or even see the vapor that comprised her soul. "They remind me of the ones on the Dorsets' patio."

Suddenly, she felt nervous, exposed. Almost as if he'd guessed the truth. The confession was on the tip of her tongue, but she couldn't force herself to tell him. She wanted to hold on to the freedom of him not knowing for another moment or so.

He spoke first. "At first glance, the garden looks strictly pure and innocent, fresh and white."

"Only at first?" Compelled to see it from his viewpoint, she turned slightly. Her arm brushed his.

He inhaled sharply as if the simple gesture caused him pain. Then he shifted, moving slowly, drawing his left arm behind her and settling his hand into the bow of her lower back. He stayed still for a moment, as if testing her reaction or waiting for her disapproval.

She pressed her teeth down into the soft flesh at the corner of her mouth, refusing to make a sound or move an inch apart from him.

His right hand lingered on the painting as he lowered his head as if to study it more closely. "Just look at those hydrangeas, how lush and full they are. You can almost see them stirring in the breeze," he said, his voice lower now, almost hoarse, his breath stirring the wisps of hair near the shell of her ear.

Tingles trailed over her flesh as if he were touching her and not the painting. Gently, he brushed over every stone, sliding his fingertip toward a bank of jasmine in full bloom on either side of the path. There wasn't a cool enough breeze coming in through the open window to diminish the heat rising from each pulse point in her body and spreading like warm honey through her veins.

Mutely, she nodded. The heat from his hand at her back caused her chemise to cling to her skin in a way that made her feel as if she wore nothing at all. As if sensing this, he moved his hand. His fingers splayed against her, drawing in a quick shock of cool air before it heated again.

His thumb swept over the curve of her hip while the heel of his hand pressed lower, against the supple flesh of her derriere. "See how they spill onto the walk here and here?"

A strangled sound climbed up her throat. She tried to disguise it as a murmur of assent by nodding. His lips grazed her temple, moving lower, following the curve of her ear to her lobe where he gently nipped her. A sigh escaped her. Ever so slightly, she tilted her head back and angled her body toward him.

Now, the warm honey transformed into tingles that started at the soles of her feet and traveled upward. She pressed her knees together to stop their progress, trying to regain her composure.

"Then, of course, there's the jasmine," he said against the pulse of her throat. He abandoned his study of the painting now, placing both of his hands on her. One, he kept at her lower back, even lower still. The other traced the curve of her waist upward to the sash tied beneath her breasts. "When you see the jasmine all clustered together, it's almost as if they're hiding something."

She waited for his hand to steal up past her sash to cup her flesh. But he held back, tormenting her with the slow sweep of his thumb, teasing the underside until she was forced to close her eyes.

In that moment, she imagined stepping into the painting with him. Overhead, the clouds seemed to gather, forcing them to look for shelter. He drew her down the path, their pace matching the quick beat of her pulse.

She could feel herself moving against him as her mind took her beyond the hydrangeas and pruned topiaries to the thick bank of jasmine. *Were* they hiding something?

Only everything she felt and all the words she'd never spoken.

Rathbun growled, the sound both feral and frustrated. He lifted his head. His breath rushed hard and fast across her lips. "And when you look further back, toward the climbing roses beneath the shadowed arbor, you catch a glimpse of pink petals in their first bloom," he said, pressing his lips to her temple. "This garden has secrets, Emma. Wanton secrets."

He lifted a hand to brush an errant lock of hair behind her ear, leaving her shaken. His fingers strayed to trace the curve of her jaw, following the line of her throat to her collarbone. Even though he didn't say a word, the question was in his gaze. Perhaps the answer as well.

At the touch of his fingertips, she swayed toward him. She'd worried about showing him the painting, knowing it would remove his grandmother's approval. Then something else entirely had happened. Now, she stood bare before him, allowing him to see what she kept hidden from everyone else.

"There's no one at all like you." His gaze dipped to her mouth with the promise of a kiss.

Her lips tingled in response and she lifted her face, a blatant invitation. *Wanton secrets . . .* Yes, she had those, too.

Yet, before he could lean in, a sharp knock sounded at the front door down the hall.

He closed his eyes and lowered his forehead to hers again. "Why is it that whenever we're kissing, there's a knock at the door?"

She released a sigh, not bothering to hide her regret. "We weren't kissing. Not exactly."

"Not exactly," he said with a chuckle. "Believe me, Emma, in some part of my mind we are *always* kissing."

As romantic as his statement was, it probably wasn't the best thing to say right before her brother barged through the door.

CHAPTER FIFTEEN

Rathburn turned just in time to see Rafe Danvers storm in.

There was no time to exchange a greeting or explain himself before a fist connected with his jaw, propelling him backward.

He might have stumbled into Emma, had it not been for his friend holding onto his lapels, preparing to punch him again. "I thought I could trust you."

He'd never heard a more lethal hiss. Blocking the second blow with his forearm, he pushed Danvers backward. There was no reason Emma should see this. "It isn't what you think."

"I wrote to you, Rafe," Emma said, coming up beside them. "I explained everything."

"That's why I came back as soon as I received your letter," Danvers said through clenched teeth, taking hold of him and leaning menacingly close. "Yet, when I do, I see my friend—someone I'd considered a brother—taking advantage of my absence. Taking advantage of my parents' gullibility. Taking advantage of my sister."

Rathburn locked his hands around Danvers's wrists.

"Let me explain." They were evenly matched in build, but his friend had the advantage of rage.

"Rafael Linden Danvers, release him at once," Emma ordered, pulling on her brother's arm to no effect. "He is your friend, and you're making a complete fool of yourself. If you think for a moment that Rathburn was compromising me in any way, you have it wrong. He isn't interested in me in that way. As I stated in the letter, this is merely a pretense."

Brave, though she was, this wasn't her fight. And her brother had a better grasp of the true situation than she did. "Emma, return to the party. Please. Your brother and I have much to discuss."

"I won't leave this room," she huffed. "Not until Rafe comes to his senses."

Her brother's gaze hardened. "Then you'd better make yourself comfortable."

"Better yet," Rathburn said with a shove toward the open door, forcing Danvers to back up. Hearing Emma misconstrue his true intentions—*still!*— and ignore everything he'd said to her, made his own anger rise. It gave him the extra adrenaline he needed. "Why don't we adjourn to my study for a private chat since our discussion isn't suitable for your sister?"

He didn't give his friend a chance to refute. Once in the hall, Danvers released his hold and went willingly. "You can't charm your way out of this one."

Rathburn closed the study door behind them and locked it for good measure. He didn't want Emma barging in. So much had changed in him in the past two weeks that he hardly knew where to begin.

"It isn't what you think."

"Oh, well, that's a relief," Danvers mocked, shoving a hand through his hair and pacing in front of the desk. "I was under the assumption that you'd asked my parents for permission to engage in a mock courtship with my sister and that somehow you'd managed to talk *her* into it. I'm glad I have that wrong. I'm glad my sister's letter, stating the stipulations of your agreement, was all a figment of her imagination." He stopped and glared at Rathburn, pressing his fists to the top of the desk. His nostrils flared in barely restrained fury. "It is peculiar though, how she stated that your reason for this sham courtship was to gain your inheritance. Since I know how you'd be willing to do anything to get it, I'm relieved to learn that this whole thing *isn't what I think*. Because believe me, if it was what I think, then you'd be a dead man."

"Everything you said is true," Rathburn said, ashamed. "At least, that's how it was in the beginning."

"Then name your seconds."

"Wait." He held up a hand. "You can challenge me, and I will appear at dawn, but know that if you do, you'll be harming Emma's reputation more than saving it. You'll also be murdering a friend who has no intention of firing a single shot in your direction. I'd never risk robbing Emma of a beloved brother. She's too precious to me now."

"Are you daring to pretend to be the man I know you're not?"

"I know how it appears." Rathburn slowly exhaled. He'd known Rafe Danvers since they were at Eton. Their close friendship was one that didn't allow for any secrets. Because of that, he knew Danvers's rage wasn't solely directed at him, but also sparked from a reminder of the woman who'd once jilted him at the altar. "I know that you are completely aware of my nature. But tell me, have I ever done anything to harm your sister? I had ample opportunity last year, being her escort in your stead."

"She gave me reports of her social schedule and how you'd behaved like a veritable bodyguard. Even worse, *she claimed*, than my behavior her first Season."

"A blatant truth"—he lifted his palms in surrender—"although, I never bothered to question my own motives until they were pointed out to me. I don't blame you for not seeing it either."

Danvers pushed away from the desk and walked to the far end of the room as if he needed the space to think, or perhaps space to keep himself from leaping across the desk and strangling him. Either way, there was a palpable shift in the energy.

"You're saying this betrothal is real for you and that your affection for my sister began last year?"

"Honestly, I don't know when it began. I feel like an idiot for not knowing, because I believe it was there all the time." A self-derisive laugh escaped. "But if I can't convince Emma that things have changed, I highly doubt I'll be able to persuade you."

"She doesn't know?"

Again, he felt like an idiot. Yet, he thought he'd made himself clear on several occasions. "I was planning to discuss it with her after the picnic."

"So, she believes you have no intention of going through with the actual ceremony?" Danvers took a few steps forward.

He nodded. "I wanted to tell her that I still wanted to marry her."

"Still?"

"My grandmother settled my inheritance. Without condition."

"You're free to do whatever you choose . . . and you *want* to marry my sister?" Danvers laughed and shook his head as if the idea were preposterous.

Rathburn straightened. "If you think to insult her in my presence then I will gladly rescind my refusal to shoot in your direction at dawn tomorrow. As you well know, I'm a far better shot."

A devilish grin spread over Danvers's face. "So, I am to have a brother after all."

"If she will have me," he said through clenched teeth.

"Yet, if you continue with your planned discussion, how will you know if she will have you, or if it is your fortune that gains her hand?"

The accusation flew off target, but stung all the same. "Emma isn't like that."

"True," Danvers mused, then lifted his brows. "However, she isn't one to risk her reputation. She might marry you simply to avoid scandal and the unwanted attention that will fall on her once you break the betrothal."

What a friend he was to point that out. This accusation hit the mark, soundly. Even though he thought he'd noticed a change in her feelings toward him as well, there was only one way to be certain. "Our altercation today gives her a viable excuse to make a clean break without risking her reputation," he said more to himself than to Danvers.

His friend's expression turned curious. "Then you're leaving the choice in her hands?"

What else could he do? He had to know.

Emma stood in the doorway of the library, listening for sounds of distress from down the hall. She'd heard a few raised voices, but nothing clear enough for her to decipher. Then shortly after Oliver and Rafe entered the study, she'd stopped hearing anything at all.

She thought about sending a footman to retrieve her parents and put a stop to whatever absurdity was happening in the study. Then she thought about how her parents would handle the situation. Each time she played the scenario out in her mind, it didn't end well. Her parents would inevitably reveal the truth of her bargain with Rathburn in front of the dowager, and Rathburn would lose his inheritance.

No. She could not involve her parents, or any of her friends for that matter. The dowager was too sharp to let anyone slip past her without questioning their reasons.

That thought brought to mind the painting lying in full view. Quickly, she tucked it back into the case and placed it on the floor, resting it against the far side of the desk.

When that was settled, she peered down the hall, worrying the corner of her mouth. What were they doing in there?

Just when she was about to rush into the library to ensure they weren't up to something idiotic like naming their seconds for a duel at dawn—her brother occasionally allowed his temper to rule his actions, after all—they emerged.

Much to her relief, they looked no worse than when they'd left . . . aside from Rathburn's reddened jaw, crumpled cravat, and wrinkled lapels.

Her brother grinned at her, making her highly suspicious. With Rathburn following, Rafe settled her arm in the crook of his and walked down the hall as if they were at their leisure. "You'll be glad to know it's all settled. Rathburn explained everything."

She'd already explained everything in her letter, but she didn't point it out. "I was afraid you were selecting dueling pistols."

"Pistols would have been a foolish choice, since Rathburn's a helluva shot. Swords would be a better option, giving me the advantage."

"I beg to differ," Rathburn said, his tone edged in amusement. "There have been a number of occasions where I could refute your claim."

"I wouldn't be much of a friend if I didn't let you win some of the times."

"*Let* me w—"

"Then you are still friends?" Emma interrupted before they ended up behaving like children again.

Her brother stopped and stared down at her. "Were you hoping I'd run him through?"

"*No!*" All the blood drained from her head, and the air left her lungs on an unsteady breath. "Of course not. That was exactly the reason I sent you the letter, to explain matters so you wouldn't get the wrong idea. And also to prepare you in case Rathburn would need you to act as best man."

"Just in case this entire farce played out." He nodded thoughtfully, making her wonder if he was going to decide he didn't like the idea of her being involved in the scheme after all. However, when he tossed a cheeky grin over his shoulder to Rathburn, she could have killed him for scaring her. "Should I *act* the part of the best man?"

"Only if you can *act* civilized," Rathburn growled as they neared the patio. "I'd hate to think what the effort would do your demon half."

"Catch fire, no doubt."

The moment they stepped foot onto the patio, the worry and nervousness of the past few minutes was swept aside. Upon seeing Rafe, her mother jumped out of her seat and embraced him. Her father rose and ruffled his unruly curls as if he was still a lad.

Surprisingly, even the dowager graced them with a smile. "I'm merely glad I wasn't forced to send a search party for the two of you."

A rush of heat swept to Emma's cheeks. Somehow, she'd become distracted from her true purpose of speaking with Rathburn alone.

Perhaps Rathburn was right. They couldn't be trusted alone. Not together, at any rate.

Yet, because of her own impulses, she'd missed the perfect opportunity to tell him about her secret. To tell him why she never should have made the bargain with him in the first place.

However, now, with Rafe's sudden appearance, another

option presented itself. She could tell the dowager of their altercation and make a clean break. Surely, a matter such as this was beyond Rathburn's control and shouldn't jeopardize his inheritance.

It was almost too easy.

So then, why was her heart breaking at the thought?

Chapter Sixteen

The following day, Rathburn had sent her flowers and a message, promising to be her escort to the Binghams' dinner. In her reply, Emma professed to having a cold. She'd sent her regrets to the Binghams, as well.

Rathburn's response had returned within the hour.

> *A cold, my darling, Emma?*
> *I suppose it is fortunate that I did not kiss you in the*
> library
> > *or else we'd both be in bed with a cold.*
> > *On second thought . . .*
> > *Yours*

She'd read the note four times and was still unable to determine whether she should laugh or blush. In the end, she did both.

Now, days later, she was still avoiding him. Even when she realized she'd left the painting behind, she couldn't contact him.

She'd completely lost the nerve to tell him about her secret. And she most certainly wasn't prepared for the conversation he'd promised—which could only have been about their future annulment. In the current fragile state of her emotions, she feared what she might reveal. If she confessed the truth of her regard for him, she ran the risk of seeing him look on her with pity as he reminded her of his true purpose for this bargain. It was not for a wife, after all.

Then, eventually—after her confession—she could lose him as a friend as well. The thought was too much to bear.

Unfortunately, when she received a summons from the dowager for a final fitting of her gown, she couldn't refuse. After all, the wedding was only a week away.

Enough was enough, Rathburn thought as he raised his hand to the doorknocker on the Danverses' townhouse. He wouldn't let Emma avoid him any longer.

He hadn't believed her *sudden cold* excuse from the beginning. However, when Parker had told him she was *indisposed* the following day, when he'd come to take her for a drive through the park, he began to worry. The day after that, he'd sent her flowers again and received a very courteous— *very Emma*—reply that revealed nothing. Then, the day after that, when Weatherstone had admitted to seeing her in fine health, he realized his first suspicion was correct all along. Emma was avoiding him.

But why?

Parker answered the door with a bow. "I'm sorry, my lord, but Miss Danvers—"

"Is *not* indisposed, I'm sure," he interrupted, gritting his teeth.

"—received a summons from the dowager," he finished.

The dowager. His blood went cold.

Without another word, he left and headed immediately to the townhouse. He couldn't let Emma speak with his grandmother before he had the chance to tell her the truth. About everything. Tethering her to him under the guise of gaining an inheritance he already possessed was too selfish, even for him.

Though it pained him to admit it, he couldn't let this farce continue a moment longer. Emma deserved a choice in the matter—not the guilt that would inevitably assail her if she spoke the words to end their betrothal.

At Grosvenor Square, he strode through the door with the sole purpose of confessing all of it. Even at the risk of losing everything he wanted.

By early afternoon, Emma stood in front of the mirror, staring at a stranger. Of course, her hair was still styled the same way it had been when she'd left her own chamber. But surely the dreamy-eyed young woman standing in the center of the blue room at Rathburn's townhouse was not the same one who'd left Number 9 Danbury Lane.

The white undergown fit her like a second skin from her shoulders to her hips. The seamstress forbade her from wearing stays because the buckram and laces would ruin the line. Therefore, she'd created a silk chemise with invisible gathers below her breasts to offer support. From her hips, the satin gown flared subtly, draping down to the floor. Over this, she wore a robe of the palest rose, trimmed in Belgian lace and needlework with flaxen thread along the lapels and sleeves. Instead of thousands of pearls, as her mother had accused, there were no more than a dozen, stitched into the centers of the embroidered swirls.

If she were ever to paint a self-portrait, she would wear this . . .

Tears stung the backs of her eyes when she thought of never having the chance to wear this gown again. But even more so when she thought of what that meant—she would never marry Oliver.

How foolish she'd been to think this bargain would ever be simple, or to imagine she hadn't always been in love with him. After all, wasn't that the true reason she had agreed to his scheme?

She sighed. Because she loved him, it was up to her to end this and plead his case with the dowager for his inheritance.

The modiste clucked her tongue and thrust a handkerchief to her face. "Not on the satin," she said in her thick French accent.

Drying her eyes, Emma stared at the stranger in the glass and felt sorry for her. *She* was going to be dealing with a broken heart very soon. As if to punctuate that certainty, a maid entered the room with a request from the dowager to join her in the drawing room as soon as she was finished.

With her mother in Lady Rathburn's private chambers for tea, there was no one to shield her or allow her to postpone the inevitable. In the end, she changed and left the blue room, regretting that she may never return.

"You seem to have recovered from your cold, Miss Danvers," the dowager said when she entered the drawing room. "Unless your red eyes are a sign I should keep to my side of the room."

"I am quite recovered," she said without even a sniff leftover from her sudden bout of tears. "The Danvers clan is very sound in both mind and body." The instant the words were out, she knew that only half of it was true. Stating that her parents were of sound mind was a small stretch.

The dowager huffed in response as she took her seat. The parlor maid bustled over and poured her tea before she disappeared into the corner. Emma glanced to the dish of sugar, but knew from her previous times at tea with Her Grace that the porcelain bowl was simply a sweet trap. One was not permitted to add sugar to one's tea in her presence without risk of severe reproach of one's character.

"The last time you were to tea, you mentioned how you weren't certain your brother would approve the match," the dowager said, getting right to the point. "The other day's kerfuffle gives me reason to worry."

Emma's throat closed. Her sip of tea was doomed to end up dribbling out of her mouth if she couldn't figure out a way to force it down. To give herself a moment to collect herself, she raised her eyebrows in question.

"Surely, you don't think my grandson's wrinkled attire escaped my notice? I've seen enough tussles between the groomsmen to know what the activity will do to a lapel."

This was it—her perfect opportunity to end the betrothal. It was happening just as she and Rathbun had discussed in the beginning. After all, a gentleman did not break an engagement. If Rathburn did, he would lose all honor.

It had to be her. It had to be now.

She set down her cup and clasped her hands. "I do not know if my brother and your grandson can overcome their differences."

"I see." The dowager lowered her cup as well and pursed her lips.

"I'm glad." Emma took a breath. Honestly she didn't know how she was going to make it through this without crying again, but she knew she had to. "It makes it easier to tell you—"

"Of course," the dowager interrupted. "It goes without saying that having two gentlemen so dear to you would set you between them, putting a strain on your relationship with your brother, as well as your fledgling marriage. After the events of the other day, one can only presume your marriage would be fragile from the outset."

A fragile marriage? No. She and Rathburn were friends first, and in being so would make a very good partnership in marriage—*if* they were to marry under different circumstances.

She'd thought about it a great deal. After all, they got along rather well. She enjoyed his wicked way of teasing her, though she would never let on. She even liked the way he looked at her, especially of late, and the way he made her think of rainy mornings alone with him, with two steaming cups of chocolate on a nearby table.

Yes, she thought with a sigh. She'd imagined marriage to Rathburn a great deal. Had even wondered what it might be like to hold an infant with ash blond hair and mossy green eyes. And right now she resented the dowager for trying to steal away those dreams.

She thought she was prepared for this. She'd resolved herself to the idea of losing him forever.

Hadn't she? After all, the sensible, practical Emma would never let romantic notions cloud her judgment. And yet . . .

Perhaps she wasn't as sensible as she thought.

Emma stood and stepped away from the low table. "Our marriage would be a strong one. After all, we are friends first. Besides, my brother would soon realize that by separating me from Rathburn, he'd be severing ties with me as well."

The dowager eyed her shrewdly. "Then you would choose my grandson over your own family?"

"I love my family, Your Grace. I love them enough to know they would never stand in the way of my happiness." Realizing her fingers were knitted together, she pulled them apart and lowered her arms to her side. "Besides, you underestimate your grandson. Rathburn would never ask me to choose, and that is exactly the reason I accepted his proposal in the first place." *A prize above all others,* was something Rathburn understood to the very core of his being.

"You seem very sure of him."

She nodded. "We know each other. We share more than an understanding of each other's characters, we share"—she stopped to catch her breath. Turning away, she faced the partially opened door that led to the gallery and lowered her voice to a whisper. "A heart."

Her heart, to be exact. He was firmly planted within the fragile, trembling walls of her heart, sharing the snug space, even if he didn't know it and perhaps never would. If she were even more honest with herself than she'd ever been before, she could admit to surrendering all of her heart to Oliver Goswick.

"He should take lessons from you, because his poetry is sorely lacking," the dowager said, letting Emma know that neither the age of the listener nor the room's acoustics had kept her admission secret.

Trying not to blush, Emma turned in time to witness a look of horror cross the dowager's face.

"Good heavens," she gasped. "You're *not* a poet are you?"

After all the tension from the past hour, she couldn't believe she managed to keep from laughing. Oh, she was much, much worse than a poet.

"Not today, Your Grace," she said smoothly and resumed her seat beside the low table.

Yet, if she didn't know any better, she'd swear that the Dowager Duchess of Heathcoat hid a smile behind her teacup.

In the gallery, Rathburn pressed back against the wall and closed his eyes, trying to ease the burning sensation from his lungs. He'd held his breath for too long, not wanting to alert either his grandmother or Emma to his presence. Everything had been fine until his grandmother gave her the perfect opportunity to break the engagement.

He saw it in Emma's eyes for a moment—her readiness to end it. That was when he'd started holding his breath. Yet, as the words flowed from her lips, something had changed. She stood, looked down at her hands, and let them fall to her sides. Lifting her head, her expression had filled with a vulnerability he'd never seen before.

Emma Danvers was always sure of herself. That quality had drawn him to her time and time again. Yet, seeing this alteration made something clench deep inside him. She was defending him—the same man who'd put her into this mess. The same man who'd yet to convince her that his plan had changed. The same man who wanted her now more than ever.

Yet, when he set his hand on the door and prepared to set her free, she spoke the words that stopped him.

"We share more than an understanding of each other's characters, we share . . ." She broke off and turned toward the door, forcing him to retreat into the shadows. His lungs burned from the effort of holding his breath, but the soft way the light spilled across her face completely arrested him. *"A heart."*

A sweeter whisper had never been spoken, he was sure.

They did share a heart. One single heart. Somehow, upon their births, half a heart had been sewn into his body, and years later, the other half sewn into hers. He hadn't known how right it sounded until she said the words.

However, it didn't escape his notice that she'd never so much as hinted her feelings to him. He'd known she was hiding something. With him, lately, she was always so careful, restrained. Yet now, with that look on her face, every doubt he'd had vanished beneath the sure, steady beats inside his chest.

We share a heart.

Yes, they certainly did. Now, the only thing left was to dare Miss Danvers to choose a life with him.

CHAPTER SEVENTEEN

"Good morning, dear," her mother said with a pat on Emma's foot as she sat on the edge of her bed.

Morning? It couldn't be. She hadn't slept a wink. Of course, having a guilty conscience *could* be the reason for that, she reminded herself. "Good morning," she groaned, draping her forearm over her eyes. This was it. In a matter of hours, she would be married.

"Nerves keep you awake?" Her mother took her non-committal grunt as a sound of assent and continued. "Don't worry, it will soon be over. Everything will work out as it was meant to."

She gave a feeble nod, appreciating her mother's way of looking on the bright side. "You're right. It *will* be over soon."

"I remember the day of my wedding," her mother said, sighing with delight, apparently oblivious to Emma's despair. "Of course, I wasn't nervous at all when I thought about marrying your father. You see, he and I had more than a long-standing friendship between us. We were deeply in love."

Her parents had openly stated their love for each other

all her life, so it came as no surprise that her mother would mention it today. However, instead of fighting the urge to roll her eyes at her mother's declaration, as she'd done for the past few years, she found herself smiling. Both she and Rathburn had been fortunate to have parents who'd loved each other.

Then again, she was sure neither of their parents had entered into marriage with the amount of guilt she was carrying at the moment. She'd had the opportunity to break their betrothal, to set him free without risk to his inheritance. Yet, instead, her foolish heart had chosen that moment to confess her darkest secret. One of them, at any rate.

Oh, Emma. What were you thinking?

Now, the wedding was only hours away. Could she go through with it? Could she really walk down the aisle, knowing that she'd had the perfect opportunity to get them both out of this mock betrothal and she'd let it slip away? Could Rathburn ever forgive her?

At the thought, she grabbed her pillow and put it over her face, hoping she might accidentally smother herself.

"I know," her mother said snatching the pillow from her. "You don't want to hear about it. Just remember this moment when your own daughter is about to get married, and then imagine me smirking at you."

A daughter of her own. Rathburn's daughter. The idea brought a tremulous smile to her lips. But wait, their agreement was to get an annulment. Why did her mother keep forgetting that part and tormenting her with what would never come to pass? For that matter, why did she?

A knock sounded at the door and Emma opened her eyes to see Lucy bringing in a tray of tea and toast. As she sat up, her mother walked around the bed and propped pillows behind her. The maid set the tray across her lap.

"Breakfast in bed?" The only time she'd had this luxury was when she'd been ill and hadn't been able to fully appreciate it. Otherwise, her parents decreed that they take their morning meal as a family in the breakfast room.

Her mother tucked a strand of hair behind her ear and smoothed the errant locks away from her forehead. "Rathburn insisted. He came to see your father and me late last night."

Emma blushed. Rathburn had sent a note earlier this week, stating that urgent business had called him away, but that he would return in time for the wedding.

The wedding. Apparently, he planned to go through with it. He must have come by last night to reassure her parents that everything was going according to plan and that their annulment would take place the instant he received his inheritance. "Oh."

Nevertheless, it was kind of him to think of how nervous she would be and insist on her having breakfast in bed. She smiled at the thought and felt a sense of calm wash over her. Curls of steam rose from the spout of a lovely turquoise porcelain teapot with silver filigree wrapped around the base and the tip of the spout. The fragrance of her favorite tea greeted her. Beside the pot sat a cup in the same color with silver filigree on the handle. "I don't think I've ever seen this service before. It's quite beautiful."

"Rathburn brought that as well," her mother said with an odd catch in her voice. When Emma looked up, she saw tears glistening in her eyes. Her mother made a face and a show of batting the tears away as she resumed her seat on the edge of the bed. "A gift for you, along with a tin of jasmine tea and a small sack of sugar."

Her heart gave a strange tug. *A parting gift.* Although, seen in a different light, it might be construed as quite the romantic gesture—as if he were determined to make her lose both her head and her heart over him, not knowing he already possessed both.

Her hand shook as she poured the tea into her cup.

"My, you are nervous." Her mother laughed quietly. Taking the pot, she poured the tea with a steady hand. Then she cleared her throat. "As your mother, it's my duty to prepare you for what awaits you in marriage. I've taught you how to manage a household. In fact, you've exceeded my instruction in that regard. As you know, the past few years, I've focused on myself. I credit your strong and capable character for allowing me that freedom, Emma. If it wasn't for your innate sense of sensibility and decorum, I never would have been able to step back and take a good look at my life."

Emma blinked. She *liked* that about her?

A sudden realization dawned. The greatest lesson she'd ever learned from her parents was that they would do anything for family. There were no limits. Even if they didn't completely agree with her choices, they'd always loved her.

A wealth of tenderness filled her. No matter what happened, she was assured of their love and acceptance, if nothing else.

Her mother stood up and began walking around the room. Stopping at the vanity table, she picked up the brush and stroked the soft bristles before she wiped away another tear. "My dear, sweet, beautiful girl," she said to Emma's reflection in the mirror. "There comes a time in every mother's life when she begins to realize her children won't live with her indefinitely. She begins to see them through new eyes, and suddenly wonders where her place will be."

"There's no need to say this now," she said, pressing a hand to her heart. This sounded too much like a farewell speech, even though nothing was going to change. Not really.

"That happened for me when Rathburn's father died. I saw how quickly everything could change," she continued, unaware of how her choice of words caused a peculiar shiver through Emma. "His mother was left alone, without the husband she loved so dearly. I saw you blossom into a woman when you decided to hold off your debut out of respect for the family that was as close as our own. It was then that I first began to see you, and I wondered how I could have missed you changing from a girl into a woman. To me, you were still the same little bundle I'd once held in my arms."

Now, Emma fought back her own tears. "Mother, I'll look dreadful if you keep this up. I'm not dying for heaven's sake. Merely changing my address for a short time." She laughed even as the tears spilled down her cheeks. "And if you ever return the parlor to its original state, I'll return sooner."

"Don't be silly, we can sit in any room," her mother said with a light in her eyes that Emma was going to miss, even for a day or two.

Suddenly, she wondered why having her mother turn the parlor into a studio ever embarrassed her at all.

"It's getting late. Drink your tea while I finish what I came in here to tell you."

She took a sip of her fragrant tea, letting the scent and flavor calm her nerves. Then, even though she wasn't the least bit hungry, she took a bite of dry toast and washed it down with more tea.

"The marriage bed can be a wonderful place."

Emma spit out her tea all over the coverlet.

Her mother paid no attention. "On the day I married your father, my mother came into my room and gave me a terrifying speech about duty and patience and a man's baser nature. To tell you the truth, the speech left me so shaken, had it not been for the fact that I was already carrying your brother, he might never have been conceived."

Celestine Danvers waited a beat while that tidbit of information settled in, and when Emma's eyes widened, she nodded. "That's right, your brother was not born prematurely. Your father and I were too much in love. For us, waiting to be together was as impossible as deciding not to breathe."

"I don't think I want to hear any more."

Her mother smiled. "Since our complete expression of love came as a surprise to me, in the best possible way, I want it to be a surprise for you, too. So, I'm not going to give you my mother's speech. I'm going to let you discover this wonderful treasure for yourself."

Emma blinked. "That's it? That's all you're going to say?"

Never mind the fact that she and Rathburn were not going to discover treasure—*wonderful or otherwise*—she was curious, and this might be her only chance to learn what married women talked about in hushed voices. After enduring this ruse and losing her heart in the process, she felt as if she deserved more.

"I think this way is better." Her mother tapped the tip of her finger against her lips the way her father did with his pipe. No doubt, she'd finally remembered the annulment at the most inopportune moment. "I'll have Tillie bring up water for a bath. Oh, and by the way, Maudette has decided to live with her sister in the country."

CHAPTER EIGHTEEN

"I never would have believed the annoying little mouse that nipped at my heels would one day turn into . . . *you*," Rafe said as she descended the stairs in her gown an hour later. A poet, he was not. However, his smile was genuine. When she took his proffered hand, he leaned in close. "If this isn't what you want, just say the word. I've ordered my carriage to follow, just in case."

If she weren't so shocked by the offer, she might have cried. For the first time, she realized how difficult this must be for him. Not once in the past weeks had she recalled the event that had changed him forever. Now, she knew how difficult it was for him to make that offer. After all, six years ago he'd been the one standing alone at the altar. His bride-to-be had fled without a word, leaving him broken in more ways than just his heart.

"Thank you," she whispered, overwhelmed by the amount of tenderness she felt for her brother. "But I want this—for Rathburn's sake."

He arched a brow at her hasty correction. "Then for *Rathburn's sake* alone, we should get you to the church."

When he laughed, the tenderness she felt evaporated in a rise of annoyance. *Really*, this was no time to tease. However, by the time she was in the carriage with her parents beaming at her as if still delighted by this deception, she realized her brother had done her a favor in stealing away some of her nervousness. She quickly forgave him.

It was a short drive to St. George's. Perhaps even too short. Her friends were all waiting for her on the stairs in front of the cathedral, each of them beautiful in her rose muslin gown. From the corner of her eye, she watched Rafe exit his carriage and say a few words to the driver. When he caught her gaze, he touched his fingers to the brim of his top hat and gave her a nod. The driver was at her disposal.

She swallowed down a tide of emotion, but held on to her composure as he quietly escorted their mother up the stairs.

Vaguely, Rathburn became aware of a twinge in his neck and the sound of hushed voices nearby. Not only that, but someone was kicking his foot. "Wake up, princess."

Danvers. He'd recognize that taunting voice anywhere. "What are you doing here?"

"I'd ask the same of you, if my sister weren't on the steps outside this very moment."

Rathburn's eyes flew open. He jolted forward, nearly toppling from the bench. The familiar walls and dark wood furnishings of the vestry came into focus. Only now did he remember arriving at the church before dawn. Everything had to be perfect. Just in case . . . she still wanted to marry him after he told her everything.

Wait. What time was it? "Emma. Here? Already?" He must have fallen asleep. Apparently, the long hours from the past few days had taken their toll.

He hadn't seen Emma for days and wasn't certain of her frame of mind. Therefore, he had no idea how she would react to what he planned to tell her.

However, by the time he'd arrived at Danbury Lane last night, her parents had said she'd retired. That was when he'd come up with the brilliant—*ha!*—plan to speak with her this morning. Only this morning had already gotten away from him, too.

"Ready for the ball, princess?"

Straightening his cravat, Rathburn glowered.

Danvers laughed. "You know, I think I'm going to like having you for a brother."

"Which isn't likely to happen unless I can steal your sister away, for a moment, before the ceremony."

"And why is that?" He arched a brow, but his amused speculation quickly turned into irritation. "Bugger! You haven't told her yet, have you?"

"There wasn't time." Rathburn was an idiot to have left the truth of his inheritance unsaid this long. But each time he'd thought it was the perfect time to tell her, something always pulled him away. Now, this was his absolute final chance.

"You think the dowager will let you cause a scene by speaking to the bride before the wedding?"

They both knew the answer to that.

Danvers was pacing now, raking a hand through his hair. "Give me a note and I'll take it to her."

"That won't do." He shook his head. "This is too important not to be said directly."

"*Too important!*" His friend scoffed at him. "This from a man who waits until the bells are ringing?"

"Point taken."

"Here's what you do," Danvers said, gesturing with his hands in a way that looked as if he held an invisible bowl between them. "The moment you see her, the instant before the ceremony, you tell her. She'll still have time then."

Incredulous, Rathburn stared. "Tell her? How the bloody hell am I going to tell her in front of everyone?"

"I don't know," he growled. "Just . . . let her know that the original purpose for your mock betrothal is no longer a factor. Let her know this is real for you."

"*No longer a factor . . .*" Rathburn nodded. It wasn't a perfect plan, but it could work. She would still have time to make her choice. "You're brilliant."

The man he'd always considered a brother let out a breath that eased the tension in his expression and then grinned at him. "It took you this long to figure that out?"

Emma turned to Penelope, Merribeth, and Delaney while her father waited a few steps away. Having forgotten their gifts at the last needlework meeting earlier this week, she presented them now, handing over three narrow boxes. The morning light shimmered over the slender strands of pearls and was accompanied by excited praises as they were admired.

While Merribeth and Delaney fastened each other's necklaces, Penelope stepped forward, and took her gently by the shoulders. "Emma Danvers," she said, keeping her voice low. "Stop, or you'll drive yourself mad."

"You're a bit too late on that account." Emma tried to laugh, but failed miserably. "I was mad to agree to this in the beginning. It was never supposed to get this far. Now, I expect the ground to start quaking at my feet. In the very least, the walls of the church will collapse on me." The words were supposed to come out as a joke. Instead, they came on a river of panic.

"I know it might feel that way, but you took a leap of *faith* in the beginning, not a leap of insanity." She offered a reassuring smile. "The most important thing to remember is the reason you trusted Rathburn enough to agree in the first place. That reason is still with you, inside your heart."

Yes, the reason filled her heart now. *Her love for him.* She trusted Rathburn to know what he was doing. As soon as he received his inheritance, they would get an annulment. Simple as that.

No. Not simple. She didn't want an annulment.

She wanted to mean more to him. She wanted her friends to be right about the way they said he looked at her and teased her. She wanted to give herself over to the dream of what their lives could be, without fear of her heart shattering to pieces. *She wanted . . .*

Emma sighed and gave Penelope a nod of understanding. For Rathburn's sake, for the sake of his father's memory, and for the sake of the hospital, she would tuck her own yearnings for this to be a true marriage away, adding another secret to the monstrous pile. She had to see this through.

Climbing the stairs with her friends, her father met them

halfway. Then, one by one, Delaney, Merribeth, and Penelope walked into the church. As Emma walked down the aisle on her father's arm, sunlight streamed in through the arched stained glass windows, blinding her to everyone around her. She feared she would faint. It was only when she neared the altar that she saw Rathburn clearly. Her gaze fixed on him as if he alone could see her through this.

Instantly, she felt herself relax.

He was quite dashing in his dark blue morning coat, silver satin waistcoat and gray breeches. His eyes gleamed like emeralds in the light. The grin he flashed matched the whiteness of his cravat and gloves as he lifted a hand to take hers. She drew in a deep breath that settled her nerves.

Her father took his cue and relinquished his hold, offering her into Rathburn's care—for the time being. When she felt the warmth of Oliver's palm beneath her fingers, every concern she had melted away.

"I want you to know," he whispered, holding her gaze with his intensity, "that the original reason for why we are here, in the church this very moment, is no longer a factor. This is real for me."

A nervous laugh nearly bubbled out. She had no idea what he meant, but it sounded lovely. "Yes, quite real for me, as well."

He seemed inordinately pleased—and relieved—by her response. His breath stirred the veil against her cheek. "Then, shall we dive off this cliff together, Emma-*mine*?"

She was surprised at how eagerly the perfect—and most foolish—response floated from her lips. "Headfirst."

CHAPTER NINETEEN

Married to Emma.

Rathbun blew out a breath and pressed a fist to the center of his chest. A tight knot of guilt churned inside him. He'd realized on the carriage ride here that he should have given her more time to decide if this was what she truly wanted. Not waited until they were standing at the altar.

He hadn't even thought about what it would be like to bring her home. Completely alone with him. *Home.* No longer his home, but *theirs.* Yes. They would make a life here. After all, he knew she loved him. *We share a heart.*

And with the memory of her sweet whisper, the knot in his chest loosened marginally.

Still, he wasn't going to remain here a moment longer, unless she was certain. Through some miracle of self-control, he hadn't touched her. If she changed her mind, they could still get an annulment.

The knot tightened again, squeezing painfully.

He'd had Woodson pack a bag of his things, just in case. Her reputation would be safe . . . but only if he left right away.

There was absolutely no more time to waste. He must speak with Emma now.

Emma stood in the viscountess's bedchamber at Hawthorne Manor. She was a fool to have believed that nothing would change between them. Then again, she'd never fully believed it. From that first moment in the study, with her parents encouraging her to embark on this calamity with Rathburn, she'd known everything would change.

She'd been right. Everything had changed, at least for her. Against all reason—against the purpose of their bargain— she'd fallen in love with him.

Not to mention, their marriage had altered her place in society and how people saw her. She was no longer looked through. No longer judged and found wanting. This morning's lavish wedding breakfast had proven as much. At last, she fit in.

But that was part of her deception, as well. They didn't know her secret.

With a sigh, Emma stared at her surroundings. The room was decorated exactly as she would have done. Rathburn had an uncanny way of knowing her thoughts, even—it seemed— before she knew them herself.

When they'd arrived, the entire staff had lined up outside the doors, ready to greet the newlyweds, not knowing that an annulment loomed overhead. Since she'd known the servants for years, there'd been no awkward series of introductions, just cheers and many felicitations for the best of marriages. Of course, after Rathburn boldly carried her across the threshold, it would make their sudden separation that much harder for everyone to understand.

An annulment would change everything again. Not back to the way it was—no, she was not foolish enough to believe that—but to some other state of existence. After all, she would be losing a husband *and* a friend who meant more to her than her mind could comprehend. However, her heart knew and it was already breaking.

How could she bear to lose him when her love was so raw and new?

Staring through the glass door that led to the balcony, she let out a shaky breath and tried in vain to win the battle over her tears. A soft knock fell on the door.

Assuming it was her maid, she called, "I'll need another moment." Then she remembered she had no maid. Though Rathburn had likely sent one of his servants to tend to her.

The door closed with a nearly inaudible click. "I find that there are varying degrees to moments."

She started at the sound of Rathburn's voice, but did not turn. The only thing worse than one of his maids seeing her this way would be to let him. She hoped he hadn't heard the catch in her voice or noticed how she used her gloves to blot the tears from her cheeks.

His footsteps approached slowly, the sound of his boots muffled on the plush carpet. "For some, a moment is a single span of a breath, a blink of an eye. While for others it can last what seems like an age."

"Three whole breaths?" she quipped, averting her face to blot her cheeks again.

"Sometimes I've even heard it drawn out to four." He

came up behind her, standing close enough so that she could feel the heat of him, along with the strength and support he offered. He was such a good friend to her. A best friend, actually. She never knew until recently how much she'd relied on him being part of her life. And now she could lose him forever.

A fresh fall of tears began and her breathing hitched with a slight jerk of her shoulders.

He placed his hands on her shoulders and turned her. With the pads of his thumbs, he gently began wiping away her tears. "See here . . . what's all this about? Did the stress of the day finally crash you against the rocks?"

She nodded at first and then shook her head before burying her face against his shoulder. "Oh, Rathburn, what have I done?"

"*Oliver,* my darling," he reminded, kissing the top of her head as he wrapped his arms around her. "And I think it's safe to say that *we've* done this, not just you."

She sniffed and rubbed her cheek against his silver satin waistcoat. Wanting to curl into his embrace, she lifted her arms, but stopped short when she remembered her gloves were soaked with her tears. But before she could lower them again, he caught her hands in his.

Lifting them, he pressed a kiss to her damp fingertips.

"Not very proper, I know. I'm glad your grandmother isn't here to see me fall apart."

"It's just us," he said, the words like a whispered promise. And then, proving there was no need for propriety, he let his hand travel over the length of her glove to the cuff above her elbow. He slipped a finger inside, teasing the sensitive flesh of her inner arm before he pinched the satin and slowly pulled it off.

A silent breath escaped her at the intimate gesture. Surely, she shouldn't allow him to remove her gloves, no matter how many times she'd imagined it. She lifted her face, prepared to say something, but the words dissolved on her tongue when she saw his tender expression.

He bent his head to press a kiss to the tip of her nose as he dropped the glove onto a chair beside them. Without a word, he followed the line of the other glove and drew it down her arm, exposing her flesh.

The last breath left her lungs.

Like before, he brought her hands to his lips—first one, and then the other—and settled both against his chest. "There," he crooned, wrapping his arms around her again.

This was a side to Rathburn she never expected to experience. He'd given everything of himself, including his pride, to gain his inheritance solely to build Goswick Hospital and to repair the manor. At his very core, he cared for people. Yet, during the years of their acquaintance, she'd only met with his flirtatious side. Of course, her cool demeanor might have been the reason for that.

Right now, she wished she hadn't pretended to be so aloof, because this was wonderful. She'd never felt so secure in her life. Resting her cheek against him again, she could hear the strong, steady beat of his heart. She drew in a breath, inhaling the clean fragrance of his clothes. If only this moment could last forever.

"I'm worried about what will happen ... after," she said quietly. "Not just with your family and my family, but with us. I don't want our ..." *friendship* wasn't the right word. What they shared was greater than that. "... *bond* to seem forced or artificial."

"That won't happen. Not with us." He said the words with such assuredness that she wanted to believe him. More than anything. Showing even more tenderness, he produced a handkerchief and dried the cheek that wasn't pressed against him and soaking his waistcoat with tears.

She felt the embroidery thread sewn into the fine linen. "You're using your wedding gift," she said, glad that he'd received the package she'd sent early this morning. After speaking with Penelope, and learning that she'd embroidered Ethan's handkerchiefs each year to show him how much she loved him, Emma had thought that was a perfect idea. Only now, it represented another enormous secret she kept from him. Her love.

His mouth curved in a smile against the top of her head. "Of course I am, but how did you know?"

"I can feel the thread of the flower I embroidered," she said, drawing in his scent and the warmth of his embrace. Both gave her a sense of peace that she'd never felt before. "I know it's hardly masculine to have a jasmine blossom on your handkerchief, so I used white silk thread to blend in. I thought you would laugh when you saw it."

"Laugh?" he asked, his voice sounding peculiar as if this was the first he'd noticed it. Now, he turned it in his hand, holding it up to the waning afternoon light coming in through the windows. "Ah. Because of the Sumpters' musicale. I stole one of your flowers."

"And tucked it inside your handkerchief," she smiled at the

memory even though it gave her a twinge of sadness. Without warning, a fresh fall of tears spilled out. "A memento of our brief make-believe courtship."

He hugged her tighter still. Then, bending down, he lifted her effortlessly in his arms. "Shh . . ." he crooned, brushing his lips across her forehead as he carried her across the room. "You're tired and overwrought. We have much to discuss when you are rested."

The annulment, of course.

He would want to discuss that immediately. They had a new plan to make, after all. She feared that it would be the last conversation they'd have.

He made a move to lower her to the bed when she stopped him, gripping his arm. "If I wrinkle this gown, your grandmother will never forgive"—her words trailed off as she looked down at her hand—"me."

He was in his shirtsleeves. How had that escaped her notice before? Through the fine lawn, she could feel the heat of his flesh. He was solid, too. *Very* solid. Of course, it made sense that as a man he was bound to be. Yet, for some reason, the knowledge fascinated her.

Rathburn set her feet down. "I'll send in your maid straight away."

Automatically, she shook her head, her attention still diverted to her hand on his arm, marveling at how the muscle flexed beneath her palm. "Maudette retired to the country. I have no maid."

He swallowed, and the sound drew her attention. She lifted her gaze to his throat, the exposed flesh above his cravat and below the line of his jaw. Standing this close, she could see the shadow of his whiskers just beneath the surface of his skin. This too was very male, very different. Fascinating.

His hand at her waist twitched, bringing her attention to precisely how close they stood. Mere inches apart, with her gown nestled against his legs. "I should send for a maid, all the same."

Reluctantly, she released his arm. "The robe is no trouble," she said, her fingers finding the delicate chain between her breasts.

She hesitated. Her gaze slowly lifted to his. Without a maid, she would undress herself as she'd done for years. Without a maid, she could keep a semblance of freedom. Yet, without a maid, she had no chaperone to ensure her reputation would remain intact after the annulment.

Emma unclasped the chain and let the garment slide from her shoulders. "It slips off without effort."

Rathbun drew in a sharp breath through his teeth. She remembered how the gown beneath clung to her like a second skin. The modiste had designed her chemise to do the same. She wore no stays or petticoat beneath it. With the robe on, it had hardly mattered. But now, he was seeing her as she'd dreamed he would.

His irises grew dark. He opened his mouth to breathe, too. "Emma," he rasped, the low sound causing swift heat to cover her flesh from head to toe, warming and tightening her skin simultaneously.

Strangely, her breasts felt full, heavy, and yet taut at once. When his gaze traveled down the white satin, a quiver pulsed through her. Even the soles of her feet tingled. She imagined that quake leaving her body through the floor because in the very same instant, he staggered back from the force of it.

Rathburn bit back a curse, gritting his teeth. Emma stood before him, barely sheathed by her wedding gown. The white satin brought to mind the petals of jasmine and the countless fantasies he'd had of her wearing nothing other than those blossoms. Of course, the reality of having her within arm's reach was far more powerful. He shook with the effort to keep his distance.

"I should leave you to rest," he said, but couldn't seem to force himself to retreat.

She lifted a hand to her throat, drawing his attention to the pulse beating as hard and fast as his. Her fingertips fluttered over that spot and her lips parted. She drew in a breath that seemed stolen from his lungs because he couldn't draw in enough air. And he needed air, not only to breathe, but to think clearly.

He'd come in here to check on her. To ensure she was faring well after what must have been an overwhelming morning. He also wanted to talk about their plans. Future plans together, he hoped. For that, he needed them both to be clearheaded.

She took a step forward and lowered her hand from her pulse to the buttons in the center of his waistcoat. "We've barely seen each other lately. As you said, we've much to discuss."

He shuddered from the intimate gesture and closed his

eyes. "Not here. I can't think in here, not when you're so tempting."

"Tempting?" She exhaled a disbelieving laugh. "You've kissed me only once."

His eyes flew open. "Don't you understand how impossible it's been for me to resist kissing you? For weeks, I've thought of your lips—their sweet flavor, petal soft texture, plump ripeness so luscious a new sin could be named for them."

Without thinking, he reached for her, his hands on her waist. He leaned in, pressing his mouth against her temple, burying his nose into the fragrant fall of curls there and drawing in a breath that threatened to unman him. When she lifted her gaze, his breath came out shaky. "Most of all, what you don't understand is that if I kiss you now, I'll take away your right to choose—"

She lifted her arms and took his face in her hands, her action surprising them both. "If my only choices are having you kiss me now or watching you walk through that door, then I choose this . . ." She rose up and pressed her lips to his.

Chapter Twenty

Rathburn pulled her flush against him. A sound of utter surrender tore from his throat at the first swipe of her tongue against his. His hands tightened on her waist, his thumbs caressing the bones of her hips, his fingers splayed over her lower back and . . . lower still, stroking the curve of her derriere.

Yes, she was the one who kissed him. Emma felt bold, daring, unwilling to release him until she'd had her fill. It was as if she'd unlocked a secret door. A door hidden to both of them until now. The force behind it refused to be ignored or shut out.

He ravaged her mouth in return, drawing her tongue deeper. She wanted to climb inside him and found herself clutching his shoulders as if preparing to do exactly that. He crushed her against him. His hands moved over her back, eliciting tingles along her spine. Further down, he cupped her, lifting her to her toes, inviting her to arch against him. She did, and *oh, yes* . . . that felt nice.

Rathburn groaned. The low sound vibrated from his body into hers, making her restless.

The heaviness in her breasts compelled her to press them hard against him. When she moved, her gown shifted. Only now did she realize that he'd unbuttoned her. Recalling how many fantasies she'd had of his dexterous fingers doing nothing more than unbuttoning her glove made her smile against his lips. This fantasy was far more salacious. Far more real. And suddenly everything she wanted.

She'd spent far too much time being cautious and sensible.

Not taking a moment to second guess, she lowered her arms and let the satin slide off her shoulders. The movement wasn't lost on him.

Rathburn broke from her kiss, but only long enough to look down at her breasts through the gauzy veil of her chemise. A feral, guttural sound escaped him as he slid his hand up along her waist, her ribs, to the curve of her breast. He covered her, pressing and kneading her aching flesh. His thumb brushed the peak of her nipple as his mouth descended on hers again, capturing her cry of surprised pleasure.

The kiss transformed even more. It was no longer about discovery, but more of possession. No one else had seen her like this or touched her. Rathburn was the first. *The only*. She felt claimed by him in the most primitive way, a fresh canvas marked by the heat of his hands.

Wanting to touch him as well, she pulled at the knot of his cravat, working through the folds until it fell away. Free, at last, to touch him, she moved her fingertips over the heated sinew of his throat, tracing the outline of his Adam's apple. A rush of pleasure spiked through her when he swallowed. It was such a basic action, but to feel the motion against her own flesh made it supremely carnal.

Driven by impulse, she nipped at his bottom lip before suckling the firm flesh. Rathburn grunted a sound of impatience. He tugged her wedding dress down from her waist and let it drop to the floor. Pulling her flush against him, he lowered her to the bed.

Emma delighted in the feel of him. He was warm, but heavy, too. His weight and deep, plundering kiss made it difficult to breathe. Then with a slow slide of his hips, she quickly decided breathing wasn't necessary.

All she needed was him. And more of this.

He moved against her again and she squeezed her eyes shut on a swift jolt of pleasure. White starlight bloomed beneath her lids. His responding groan told her this felt as good for him. His hips rolled against hers again and again, faster each time.

"Emma. Emma. *My Emma*. Please, tell me to stop," he rasped in between kisses. He attempted to lift himself off her, taking away the pleasant weight of him. "There are things we should discuss . . ."

Her body quickened. She held fast to his shoulders, shaking, trembling. "Later." Why would she tell him to stop when this felt so wonderful? She wanted more. "Please stay."

A startling feral heat darkened his gaze as he claimed her mouth again. His hands skimmed down her body, teasing the sensitive peaks of her breasts through her silk chemise. Feeling brazen, she arched into his palm, not afraid to let him know that this was what she wanted. Not afraid to tell him without words how desperately she loved him. How she would die if he left her. How she would die if he ever . . . stopped . . .

Before she could finish the thought, her back bowed off the soft mattress. Every muscle in her body locked. Her breath seized in her throat. A sudden shower of tingles washed through her, converging deep in her core. Her body contracted sharply, clenching, writhing against him in helpless, wanton pleasure.

The spasms went on and on until she felt as if the last vestiges of her life might drain away. Still, she clung to him, refusing to leave this earth without him. If she were to die from pleasure, she wanted to take him with her.

Remotely, as if she were both locked here in his embrace and also floating above herself, she realized the air felt cool on her legs. His hold had shifted. His hand moved down her body, caressing her, sliding over her hip, down her thigh to the edge of her chemise and back up again.

He shifted away from her for a moment, but only long enough for her to murmur her displeasure at having him gone. "Don't leave," she whispered.

This time when he lowered onto her, it felt different. Hotter. A scorching heat touched her where her body still throbbed.

"You're so wet for me," he groaned into her mouth.

She made a sound of agreement without fully understanding what he was saying. She wanted more. More of his kiss. More of his weight. More.

Rathburn gave into her unspoken demands and pressed against her. The scorching heat of him burned her at her core. He hissed as if he felt the heat of it, too. The burn continued as she felt her body stretch and feel uncomfortably full. She fought the urge to tell him that she wanted him to return to whatever he was doing before. She'd liked that quite a lot.

This new sensation was too complex. She could feel him everywhere, her breasts flush against his chest, his weight pressing her into the soft mattress, his heat filling her. It was too much.

As if he sensed it, he shifted marginally, effectively easing the burning, stretching sensation. His kiss gentled. His tongue caressed hers slowly, deeply, their breath mingling. She hummed in approval and slid her fingers into the cool strands of his hair. He moved again, letting her get used to the full feeling as he rolled his hips. A wanton purr rose from her throat.

He groaned. "Em . . ." he said brokenly against her lips. "You're so—" He shifted again. The hard, scorching heat of him pushed deeper inside. Impossibly deep.

She gasped at the sharp tearing sensation. Her body went rigid. All at once she had the urge to push him away and yet cling to him. It was too much. She was too full. Her body refused to stretch anymore. This felt foreign. Not at all the way it had a few moments ago.

Rathburn stilled and looked down at her, his expression grave and tense. "Darling, are you hurt . . ." he began but broke off to brush a tear from the corner of her eye. His expression turned tender, a gentle smile curving his lips. "I'm a cad."

Emma wanted to agree, but couldn't be sure it was entirely his fault. "I think we did something wrong," she confessed in a whisper. "It doesn't feel the same." Was this the surprise her mother had warned her about? It certainly didn't feel wonderful at the moment.

"There was no other way, my love. Not when I've wanted you like this for an eternity." He lowered his head and kissed her. "I needed to be inside of you."

Her body tingled at his confession, quick to forget about the pain. Yet, she still felt stretched and too full and wasn't sure what to think about it. Even though she didn't know what to expect from making love, she knew she never expected this confused mixture of sensations.

Without waiting for her to be certain, he rolled his hips against her, edging even deeper inside. She held her breath, expecting another stab of pain. However, this time there wasn't. Only heat and fullness. Her eyes widened as she gazed up at him. The look he returned to her was full of feral promises as he drew her legs around his hips.

Emma closed her eyes and returned his kiss, giving herself fully to Rathburn. No—to *Oliver*. He was hers now, and she could claim him as her own.

"Oliver," she whispered, winding her arms around his neck and arching against him. Her breasts strained against her chemise, aching as she crushed them into his chest. The taut peaks of her nipples shot ribbons of fiery tingles deep inside her body where he filled her.

He growled, breaking from the kiss and burying his face against the side of her neck. His mouth opened over her flesh. The warm, rough texture of his tongue stroked her frenzied pulse, sending another shock of tingles through her. He moved again, rolling his hips and surging forward until their bodies were flush. Her head tilted back on a moan and his name followed by a plea for him to do that again.

He did. Over and over again, until the room grew suddenly dark and the rumble of distant thunder was the only sound to drown out her cries. Wind blew in from the open windows, cooling the perspiration from her body and making the heat between them more intense. The storm was within her, quaking and threatening to unleash a torrent. She felt it keenly, building without expectation. Only promise.

When he lifted his head and took her mouth again, the storm broke free. Oliver swallowed her cry as the deluge rolled on and on.

Above her, holding her fiercely, he stilled. She opened her eyes and their gazes locked. His intensity struck her hard, filling her with awe. Deep inside, perhaps even into her soul, she felt his release.

Without a doubt, nothing would ever be the same again. She only hoped he could forgive her.

R athburn reluctantly lifted away from Emma and walked to the washbasin at the far corner of the room. The afternoon light had dimmed with the approach of a storm, yet he could still make out the bloodstain on the fall of his breeches. His valet would be furious . . . at first. Then Woodson would likely make a comment on his wooing prowess, or lack thereof.

He'd behaved like a beast with his new bride. Hell, he hadn't taken the time to undress either of them. Yet, as much as he attempted to give himself a stern lecture, he couldn't stop the utter joy and exhilaration he felt.

Emma Danvers—*correction*—Goswick, Viscountess of Rathburn, was truly his.

Without bothering to hide his triumphant grin, he strode back to the bed with a damp cloth. His bride had pulled down her chemise, and the apples of her cheeks were suffused in a very becoming blush.

"Has my buttoned-up Emmaline returned?" he teased, noticing how she kept her head turned to the side and pulled on the corner of her mouth with her teeth. He bent down to kiss her. "I'm afraid it's far too late for modesty, my darling. Your cad of a husband made sure of that."

She shook her head, the motion bringing her lips to his. "You're not a cad."

He put it more plainly. "There'll be no annulment now. I'm afraid you're stuck with me."

"Are you . . . disappointed?"

He knew she wasn't asking if he was satisfied with their lovemaking. The evidence was clear in his undoubtedly sappy grin and primitive gleam in his eyes. She was asking if he was disappointed in his choice of bride. "If you'll recall, I'm the one who proposed to you."

"You proposed a mock courtship, Oliver. Not this."

At first, but at the church he'd made his intentions perfectly clear and now everything was absolutely perfect. All he needed was Emma . . . and perhaps hearing her admit her true feelings.

Because he loved the sound of his name on her lips, he kissed her again. And lingered. *Her luscious mouth will be the death of me*, he thought, imagining that he'd sooner starve than stop kissing her. His body stirred.

Now, he wasn't familiar with the protocol of deflowering virgins, but it was a time-honored belief that they were fragile creatures. Most likely, it was too soon to seduce her again before nightfall.

Reluctantly, he broke the kiss and kneeled on the bed beside her. "This will be cool," he said as he lowered the cloth to the apex of her thighs—a place of rapture more divine than he'd ever experienced before.

She gasped and sat up part way, taking hold of his wrist as he administered loving strokes across her sensitive flesh. "Surely, I should do this."

"And deny me the pleasure?" To make his point, he made a slow circle with the pad of his middle finger.

"*Oliver.*" Instinctively, she closed her thighs. Her lashes lowered, but not before he saw her eyes darken with desire. His body responded elementally to that knowledge.

Yet, before passion ran rampant again, he eased his hand away. Standing, he walked back across the room to put the cloth back in the basin. "There is one part of our altered bargain that we haven't discussed," he said casually as he returned and sat on the edge of the bed, pulling her onto his lap.

"Surely, you shouldn't—" She put up a meager protest for modesty's sake, then settled her hands on his shoulder and chest. Her brows lifted in curiosity, yet her gaze lingered on his mouth. "Have we altered our bargain?"

His mouth twisted in a wry grin and lifted her chin with the crook of his finger. "Everything has changed now, Emma."

The moment he saw her expression change to uncertainty, eclipsing the passion from an instant ago, he leaned down and kissed her, drawing on her lips until he felt her body relax into his. Since he didn't want her to ask a follow up question, he distracted her by deepening the kiss.

Settling his hands at her waist, he turned her so that she would straddle him. However, the distraction worked to his disadvantage. Feeling the welcoming heat of her body made him hard and ready to take her again. Her soft purrs were driving him mad. It was too soon for her, surely.

He broke away from her tempting lips to her cheek, peppering kisses along her jaw and down her throat. At the hollow between her collarbone and shoulder, he paused and asked his question. "Do you like children?"

She drew in a quick breath, tenderness and wonder in her expression. "I think so," she said quietly, searching his face.

Rathbun lifted his hands to her hair and began to remove the pins he'd thoughtlessly left in before. "I think so, too. A little girl with your brown eyes would be lovely."

She smiled. "Or a boy with mossy green eyes flecked with gold," she said, apparently without realizing how much she'd revealed. It was obvious to him that this wasn't the first time she'd thought about their child ... their *children*. If she'd thought about that, then clearly she'd imagined a life with him. A true marriage.

He continued removing the pins, letting them fall on the floor beside the bed. "You bring up a valid argument. We'll have to have one of each to be sure." He drew the long locks of her hair forward. He'd imagined her just like this—unbound and uninhibited—dozens of times. How could it be that in so short a time she'd come to mean everything to him? It didn't seem possible, and yet his heart told him it was the truth. "I always wanted a brother. So, we should probably have at least two boys."

She grinned back at him. "And I always wanted a sister."

"Of course." He nodded sagely. "Then two boys and two girls ... to start."

She giggled, a sound he was sure he'd never heard from

her before. It hit him like the blast of cupid's arrow. A super-fluous shot, since his entire heart was already hers. He knew she was adept at hiding her feelings from him, but this gave him hope that it wouldn't always be the case. Already she was freer and happier than he'd seen her before.

"I'm not certain it will be that easy," she said, naively presenting him with a challenge.

"No. It won't." He twisted a heavy lock around his finger. Releasing the mahogany curl slowly and drawing it down until his knuckles grazed the dusky pink tip of her breast, still veiled beneath the chemise. Her sweet breath came out in a long exhale as she looked down to his hand, and to the way the bud strained against the insubstantial fabric. "We'll have to work tirelessly to achieve our goal. Slaving away for hours each day until the weeks draw into months and then years."

Emma licked her lips, her fingers straying to the buttons of his waistcoat. "Who'll manage the house?"

He sighed, pretending it was for dramatic effect, but in truth, he was nearly undone by her boldness. This was a side to Emma he'd never expected to live outside of his fantasies. The reality was much sweeter. "It will fall into disrepair."

"After all the work you've done, it would be a shame." Her hand slipped into the gap she'd exposed and swept over his nipple. She smiled when he hissed between his teeth.

Realizing that she was learning by mimicking his actions sent another rush of blood to his already engorged erection. If this went on much longer, neither of them would be undressed for the second time they made love either.

Rathburn needed to slow things down. He didn't want to risk hurting her by letting his animalistic appetite rule him again. No, this time he was going to keep the fall of his breeches buttoned and worship her with his mouth.

"Perhaps." He started by pressing his lips to her throat. Distracted from her lesson, her hands moved to his shoulders. She arched her neck to allow him better access. "But we would have four children, in the very least, to play in the rubble with us."

She went still. "Then you don't mind . . . about . . . the way our plan changed?"

He met her gaze, disturbed by the uncertainty he saw. Could she still doubt him, or was there something more? Trying not to let doubt cloud this moment, he brushed his lips over hers. "I rather enjoyed the reason."

"Mmm," she murmured, shifting closer in a way that made him abandon thought. "It was very nice."

"*Nice?*" His prowess took a hit. She didn't know how such a bland word could wound a man. Well, he was going to have to show her just how nice he could be.

Slipping his hands beneath the hem of her chemise, he lifted it over her head and tossed it to the floor. Not allowing her a moment to gasp, he covered her mouth with his and eased her back onto the bed.

CHAPTER TWENTY-ONE

"Not married five days and we already have a routine," Rathbun said from behind her, his footfalls echoing in the empty ballroom.

Emma turned from the windows in time to catch his grin. Her heart filled with fireflies at the sight of him and gave a tremulous flutter as he neared. This seemed easy for him, the wedding, the alterations in their plans . . . everything. He was much the same as always. Teasing and shamelessly flirting while she was constantly worried that she'd selfishly squandered her chance to free him from their arrangement before it was too late. Well, not *constantly*. When they made love, she allowed herself to let go.

He cupped her shoulders and gave her a gentle squeeze. Slowly, his hands descended down the length of her arms before he threaded his fingers through hers. "First, we breakfast in bed—which, just this morning you deemed *suitable* for a newly married couple." He grinned, looking pleased by this.

"Though, I'm certain, when we are in our dotage, sitting in chairs will be a requirement for our health."

"I look forward to testing that theory. Yet, you may be right." He made a show of placing a hand to his lower back and pulled a frown. "After our lengthy . . ." He paused to waggle his eyebrows at her. ". . . *repast* this morning, I am in need of a stiff backed chair."

Would he ever cease making her blush? "The morning room hosts many comfortable chairs," which was where she adjourned each morning when he went to his study. And each morning, she wished he would join her. "It's a lovely room."

"Perhaps," he mused. "Although, it would be a truly lovely room if it were not such a distance from the study."

She was surely making calf eyes at him, but there was no help for it. "You are welcome to write your correspondence alongside me, if you so desire."

He grinned and lifted a hand to tuck a lock of hair behind her ear. "Then the estate would surely fall into ruin, because I would accomplish nothing other than a thorough study of my bride's elegant scrawl upon each page, and the way the light caresses her hair, her cheek . . ."

Her eyes closed as she nestled her cheek into the palm of his hand. "My, you are easily distracted."

"Not always, as you well know," he said in a low whisper across her lips, before he pulled back. "Now, where was I in my account of our daily life . . . Ah yes. With your letters in hand, you slip quietly downstairs and place them on the salver in the foyer next to mine. Then, while I meet with Harrison in my study, you meet with Mrs. Stillson in the drawing room to discuss the day's tasks."

"She was good enough to inform me of your fondness for

lamb stew. I've arranged that for dinner, among other things, including brandied pears for dessert."

"Mmm ... I haven't had those since"—he gave her a look—"I last dined at your parents' home."

"You said they were your favorite," she admitted.

He stared at her as if waiting for her to continue, as if anticipating more. Then, after a moment, he gave her what seemed to be a patient smile before turning her in his arms so that they were both facing the windows.

"I have heard it from Mrs. Stillson that you are perfect in every way. I'm inclined to agree. The only flaw I can find is that you are too much of a distraction." He pressed a kiss to her temple and wrapped his arms around her waist. "I find myself thinking about where you are each minute of the day. And, just now, I found comfort in knowing I would find you here, gazing out at the garden."

She leaned back against him, placing her arms over his. "I'd expected the new buds to have bloomed by now, but they seem stilted. I wonder what they are waiting for."

"Perhaps, the fragile blossoms dare not open up in such a deluge." He nuzzled into her hair and drew in a breath. "Don't worry. Soon our garden will be full of color and life."

CHAPTER TWENTY-TWO

Rathburn jolted awake. An icy sweat covered him from head to toe. "It wasn't real," he said, breathing hard and fast. It was only a dream. A nightmare. Only this nightmare was coming all too frequently.

Emma stirred beside him, laying a cool hand against his bare shoulder. "Was it another dream?"

He turned his head and kissed her fingertips, grateful to have her beside him. Safe and sound, unlike in his nightmare. "Yes, darling. Just a dream."

She roused from sleep and snuggled closer, pressing her lips where her hand had been. After only two weeks of marriage, it seemed as if she'd grown accustomed to this new intimacy between them. In addition to his waking abruptly from sleep. However, she was always there beside him to offer reassurance and sweet relief in the form of distraction.

Even now, her hand flitted over his collarbone. Then, through the sprigs of hair dusting his chest. She paused briefly to circle each flat nipple before roving downward over the ridges of his abdomen and, finally, to the unyielding length of him pulsing in expectation just below his navel. He hissed out a breath when her delicate hand circled him.

"Are you always in this state?" she asked, her mouth pressing kisses along the same path her hand had taken. She circled his nipple with the tip of her tongue before she nipped him with her teeth.

He arched against her hand, hissing again when her grip tightened and slid to the hilt. While he'd been the first to teach her of pleasure, she was an incredibly quick study and surprised him time and again. Even though her course was plotted, as her kisses over his abdomen told him, this was not the night for slow exploration. He needed more. He needed reassurance that he was no longer in the nightmare. He needed to know she was here, she was safe, she was his.

Rathburn reached for her, lifting and turning her so that she lay beneath him. Automatically, she welcomed him, wrapping her arms around him, sliding her hips against his. She was already wet for him. She kissed the column of his throat, trailed her tongue over the line of his jaw, and gently sank her teeth into his chin.

He growled and entered her in a single thrust. Her body clenched around him, stealing his breath. "If I am always in this state, then you have only yourself to blame," he said against her lips, losing himself in the healing power of her kiss. Only she could chase away the demons that plagued his nightmares. Only she could restore his soul and make the world right again. "You've given me more pleasure than I've ever imagined. I've gorged myself on the taste of your mouth and the delectable heat of your body, and still I cannot get enough."

Her dark gaze glittered in the moonlight shining in through open curtains. She lifted her hands to his face, the intensity in her expression telling him more than she'd ever spoken. "I would never impose limits on you. I am yours to consume. Take what you will and leave nothing behind."

Still, he wanted more. He moved within her, filling her, making her gasp his name. His name, but not the words he'd longed to hear. Even though she didn't admit it, she still withheld something from him. She held those words ransom, using her body to tell him instead. But he was going mad for want of them. Mad to hear her tell him she loved him.

In his nightmare she wouldn't tell him either. Her words were swallowed by the flames that surrounded her. He was desperate to hear them. Desperate to know that she wanted this marriage and hadn't merely resigned herself to a life with him.

He thrust harder, faster, driving into her as her cries of ecstasy blew across his lips. She held his gaze even as her body tightened around him and a flood of slick heat coated him. Her lips parted on an endless river of his name.

His name was so close to what he wanted to hear. *Please*, he nearly begged, lifting her hips higher so that he could sink deeper inside her. He wanted to touch her soul.

Sweat dampened his skin. The fire from his nightmare lived within him, consuming both of them. "It's all right, love. Say it. Tell me."

She arched back. Her nipples tightened to pebbles against his flesh. *"Oliver, I—"* Her words transformed into a guttural moan, ripped from the very core of her as her body shuddered.

Knowing that the words he longed for were so close, he

lost control, spending every ounce he had left of himself inside of her. For now, the knowledge that she nearly told him would be enough. But he couldn't wait for long.

It had rained in the early morning hours, every day, for the past two weeks. And every morning for the past two weeks, Rathburn woke her with tender kisses and a slow exploration of her body until she was wanton and writhing beneath him . . .

Or sometimes lifting her to straddle him, his hands touching every inch of her flesh, eliciting whimpers from her until she crashed in ecstasy over him . . .

Or sometimes he would simply roll to his side, his chest against her back, his hands liberating her from sleep as he entered her, unhurried, making love for hours with the rain sounding like music against the windows.

Now, that sound aroused her. The rain, she realized, was like her. For weeks the deluge held back, accumulating an endless river of unspoken desires and longing. Then, finally, it broke free. Marrying Oliver had brought on a storm of emotion in her that she could only release while making love.

Emma likened herself to a blank canvas. Rathburn's hands, fingers, mouth, and tongue were the brushes he used to bring her into being. He'd spent days proving what a master artist he was. Now, she felt as if she were on the cusp of emerging as a new woman.

However, the idea of becoming a stranger to herself was still a bit frightening.

Beneath the covers, she turned, ready to wake him with

her mouth as she'd intended last night. She'd recently discovered this had the ability to turn his speech into an incoherent jumble of sounds, but always ended in a passionate groan of her name. With her eyes still closed, she reached for him—

But he wasn't there.

Her eyes opened. The bed was still warm, telling her that he'd slipped away a moment before she'd woken to the sound of the rain. "Oliver?" Holding the sheet to her, she sat up and looked around the empty chamber. The door leading to her dressing room—and beyond that, his bedchamber, which he never used—stood ajar.

Hearing her, he strode through the door, shrugging into a gray morning coat that made the green of his eyes more pronounced. "You've trained me well, my darling," he said with his almost grin. Yet, for some reason amusement did not reach his gaze. "My name from your lips sends me scurrying to your side."

Stopping beside the bed, he leaned down and kissed her. On the forehead. She felt slighted. For that matter, why was he dressed already? He hadn't mentioned any plan to leave at daybreak.

Yet, instead of asking him directly, she pointed out the obvious. "It's raining."

He made a show of looking to the window and back to her, one brow raised as if to ask why this was supposed to be significant. "So it is."

If she'd had a cup of steaming chocolate on the bedside table, she would have taken a sip, hoping to remind him of that elicit promise he'd made a month and a half ago. Instead, she was forced to be more direct. She lifted her gaze, already feeling a blush creep to her cheeks. "You're not in bed."

He turned away, his fingers busy with his cufflink instead of her body. "I have an errand to run."

Emma felt a chill of uncertainty sweep the length of her spine. He was different today. Distracted. His cool regard didn't sit well with her, especially after last night. There had been moments when she felt bonded to him like never before, as if they'd exchanged pieces of their souls. She wanted to feel that way again. Always.

Yet, now something had changed. "So early?"

"Yes. I'll likely be gone most of the day, as well. However, I thought you would enjoy a day free to attend your needlework group. I can drop you at the Weatherstones' if you are ready within the hour. Otherwise, I'll order a second carriage brought around."

From the clock on the mantle across the room, she noted it was already half passed. There wasn't much of a chance for her to get dressed *and* seduce him properly in such a short span of time. Then again, she was willing to have him any way she could get him.

Needing reassurance, she let the sheet and blanket fall down to her waist, exposing her bare breasts. Even without looking down, she knew her tender nipples were taut and eager for his attention. "Perhaps you could help me dress."

His back to her, he stilled as if his ears were tuned to the quiet whisper of the sheet sliding over her skin. She could tell by the way his shoulders strained the fabric of his coat that he tensed. "I'll be more than happy to summon your maid," he said, his voice a low rumble, letting her know he knew *exactly* what she wanted.

Not only that, but the husky timbre let her know he wanted the same thing. So, why didn't he turn around?

His rejection stung, a sharp stab in the center of her chest.

Reaching for her dressing gown draped over the foot of the bed, she slipped out of bed and pulled it on. She stepped toward the window to watch the raindrops snake haphazardly down the diamond panes. His distance and reluctance to come back to bed shocked her, unsettling her in more ways than she wanted to think about. Their bargain, the quashed annulment, and all the things they hadn't said were in the room like an abyss yawning between them.

Then again, perhaps there was another errand that was of the utmost importance. A task he'd been neglecting the past two weeks—

It came to her suddenly. *The hospital, of course!* That must be where he was going. After all, he'd been absent since their wedding day.

Emma expected to feel relief. Yet, if he were spending the day readying the hospital for completion, then why wouldn't he simply say so?

It was impossible not to wonder at his reason, and not to feel wounded by being left out of something that was so important to him.

"It's fine," she said, not wanting to imagine the worst, not wanting to think that maybe he wasn't going to the hospital at all, but somewhere else he didn't want to divulge. "Go on with your plans. I'll have the carriage ordered after I have a bath. Oh, and don't forget our dinner this evening."

Their first dinner as a married couple with his mother, his grandmother, and her parents. Her parents, she was sure, were expecting to see evidence of a perfectly content union.

The dowager was *merely* expecting perfection.

Emma was afraid of letting everyone down.

"I won't," he said, his voice across the room. "And, Emma?"

Afraid that her expression would reveal too much, she didn't turn. "Yes?"

"There are things"—he drew in a breath—"things we should have discussed before all this, I'm sure. It might be too late now, but perhaps before dinner we could . . ."

Too late now? Her heart stopped.

"Of course." She couldn't catch her breath. This was the first time in weeks that she'd felt as if she was nothing more than a means to an end. A way to gain his inheritance. Surely, she meant more to him than that by now. But perhaps, if he knew how she felt, how much she loved him . . .

"Oliver," she said with quiet uncertainty, exhaling a breath that fogged the glass. "There's something I need to tell you as well." She turned, hoping the sight of him would give her the courage to continue. However, when she did, she found herself completely alone in the vast chamber.

CHAPTER TWENTY-THREE

By the time Emma stepped into the Weatherstones' parlor, all her friends were present.

A sudden burst of glee and welcome came at her unexpected arrival. They each rose to greet her. Though Penelope a bit more carefully than usual, as her faintly rounding form decreed.

"I'm so glad to see you," Penelope said with a smile and warm embrace. Then in a whisper, she added, "Since you've been absent for the past two weeks, I trust marriage suits you well."

Even though this morning's rejection had left her confused and admittedly hurt, memories of the last two weeks brought a blush to her cheeks. Whatever was lacking in their marriage, passion certainly filled the void . . .

Or at least it had. Until this morning.

She refused to think about it now. "It's been . . . unexpectedly wonderful."

"Lady Rathburn, do sit beside me," Delaney said with a cheeky grin as she patted the cushion beside her on the settee.

Emma drew off her bonnet and gloves and laid them on a side table. Taking the opposite chair, Merribeth smiled, though her usual brightness was somewhat diminished. "It's good to see you, Emma."

"It's nice to be back," she said, meaning it. She'd missed the familiarity of their group and visiting with her friends. Especially today when she felt as if she'd lost her *best* friend.

Stepping around the table, she took her place beside Delaney. The group was unusually quiet. Normally, by now they'd have resumed talk of the latest gossip. Instead, there was a very pregnant silence, telling her that she'd missed a great deal in the past two weeks.

Her gaze stayed with Merribeth. "What's happened?"

Her friend tucked the needle into a bare scrap of cambric and set her embroidery hoop aside. "I suppose it's best if I simply come right out with it," she said with a sigh of resignation. "Mr. Clairmore and I . . . have ceased our involvement. But no—that makes it sound like I had a say in the matter. I'm botching this already, and I told myself I wasn't going to let it bother me for another minute." She huffed out a breath and a flash of anger lit the sky blue depths of her eyes. It was startling to witness only because Merribeth never got angry. "*He* has ceased our involvement. And furthermore, he's also decided to marry Miss Codington."

"The vicar's daughter?" Emma gasped, stunned. Merribeth had known Mr. Clairmore for most of her life. More years than Emma had known Oliver, and even longer than Penelope had known Ethan. It wasn't possible. It was so unexpected. So sudden.

She never would have believed such a thing could

happen ... until today. Until Rathburn's obvious change in demeanor. Now, she feared she was experiencing firsthand how unpredictable a man's heart could be.

Tears sprang to her eyes, and she was certain they weren't all for Merribeth. She reached forward and took her friend's hand. "I'm devastated for you."

Merribeth batted away her own tears as if refusing to let them fall. "As you can imagine, I was devastated, too ... for about three minutes." Her eyes narrowed and the infamous Wakefield brow made an appearance. "Then I made the mistake of asking him how he could be so certain of his affection for *her* when we'd spent years planning to marry. Oh, why didn't my aunt ever teach me that I should only ask questions I truly want answered?"

Emma understood this too well. Hadn't that been the reason she avoided asking Rathburn about his inheritance? She didn't want to risk having him tell her outright that it was all settled because of their bargain and thanking her for her part of the deception.

"Mr. Clairmore responded by saying," Merribeth continued, her tone incredulous, "that her lips tasted *like summer wine* and her skin was *soft as butter.*"

"Summer wine?"

"And butter." Merribeth jerked her head in a nod and then lifted her hands in an angry gesture. "How could I have trusted my heart to a man who delights in ... in fondling dairy?"

"I think he meant to say—"

Another flash ignited. "I understand the inference, Delaney. I've turned his words over so many times in my mind that I know quite clearly how he knows her skin has the same texture as butter."

"Slippery," Penelope added in a rush.

Emma nodded. "Greasy."

"Her face must be covered with pockmarks," Delaney said.

Merribeth let out a slow breath. "Thank you. I'm certain she's quite hideous, as well. It will serve him right if he does marry her."

"You believe he doesn't intend to marry her?"

"How can I when we've been engaged to be engaged for five years? He will probably string her along for a time before he realizes his mistake in losing me," she said with an edge of her old certainty returning. "By then it will be too late. I'm not going to waste another thought on Mr. Clairmore. I've wasted years on him already."

"Brava," Delaney said. "We'll find you a far better candidate for husband before the Season ends."

"Yes," Penelope added. "I'm certain he's out there."

"This is my third Season," Merribeth pointed out. "I haven't been courted by a single gentleman."

"That's because every eligible gentleman assumed you were nearly betrothed. Perhaps you've known him all along but he's been too shy."

"Shyness is the last trait I'd ever look for in a husband again. If there were a suitable gentleman out there, he'd have found me by now, nearly betrothed or not. I've given it a great deal of thought," she said with a firm nod. "I've decided that I'd rather meet a man who's impulsive, passionate, and completely irredeemable than to waste any more time on fools."

"Don't make any rash decisions," Emma said, reminded

of her own. The rash decision to go along with Rathburn's scheme was only leading to her heartbreak. Then again, it had also given her the best two weeks of her life, as well.

"Since my social calendar has been cleared, due to recent events, rash decisions are nearly all I have left." She released a sigh and then shook her head as if to pretend she hadn't just said something completely out of character. "Oh, you know me better than that. Clearly, I've allowed my romantic sensibilities too much freedom. What I need is certainty. Right now, the only thing I'm certain of is that my aunt and I are attending a house party in Suffolk at Lady Eve Sterling's estate. After that . . . I'm not certain of anything."

"I think we can all agree that Mr. Clairmore was undeserving of your affection and devotion," Penelope said, earning nods of agreement from Emma and Delaney. "But don't allow his behavior to dictate your life."

"She's right," Delaney chimed in. "You deserve to find a man who'll sweep you off your feet. A man who'll write sonnets about your lips—and good ones, too, not paltry comparisons to summer wine. You deserve to find love and settle for nothing less."

Merribeth blinked back tears again. "Since when did you become a romantic?"

"*Romantic*," Delaney snorted, but two spots of color rose to her cheeks, turning all attention to her. "I'm merely supporting my friend in her time of distress. Helping her to find a worthy candidate."

None of them believed her, but they didn't press further. After all, Delaney could be inordinately stubborn when she wanted to be.

"I'm certain even the most worthy candidate would choose a bride with a dowry as opposed to one with none."

"At least without one, you're certain to find a man who loves you and not your fortune," Delaney said quietly.

Or marries you in order to gain his inheritance, Emma thought. Although she didn't speak the words aloud, Penelope seemed to guess what she was thinking. They exchanged a look. Hers filled with doubt and her friend's with reassurance.

It wasn't fair to her, with the way she felt and doubted everything about her marriage to Rathburn. And it certainly wasn't fair to him, having waited so long for his inheritance only to have it withheld by his grandmother when it should have been his years ago.

Emma's heart broke for Merribeth, but she also admired her certainty. Her friend had a plan and was determined to follow it, rash though it may be. Yet, she couldn't stop thinking about what Delaney had said, as well. Didn't they all deserve to find love and settle for nothing less?

Her hands shook when she picked up her needlework. She knew instantly that she wouldn't be able to sit here for the next hour or two and pretend her nerves weren't frayed. Pretend that her heart wasn't breaking.

"Emma, is everything alright?" Penelope asked.

She placed one hand over the other and affected a small laugh. "Perhaps I am out of practice."

"Do you know what I think?" Delaney offered, hastily stuffing her needlework back into her reticule. "I think we could all use a distraction. After all, new ribbons arrived at Haversham's today and I'm dying to see if I can convince my newly married friend to buy the crimson. It would look splendid with your coloring."

"Crimson?" Emma had never worn such a bold color. Surely, the dowager wouldn't approve.

Merribeth tucked her needlework away and sat on the edge of her cushion. "It would be lovely. Besides, now that you are married, a whole world of color is yours for the taking."

"Or the *wearing*," Penelope added with a grin. "I think it sounds like a splendid idea. After all, the rain has stopped."

Mention of the rain only reminded her of this morning. Melancholy threatened to return. Yes, she needed a distraction.

"Then, it's settled." Emma was determined to put her fears in her reticule with her needlework and synch it closed for the remainder of the day. Perhaps a bit more color in her life was all she needed.

They spent most of the afternoon at various shops, in addition to stopping by a tea room.

At Haversham's, Emma chose the crimson ribbon, a peacock blue, an emerald green, and a yellow so bright it reminded her of daffodils and one of her mother's more garish gowns. Although it was all wrong for her coloring, it was too cheerful to leave behind. She needed all the cheer she could get.

As the afternoon progressed, she kept careful watch of the time, not wanting to return too late. Even though she'd planned every detail and left her orders in Mrs. Stillson's capable hands, she had to arrive in time to dress for dinner and make certain everything was perfect.

Tonight was a night to prove herself worthy.

They were just leaving the flower shop with a dozen pink roses Emma wanted to use as a centerpiece, when they crossed the path of Elena Mallory on the busy street.

Their nemesis stopped instantly, her dark eyes going wide and her mouth open like a fish at market. "Why, Lady Rathburn, what a coincidence. Imagine who I should find after just having received the most delicious morsel of news only moments ago."

Emma bristled, but inclined her head. She had gall in abundance, this one. Only a month past, she'd tried to embroil both her and Oliver in a terrible scandal. "Miss Mallory."

"Such formalities when we are all friends." She tutted.

Delaney scoffed and stepped forward, as if acting as a buffer. "Your news, *cousin?*"

"I heard it directly from Lady Amherst, who stopped her carriage in order to tell me." She preened, pressing her splayed fingers to her chest. "I just knew I had to tell you, Lady Rathburn, for I'm sure it must be of the utmost importance to you."

Don't dare ask, a voice whispered in her mind. Unfortunately, the dread in the pit of her stomach demanded an answer. "Why me, in particular?"

"Oh . . . because it involves a certain actress and a newly married gentleman, whom it is said used to *keep* her." Her eyes brightened in wicked delight. "I believe you might recognize her by name, a Miss Lovetree?"

Merribeth and Penelope moved beside Emma, slipping their arms through hers, as if they'd sensed the amount of strength it required of Emma to continue standing here—all the while pretending she was unaffected.

Delaney set her hands on her hips. "Bad form, cousin. Besides that's old news."

"Part, perhaps. However, the fact that she ran away with her gentleman shortly after dawn this morning, is quite new, I assure you."

This morning?

"From what I hear, he'd just come into a large sum of money."

His inheritance. Emma couldn't breathe. Had Oliver left her? After everything, was this how it was to end between them?

Chapter Twenty-Four

Archie sank down into the overstuffed wing-backed chair in the small parlor at the back of his shop. "If the good doctor's goal is to exhaust me with exercise and cold water baths, I'd say he's doing a fair job of it."

"I met a few of his patients when I visited Austria, and the water therapy was showing signs of success," Rathburn said, concealing his amusement when his friend raised a speculative brow. "Although, I'm sure it takes some getting used to. The hospital should be finished by the end of summer, at which point he'll have the rest of the treatments in place."

"The torture devices, you mean." Archie scrubbed a scarred hand over the top of the other. "What was that paste he put on me made of, anyway? Crushed brimstone from Satan's hearth? Burned like the devil . . ." he muttered and then lifted his arm to get a better look. "But it seems to be doing something. Not sure what just yet."

In the same moment, Penny walked into the back room and set down a tray of fragrant brown bread, sliced ham, a hunk of cheese, and two pints of ale onto a side table. "You need to give the good doctor your trust, *that's* what, Archie Smith," she scolded, but then ruined her set-down by gently brushing back a lock of hair from her husband's forehead.

Archie grabbed his wife's gloved hand and kissed it, gazing up at her adoringly. "I'll do that, pet, but only if you're brave enough to come with me next time. Maybe you won't need these forever," he said, tugging at the finger of her gloves. Just then, Rathburn noticed something familiar in the embroidery—an ivy-trimmed border in a russet brown.

She let out a flustered sound, as if they'd had this conversation before, and pulled her hand from his grasp. "These are my favorite pair, as you well know. A gift from *Miss Danvers*—but, no, she's Lady Rathburn now."

He'd known for years that Emma came here. While both of them knew of the other's involvement with the Smiths, they never spoke of it until recently. Yet still, he hadn't told her how he'd always looked out for her, even before Rafe Danvers had asked him to act as her chaperone in his stead. He didn't like her coming so close to the rookeries with only an elderly maid as her chaperone. So, he'd arranged for one of his footmen to watch over her. He'd even taken to scheduling his own surreptitious jaunts down the street on the days she'd come here. And not once in all that time, had he ever taken account of his strange, proprietary behavior.

However, now it all made perfect sense.

"And what of her ladyship? How is she faring with her new circumstances?" Penny asked with a smile as she handed him a mug of ale. "I know last Season she'd lamented on ever finding a husband, but I could always tell she held a soft place for you in her heart."

Stunned, Rathburn stared at her. "You could?"

"Aye. Though she's reserved in her way, it was always been clear to Archie and me."

One look at his friend's easy grin confirmed it.

Huh. Rathburn lifted the mug to his lips and took a hearty swallow. Perhaps he'd been unfair, leaving the way he had this morning. He hated to admit that a degree of selfishness had driven him to this point. It had taken every ounce of control he had, not to cross the room and pull her into his arms. He knew he'd hurt Emma, and felt terrible because of it. However, at the same time, she infuriated him.

All those unspoken words! She hadn't even demanded to know where he was going. Furthermore, she never once brought up their future. She hadn't mentioned children since that first day. Yet, she was more than willing to share her body with him, surpassing even the fantasy he'd had of her. In her eyes, he could see the love she felt for him . . . and yet she still held back from telling him.

"All she needed was to have you draw her out, and now look at you." Penny lit up the small parlor with her smile.

Yes, look at him and Emma. While he had a wife who selflessly gave everything she could, she had a husband who still wanted more. Damn, but he'd been right prig this morning.

Perhaps Penny was right. All he needed was to draw her out.

She'd told him once that she'd be a fool to lose her head over him. But that was exactly what he wanted. Her head. Her heart. He wanted everything Emma kept locked inside. And he was determined to get it.

CHAPTER TWENTY-FIVE

Emma stared out the carriage window the entire way to Hawthorne Manor, willing the horses to gallop faster. The instant the regal façade came into view, her heart ran at breakneck speed. The moment of truth was upon her.

However, the driver slowed his pace too early for her liking. So before he'd come to a complete stop before the stairs, she opened the door and leapt out. Propriety be damned.

Leaving every parcel behind, she rushed up to the door and flung it open—only to see Oliver standing in the foyer. Her half boots skidded to a stop on the marble tiles. She was out of breath.

"You're here." It was then she noticed the hat in his hand and was unsure if he was just arriving or just going out. She didn't see a satchel waiting. Yet, it could already be packed and inside his carriage. Perhaps Miss Lovetree was waiting as well . . . "Were you going out again?"

For a long moment, he simply stared at her, his expression changing like the sky in inclement weather—darkening, shifting, churning. "Not any longer," he said at last and then laid his hat atop the table. "I was on my way to Danbury Lane to ensure that you were—or rather that your group was"—he drew in a breath—"I'd no notion that needlework could occupy so much of your afternoon."

Was that concern in his gaze? She dared to hope. "We were a restless lot. I'm afraid we decided our time was better spent in the shops . . . And you? I hope you kept good company today."

An eternity passed before he answered.

"I did. A mutual acquaintance, in fact. Mr. and Mrs. Smith."

"Oh," she said. A bud of hope had an inkling to blossom. "The whole day?"

"Yes."

A startled sob bubbled up from her throat. *It wasn't him!* He wasn't the one who ran away with Lily Lovetree this morning. Though she tried to smother the sound with her hand, she was too late. Tears pricked her eyes and flooded her lower rims. Her vision of him rapidly turned liquid, giving her the sense that she was drowning.

For the past two weeks, it had taken every ounce of control not to reveal the depth of her feelings. Her only outlet had been while making love. Time and again, he'd whispered his desires for her to let go. And she did. While in his arms, it was safe to give him everything. But afterward, while he held her so tenderly, she still had this terrible restlessness inside her. It made her want to leap out of bed, fling open the doors of their balcony and shout her love for him for all the world to hear. She wanted to make love to him with the rain pouring over their skin. She wanted to sip chocolate from his lips. She wanted to crawl inside of his skin so she would never be apart from him.

The depth of her feelings terrified her.

Oliver took a step toward her. "Emma, darling, what is it?"

Emma's cool head had helped her get through many moments when the world around her turned to complete and utter chaos. Only now, the chaos was inside her, threatening to expose her. "I'm afraid . . ." The words were there, waiting to spill out. And yet, they shied away at the last moment. "That I won't be ready in time for our guests, if I don't hurry."

Like the coward she was, she rushed past him and up the stairs.

Emma's sudden tears had robbed Rathburn of speech. He'd hurt her, obviously. More than ever, he wanted to comfort her and apologize for being such a cold-hearted ass this morning. Unfortunately, the moment she'd disappeared up the stairs, the carriages arrived, bringing their guests of honor.

Now, inside the drawing room with his grandmother, mother, Cuthbert and Celestine Danvers, and Emma, he felt as if he were about to burst out of his skin. Each time he checked the mantle clock, it was as if the hand never moved. He wanted dinner over with as soon as possible, and yet the opposite seemed to be happening. They were still chatting while sipping aperitifs in the drawing room, and the meal was not scheduled for another quarter hour.

". . . take Harrison for instance," his father-in-law continued. Although, whatever he'd said before was a mystery. "His jowls are positively inspiring."

Rathburn shook himself out of his distraction. Once he saw Emma rise and walk toward the sideboard to refill his grandmother's sherry, he started to think of a dozen ways to get her alone. "Quite right," he said absently. "Can I offer you another splash of whisky?"

It was only when he started to walk away without Danvers's glass in hand that he turned back. His father-in-law chuckled. Biting down on the tip of his pipe, he offered a nod. "A prize above all others, son."

Rathburn smiled at this exchange, and turned to join his bride at the sideboard.

"Faring well?" he whispered, leaning in to catch the scent from one of the jasmine flowers tucked in her hair.

She angled her head toward him and kept her voice low. "I can't imagine what you must think of me after how I'd behaved earlier."

"No, darling. I was the cad. I never should have—"

"I've changed my mind, dear," his grandmother interrupted. "I don't think I will have another. Too much sherry can cause a headache, and after the news I learned earlier, I shouldn't take the risk."

"Mother, surely now is not the time to mention such things," his mother said with very uncharacteristic reproof. It was enough to draw his curiosity, as well as, it seemed, Emma's.

They both turned.

"I believe the news left our dear Emma shaken as well. After all, she didn't even notice our carriage pass her in the street this very afternoon."

Emma drew in an audible breath. "I didn't realize. For-

give me. I was unsettled by an encounter with an old friend."
Before he could ask whom and threaten to run them through
for causing her any moment of distress, she glanced up at him.
"Miss Mallory."

"Ah." He thought he was beginning to understand. However, when his grandmother continued, he realized it was
much worse than he imagined.

"No doubt the news of Captain Burns—our neighbor and
the recently deceased Lord Sturgis's nephew—running away
with that actress was enough to unsettle anyone with high
morals. Though at this moment, her name slips my mind . . ."

"Miss Lovetree," Emma supplied.

"Thank you, dear," his grandmother said with a nod that
seemed more of admiration at his bride's character than appreciation at having a name supplied. In fact, he believed
his grandmother wanted to make certain *he* knew exactly of
whom they were speaking.

Recalling the way Emma had rushed into the foyer a short
while ago, the way that she was surprised to see him, how she
asked him if he was planning to go out again, and if he'd been
with the Smiths the *whole* day, it all started to make sense.

"You thought that I—"

"Of course not." Facing him, she shook her head. Then,
she lifted her gaze and the truth was there as she worried the
corner of her mouth. "Not for longer than the briefest of moments."

He blew out a breath that ended in a chuckle. Lifting a
hand to his brow, he pressed the pad of his thumb and forefinger to his temples. "And I'd worried that you might have met
with the vicar to seek an annulment."

"Annulment?" His grandmother scoffed. "I'll not hear of it. The truth of your bride's altered state is far too obvious in the glow of her cheeks and brightness of her eyes. As are yours, for that matter. Therefore, she cannot give you back."

He expected Emma to gasp at his grandmother's frank speaking. After all, he'd had years to grow used to her ways when she hadn't.

Yet, Emma didn't gasp. She laughed instead, though her cheeks were suffused with bright color. "I would not wish to," she said quietly, still holding his gaze. "He is very dear to me."

Rathburn was the one left struggling for breath. There was no steadying the sudden leap of his pulse.

"I'm sure I do not need to tell you what a remarkable man he is."

"Nothing escapes my notice," his grandmother declared arrogantly. "After all, I've known about his plan to build that hospital since the inception, or thereabouts."

Stunned, Rathburn blinked. *The hospital.* "You knew?"

His attention focused on his grandmother—the same woman who'd withheld his inheritance for years. The same woman who'd practically beaten him over the head with the notion of marrying Emma when he was too blind to see how much he loved her. And now, she was the same woman who'd known his secret all along.

She huffed as if disappointed that he hadn't figured it out. "There is no secret you can keep from me. Besides, didn't it occur to you that Collingsford would come to me for payment when he knew I held the funds? He even tried to plead your case."

His gaze veered to his mother and he noted that she, too,

was unsurprised, albeit tearfully happy. However, the Danverses were sufficiently shocked. In that he felt moderately mollified.

"A hospital. What a wonderful way to honor your father," Celestine Danvers said, tears brimming in her eyes. "Why ever would you keep it a secret?"

Emma slipped her hand in his. "Because he is too modest for his own good. If I hadn't found out by accident—"

"You mean you didn't tell her?" his grandmother asked. "When you schemed with her in order to gain your inheritance, you should have told her everything."

His mouth fell open. She'd known about that as well?

Grandmamma heaved a great sigh of exasperation and turned her focus to Emma. "Forgive my grandson, dear. He can be rather thickheaded at times. He was so focused on repairing the manor, building the hospital, and keeping it a secret that he never saw what was right in front of him. Therefore, I felt compelled to give him a reason to open his eyes, first by nudging him in the direction of your *false* courtship. Then, by releasing his inheritance without condition, he was free to decide what his heart truly wanted."

Emma went still. "Released . . . his . . . . inheritance?"

"Over a month ago," she said offhandedly. "Plenty of time for the two of you to call off the ruse. I even gave you the perfect opportunity to break your betrothal, if you'll recall."

She turned and searched his gaze. He hoped she saw what his heart truly wanted reflected in his eyes. "Oliver is a very honorable man. I'm sure he was only worried about my reputation if we would have broken our engagement."

"You're rather thickheaded too." The dowager issued an uncharacteristic chuckle as if this were the most entertainment she'd had in years. "Heaven help my great-grandchildren."

Emma blinked out of her momentary haze as all the news slowly spread through her. "Released your inheritance ... a month ago?"

When her hands went slack, Oliver took them in his. "I told you at the church. Don't you remember how I said that the original reason we were there was no longer a factor, that it was real for me?"

Incredulous, she simply stared at his confused expression. "*That* was your way of telling me you'd received your inheritance?"

"Well"—he shrugged—"yes."

Was it possible that he'd loved her all this time? "You never intended to get an annulment."

He grinned at her and shook his head. "Never. Did you?"

She held his gaze, a pleasant warmth filling her. If she had a modicum of doubt any longer, she wouldn't be able to speak at all. "I had no foundation for an annulment."

He radiated a palpable energy while remaining perfectly still. His eyes glittered with those gold flecks as he drew in a breath. "And your vows?"

"Were spoken with sincerity and a full understanding of their significance." She had not ventured into this marriage lightly.

He huffed in frustration and looked up to the ceiling as if seeking council. "You are determined to make me question my sanity. You know very well what I'm asking of you."

Emma didn't know why the sight of him so flustered amused her, but it made her feel giddy. She replayed all those years of his teasing her, his quips of how buttoned-up she was, his own flirtations that had left her flustered time and again.

"You and I have gotten too used to keeping secrets," he said with an edge to his sincerity.

She squeezed his hands. "I'd like to be done with all that now."

"Are you sure?"

There was a distinct challenge in his expression. But she didn't back down. Emma decided that it was time to banish all secrets between them. This was her home. Rathburn was her husband ... *by choice*. There was power in that knowledge. It changed her. "Yes."

He grinned in a way that made her question if she would regret her acquiescence.

"Everyone, I believe dinner is ready," he announced, glancing to Harrison's presence near the door. "However, if you would follow me to the study first, I have something I'm certain you'll all want to see."

This was not what she expected. Then again, she didn't know what to expect. In the end, she indulged her curiosity. What was he up to?

As a group and without an ounce of ceremony, they crossed the hall and stepped into the study. She was just about to ask him the reason for their detour when she saw it hanging on the far wall.

"You—" All the air suddenly left her body. "You framed the painting."

She couldn't tear her gaze away. The frame was a work

of art in itself, looking to be hand carved from a dark cherry wood that altered the focus of her painting. Now, the eye naturally sought the pink blush of roses hidden in the shadows of the arch at the end of the path.

Only then did she realize—only then did she know with absolute certainty—that Oliver knew her secret. Or secrets, rather. All of them. And from the smug look on his face just now, he'd known for quite a while.

"Of course." That smug look didn't waver as he stepped around the desk and stood within arm's reach of her.

He knew. She felt lightheaded. "Why?"

"Because it's remarkable," he said with a secret smile. "Especially the jasmine and the topiaries . . ." His words trailed off, letting her know how utterly obvious she'd been.

She felt exposed. Even though he'd stripped her bare dozens of times in the past two weeks, she felt far more vulnerable this time. After all, this was part of her that no one knew about.

"Is there something you want to tell me?" he asked as he drew her against him. "Or is this another part of you that you're determined to keep hidden, maddeningly out of reach?"

She didn't want to hide anything from him. "Oliver . . . Everyone . . ."

His gaze was intense, boring into hers with expectation. "Yes, my darling?"

"I painted it," she confessed.

"Oh, Emma!" her mother exclaimed, tears glistening in her eyes. "It's magnificent. The flowers are so alive."

Studying the painting closely, her father looked over his shoulder at her and nodded. His eyes misted over and crinkled at the corners. At the simple gesture, it was all she could do not to run across the room and hug him. "I always knew you had it in you."

"My dear, what a remarkable talent you have," her mother-in-law said, embracing her. "Why ever would you keep such a gift a secret?"

Emma swallowed and shrugged without knowing what to say. Should she admit to never imagining praise or acceptance, but always scorn and censure?

"Clearly," the dowager said, her lips pursed. The tip of her cane tapped against the floor.

During the moment when her gaze traveled from the painting and back to her, Emma held her breath.

"I was right to encourage the match all along."

"Then you aren't terribly disappointed?"

"That depends. How long must I wait until I have a painting of my own to place in my sitting room where I can brag about my granddaughter-in-law?"

Emma felt her shoulders relax and her lips curve into a smile. "Not long."

"Good." The dowager winked at her. *Winked!* "Now, let us see what artful creations your cook has in store for us."

Her parents beamed as they followed the dowager and Oliver's mother out into the hall. She was still grinning when she felt him take hold of her hand and pull her back into the study, closing the door the behind them.

"We'll only be a moment," he said, pulling her close.

She slipped her hands beneath his lapels and gazed up at him. "Should I have confessed the way I take my tea with sugar instead of lemon, do you think?"

"You do not want to incur my grandmother's wrath," he teased.

His expression told her that he was still waiting for a different confession.

Wanting to bare her soul to him, she said, "I haven't painted anything in years, but in the weeks leading up to the wedding, I couldn't help myself. When you asked my opinion about the garden, I thought it was the perfect opportunity to show you how I feel . . . when I wasn't brave enough to tell you."

He smiled. "That painting shows me how passionate you are and how much you love . . ."—he lowered his mouth, stealing her breath with a kiss—". . . the garden."

"I knew that an association with another artist in the Danvers clan would not bode well for you. I didn't want to say anything for fear of you losing your inheritance."

"Because you thought our marriage had everything to do with my inheritance and nothing to do with how much I love you."

She gasped. A delightful airy feeling rushed into her heart, as if the fireflies in his gaze were fluttering there. She circled his neck with her arms and leaned against him.

"How I've loved you all along," he continued, pressing his lips to one corner of her mouth and then the other. "At first, I was going to leave the decision up to you. After all, you had the perfect excuse to end our pretense when your brother swept into the library with every intention of murdering me." His lips lightly brushed over her jaw. "The next day, when you met with my grandmother, I was fully prepared to stop you and confess the whole truth."

She arched her neck, encouraging his exploration of her throat. "What stopped you?"

"I heard you whisper"— he lifted his head and gazed down at her with enough intensity to stop her heart and start it all over again—"and I'm certain, sweeter words have never been spoken. I knew in that moment I had to marry you, Emma. For my sake as well as yours. You said it best. *We share a heart.* A statement so true that I had the jeweler inscribe it inside your wedding band."

It took her a moment to recover from the joy rushing through her. "You're right, you know. You've been right all along. I do love"—he took a breath—"your garden."

"Emma . . ." He growled at her, taking her mouth in a fierce kiss of total possession, demanding her complete surrender, and leaving her dizzy.

"But not nearly as much as I love you, Oliver."

Acknowledgments

Thank you to my amazing editor, Chelsey Emmelhainz, for your insight, dedication, support, and most of all for making my dream a reality.

Thank you to the art department at Avon Impulse for my swoon-worthy cover.

Thank you to my sisters—Deanna, Cyndi, and Katie—and to my sisters of the heart—April, Gwen, Lora, and Robin—for listening to me ramble on about fictional characters, and even more for the times when you believe in them too.

Thank you to my parents for helping me to become the person I am.

Thank you to the incomparable Cindy C, the best research librarian I know.

Thank you to Lynne for making the day of "the call" even more incredible.

And to Mike, thank you for years of love and laughter.

See how Vivienne Lorret's Wallflower romances began
with an excerpt from

"TEMPTING MR. WEATHERSTONE"

available now in FIVE GOLDEN RINGS:
A Christmas Collection.
And continue reading
for a sneak peek at

WINNING MISS WAKEFIELD,

coming June 2014 from Avon Impulse.

An Excerpt from

"TEMPTING MR. WEATHERSTONE"

*Responsible Ethan Weatherstone is determined to save Penelope
Rutledge—and her reputation—from her silly scheme, but can
he save himself from the temptation of her lips?*

Ethan Weatherstone was due for a piece of her mind. It was
about time he understood that he had no right to interfere
with her life.

Mind made up, she took one last look at the mail coach
and shook her head. She reached down for her satchel and
stormed over to Ethan's carriage.

Penelope threw open the door and climbed inside, seeth-
ing as she sat across from him. He didn't even have the courtesy to look at her. Instead, he sat back against the squabs, his
head turned to the window. The only reason she knew he was
aware of her presence was from the way he clenched his jaw, a
muscle twitching just beneath the surface of his skin.

"Were you waiting to humiliate me? Waiting until I was
already seated before you dragged me away from the mail

coach? Or perhaps you planned to follow me all the way to Portsmouth?"

He refused to respond or even so much as look at her. If she hadn't been angry before she entered the carriage, then she certainly was fuming now.

"Truly, Ethan, for someone who cannot live outside the lines of your carefully crafted order, your sameness that covers you like a shroud, this is quite surprising behavior," she hissed, baiting him. "I only wish your concern for my happiness were as great as your concern for my reputation."

At that, he glared at her sharply. Ah, so she'd struck a chord.

Good. Yet still, he did not say anything.

There he sat, perfectly groomed, his cravat perfectly pleated, his temper perfectly managed. She wished just once he'd lose some of that control. Because here she sat, with her eyes, most likely puffy and red from having cried most of the night instead of sleeping. She was certainly not perfectly groomed, since she could feel a soggy tendril of hair plastered to her cheek. Her cloak was damp from rain. Her nose was cold and likely red as well.

"How can you be so . . . so *unaffected* all the time?" Her voice rose with her accusation. "Haven't you ever dreamed for something outside the realm of possibility? Or are you content with each day so long as your cravat is perfectly pleated?"

She glared at the offending garment, struck by a ridiculous notion to crumple it. No sooner had the idea formed that she gave in to the impulse and moved forward on her seat, her arm reaching forward.

Ethan stopped her, taking hold of her wrist. His eyes

flared. Before she could react, he yanked, propelling her forward to land clumsily on his lap.

"How dare—"

His mouth covered hers, silencing her outrage. Her head spun, reeling from the sudden scorching heat of his kiss.

This was a kiss, wasn't it? Yet, it was nothing like her dreams, where his rehearsed request was followed by carefully controlled actions. No, this was no gentle dream. This was hard and demanding. His tongue didn't request entrance but swept in and plundered.

His arms were not gentle either. In fact, he held her so tightly she couldn't move, and grasped her wrist so she couldn't touch him or push him away.

But she'd never push him away.

Instead, she wanted to cling to him. Her anger evaporated in a rush of steam. Her mind cried out for more of this glorious punishment. She wanted his kiss to burn her, through and through. This was the first time she'd been warm in months.

An Excerpt from

WINNING MISS WAKEFIELD

When her betrothed suddenly announces his plans to marry another, Merribeth Wakefield knows only a bold move will bring him back and restore her tattered reputation: She must take a lesson in seduction from a master of the art. But when the dark and brooding rake, Lord Knightswold, takes her under his wing, her education quickly goes from theory to hands-on knowledge, and her heart is given a crash course in true desire!

"Now, give back my handkerchief," Lord Knightswold said, holding out his hand as he returned to her side. "You're the sort to keep it as a memento. I cannot bear the thought of my hand-kerchief being worshipped by a forlorn Miss by moonlight or tucked away with mawkish reverence beneath a pillow."

The portrait he painted was so laughable that she smiled, heedless of exposing her flaw. "You flatter yourself. Here." She dropped it into his hand as she swept past him, prepared to leave. "I have no desire to touch it a moment longer. I will leave you to your pretense of sociability."

"'Tis no pretense. I have kept good company this evening." Either the brandy had gone to her head, impairing her hearing, or he actually sounded sincere.

She paused and rested her hands on the carved rosewood filigree, edging the top of the sofa. "Much to my own folly. I never should have listened to Lady Eve Sterling. It was her lark that sent me here."

He feigned surprise. "Oh? How so?"

If it weren't for the brandy, she would have left by now. Merribeth rarely had patience for such games, and she knew his question was part of a game he must have concocted with Eve. However, his company had turned out to be exactly the diversion she'd needed, and she was willing to linger. "She claimed to have forgotten her reticule and sent me here to fetch it—no doubt wanting me to find you."

He looked at her as if confused.

"I've no mind to explain it to you. After all, you were abetting her plot, lying in wait, here on this very sofa." She brushed her fingers over the smooth fabric, thinking of him lying there in the dark. "Not that I blame you. Lady Eve is difficult to say no to. However, I will conceal the truth from her and we can carry on as if her plan had come to fruition. It would hardly have served its purpose anyway."

He moved toward her, his broad shoulders outlined by the distant torch light filtering in through the window behind him. "Refresh my memory then. What was it I was supposed to do whilst in her employ?"

She blushed again. Was he going to make her say the words aloud? No gentleman would.

So, of course, *he* would. She decided to get it over with

as quickly as possible. "She professed that a kiss from a rake could instill confidence and mend a broken heart."

He stopped, impeded by the sofa between them. His brow lifted in curiosity. "Have you a broken heart in need of mending?"

The deep murmur of his voice, the heated intensity in his gaze, and quite possibly the brandy—all worked against her better sense and sent those tingles dancing in a pagan circle again.

Oh, yes, the thought as she looked up at him. *Yes, Lord Knightswold. Mend my broken heart.*

However, her mouth intervened. "I don't believe so." She gasped at the realization. "I should, you know. After five years, my heart should be in shreds. Shouldn't it?"

He turned before she could read his expression and then sat down on the sofa, affording her a view of the top of his head. "I know nothing of broken hearts, or their mending."

"Pity," she said, distracted by the dark silken locks that accidentally brushed her fingers. "Neither do I."

However accidental the touch of his hair had been, now her fingers threaded through the fine strands with untamed curiosity and blatant disregard for propriety.

Lord Knightswold let his head fall back, permitting—perhaps even encouraging—her to continue. She did, without thought to right, wrong, who he was, or who she was supposed to be. Running both hands through his hair, massaging his scalp, she watched his eyes drift closed.

Then, Merribeth Wakefield did something she never intended to do.

She kissed a rake.

ABOUT THE AUTHOR

VIVIENNE LORRET loves romance novels, her pink laptop, her husband, and her two teenage sons (not necessarily in that order . . . but there are days). Transforming copious amounts of tea into words, she is the author of Avon Impulse's "Tempting Mr. Weatherstone" and the Wallflower Wedding series. For more on her upcoming novels, visit her at www.vivlorret.net.

Visit www.AuthorTracker.com for exclusive information on your favorite HarperCollins authors.

Give in to your impulses . . .
Read on for a sneak peek at two brand-new
e-book original tales of romance
from Avon Books.
Available now wherever e-books are sold.

FALLING FOR OWEN
Book Two: The McBrides
By Jennifer Ryan

GOOD GIRLS DON'T
DATE ROCK STARS
By Codi Gary

An Excerpt from

FALLING FOR OWEN
Book Two: The McBrides
by Jennifer Ryan

From *New York Times* bestselling author
Jennifer Ryan comes the second book in an
unforgettable series about the sexy McBride
men of Fallbrook, Colorado. Reformed bad boy
Owen McBride will do anything to protect his
beautiful neighbor when she gets caught in the
crossfire between his client and her abusive ex.

Claire woke out of a sound sleep with a gasp and held her breath, trying to figure out what had startled her. She listened to the quiet night. Nothing but crickets and the breeze rustling the trees outside. A twig snapped on the ground below her window. Her heart hammered faster, and she sucked in a breath, trying not to panic. Living in the country lent itself to overactive imaginings about things that go bump in the dark night. The noise could be anything from a stray dog or cat to a raccoon on a midnight raid of her garbage cans, even an opossum looking for a little action.

Settled back into her pillow and the thick blankets, she closed her eyes, but opened them wide when something big brushed against the side of the house. Freaked out, she got up from the bed and went to the window. She pulled the curtain back with one finger and peeked through the crack, scanning the moonlit yard below for wayward critters. Not so easy to see with the quarter moon, but she watched the shadows for anything suspicious. Nothing moved.

Not satisfied, and certainly not able to sleep without a more thorough investigation, she padded down the scarred wooden stairs to the living room. She skirted packing boxes and the sofa and went to the window overlooking the front yard. Nothing moved. Still not satisfied, she walked to the dining room, opened the blinds, and stared out into the cold night. Something banged one flower pot into another on the back patio, drawing her away from the dining room, through the kitchen, and to the counter. She grabbed the phone off the charger, went around the island, and tiptoed along the breakfast bar to the sliding glass door. She peeked out, hiding most of her body behind the wall and ducking her head out to see if someone was trying to break into her house. Like she thought, the small pot filled with marigolds had been knocked over and broken against the pot of geraniums beside it. Upset that her pretty pot and flowers were ruined, she moved away from the wall and stood in the center of the glass door to get a better look.

With her gaze cast down on the pots, she didn't see the man step out from the other side of the patio until his shadow fell over her. Their gazes collided, his eyes going as wide as hers.

"You're not him," he said, stumbling back, knocking over a potted pink miniature rose bush, and falling on his ass, breaking the pot and the rose with his legs. She hoped he got stuck a dozen times, but the tiny thorns probably wouldn't go through his dirt-smudged jeans.

In a rage, she opened the door, but held tight to the handle so she could close it again if he came too close. She yelled, "What the hell are you doing?"

"I'll get him for this and for sleeping with my wife," the guy slurred. Drunk and ranting, he gained his feet but stumbled again. "Where is he?" The man turned every which way, looking past her and into her dark house.

"Who?"

"Your lying, cheating, no-good husband."

"How the hell should I know? I haven't seen or heard from him in six months."

"Liar. I saw him drive this way tonight after he fucked my wife at his office and filled her head with more bullshit lies."

"Listen, I'm sorry if my *ex* is messing with your wife. I left him almost two years ago for cheating on me. Believe me, I know how you feel, but he doesn't live here."

"You're lying. He drove his truck this way and stopped just outside."

"He doesn't drive a truck."

"Stop lying, bitch."

"I'm not. You have the wrong person."

"You tell that no-good McBride he better stop seeing my wife. If he thinks a bunch of papers will ever set her free from me, he doesn't know what I'm capable of, what we have. He'll be one sorry son of a bitch. She's mine. I keep what's mine."

"You don't understand."

"No. You don't understand," he said, almost like a whining child. "You tell him, or I'll make him pay with what's his." He pointed an ominous finger at her. "You tell him if he doesn't leave my wife alone and let her come back to me like she wants, I'm going to hurt you before I come after him."

An Excerpt from

GOOD GIRLS DON'T DATE ROCK STARS
by Codi Gary

Gemma Carlson didn't plan on waking up
married to her old flame—and her son's
father-turned-country rock star—Travis
Bowers, following a night of drunken dares.
So she does the only sane thing: she runs!

Travis finally has a second chance, and he doesn't
plan on losing Gemma again—or the son he didn't
know he had. He's in this for the long haul. Even if
it means chasing his long-lost love all over again . . .

"What are you doing here, Travis?"

The rage and frustration that had been simmering below the surface of his skin started to burn. "Why wouldn't I come here?" He turned around and faced her, crossing his arms over his chest. "You're my wife. We spent a magical night together, and I just happen to have a break in my tour that allows me to spend several weeks with you."

"I thought you would—"

"What, Gemma?" His voice was low and dark as he approached her. Grabbing her shoulders, he gave her a gentle shake. "What? You thought I'd just read your letter and be grateful? That I'd think, 'you know what, she's right' and leave you alone, just disappear from your life again?"

She stopped struggling, and he could tell by her expression that was exactly what she'd been thinking.

"This is my home, Travis. You can't just show up here and disrupt my life," she hissed.

"I'm not trying to disrupt your life. I just want to know why you left without talking to me. At least trying to work out what happened," he said.

"What happened is we got drunk and did something stupid. End of story," she said.

"No, that's not the end of it, sweetheart," he snapped before he could rein in his temper. "Like it or not, we're married. It wasn't something I planned, but that's the way things are, and you could have at least given me the courtesy of waking me up and talking about it."

"What's there to talk about, Travis? We haven't seen each other for ten years, and yes, I had fun with you, but we want totally different things," she said, sounding almost disappointed. "You and I . . . we don't work anymore. We're too different. Our worlds are too different."

He took a calming breath and thought about her words. It was true that their lives were different, but that wasn't a kill switch for a future. People called alcohol "truth serum," and if he'd stood up and pledged himself to Gemma legally, deep down he must have wanted it. Which led to a whole new line of crazy he could sift through later, but right now, he needed to make her understand that he took what they'd done seriously. He wasn't going to let her just sweep it under the rug as a drunken mistake.

Especially since it took two to say "I do."

He had been developing his strategy the whole drive, and he'd come up with an idea he was going to propose—before he'd lost his cool. He needed to prove that there was more to what happened than a wild weekend gone wrong. Gemma had said he didn't know her; well, what better way to get to know someone than to date them?

She'd never agree to it, though, until she got over whatever had her in a panic. He needed to show her that it wasn't over, not just like that. There was too much left between them for "closure" or whatever her letter had said.

And he would prove it to her.

"I thought we were working really well together," he said softly, his tone seductive. He took her hand, holding it gently when she tried to pull away and caressing the back of it with his thumb. He saw her shiver and smiled as he brought her fingers up to his mouth, his lips hovering above the knuckles as he spoke. "When we were in your hotel room, and I had my hands on your body, running them over your skin . . . you felt so good." She licked her lips and closed her eyes. He pulled her closer, trailing his lips from her wrist to her elbow. "And the taste of your skin . . . all the little sounds you made when I played with your breasts . . . or when I was deep inside you."

He wrapped his arms around her, his large hands splaying across the curve of her ass, using it to pull her against him. Her breath whooshed out as he pushed himself against her, knowing she could feel every inch of his erection between them. He felt her relax into him, and her hand held onto his bicep, her eyes opening slowly, meeting his. He saw the matching desire in those mossy depths and dropped his lips to her temple, traveling over her skin until his mouth reached her ear. He nipped the small shell teasingly, and her body tightened against his, making him smile as he added, "I can show you again, if you don't remember."